Eric Gallagher was born in 1913 in Ballybay, Co. Monaghan. He is a graduate of Trinity College Dublin in Modern Languages and Divinity, and continued his theological education at Edgehill College, Belfast. He was superintendent of Belfast Central Mission from 1957 to 1979 and chairman of the Mission Board of the Methodist Church from 1971 to 1977. His former appointments include: minister at Woodvale Methodist Church (1938–42); chaplain and senior resident master at Methodist College, Belfast (1942–50); minister, Cregagh Methodist Church (1950–4); minister, University Road Methodist Church and chaplain to Queen's University Belfast (1954–7); secretary of the Methodist Church in Ireland (1958–67), president (1967–8). He also has been chairman of the Irish Council of Churches; vice-president of the British Council of Churches; a member of the Press Council of the United Kingdom; and at different times, a member of the Religious Advisors' Panel of the Independent Broadcasting Authority, of the British Broadcasting Corporation, Northern Ireland, and of Ulster Television. He was awarded an honorary Doctorate of Divinity from Queen's University in 1971, and appointed OBE for services to Belfast in 1972, and CBE for services to community relations in 1987.

Other publications are: *Violence in Ireland: A Report to the Churches* (1976), which he co-chaired with Bishop Cahal Daly; and with A. Stanley Worrall, *Christians in Ulster, 1968–80*, published by Oxford University Press in 1982.

GW00469809

# AT
# POINTS OF NEED

# AT
# POINTS OF NEED
–o–

## THE STORY OF THE BELFAST CENTRAL MISSION
## GROSVENOR HALL
## 1889–1989

## ERIC GALLAGHER

BELFAST CENTRAL
MISSION

———

THE
BLACKSTAFF
PRESS

## ACKNOWLEDGEMENTS

Grateful acknowledgement is made to Robin Bryans for permission to quote from *Ulster: A Journey Through the Six Counties* (Blackstaff Press, 1989), and Barbara Gallagher for permission to quote from *Embers: From the Fires of Ulster* (Christian Journals, 1977).

First published in 1989 by
Belfast Central Mission
Grosvenor Hall, 5 Glengall Street, Belfast BT12 5AD
and
The Blackstaff Press Limited
3 Galway Park, Dundonald, Belfast BT16 0AN, Northern Ireland

Printed by The Guernsey Press Company Limited

British Library Cataloguing in Publication Data
Gallagher, Eric, *1913*–
At points of need.
1. Belfast. Methodist missions, Belfast Central
Mission, history
1. Title
266'.754167

ISBN 0-85640-424-1

*for those named and the many more unnamed,*
*who, under God, were and are the*
*Mission*

# CONTENTS

# FOREWORD

We are not the first generation of Christians to be concerned about the inner city. A hundred years ago the big cities of Britain were scenes of poverty, slumdom and vice, which moved our grandfathers and grandmothers to action. The Methodist contribution to that action consisted, in city after city, in the building of large central halls. It was hoped the unchurched masses would not be averse to entering such a building. In it novel and unconventional ways of communicating the gospel could be explored. Large scale ancillary premises would form the base of compassionate work among the needy. The very scale of the operation would give Christianity a significant presence in a very grim environment. For two or three generations this formula worked well. Now with changing conditions, the great halls, if not the missions, are being called into question.

In Belfast the need was all the greater and the difficulties more severe because of the division of the city between two hostile communities who used religious terminology as their badges of identity. Three times in this century the underlying tension has broken out into extended periods of civil unrest, compounded by organised campaigns of terrorism in support of cherished causes. On both sides of the divide the causes have been worthy of respect, but the methods used to pursue them have lacked any justification. The task of ministering to the victims of urban deprivation is made vastly more difficult when organisations aiming to achieve their political ends by force are also engaged in the protection and succour of those whose support they hope thereby to gain.

It was in 1889 that the Belfast Central Mission was set up. To mark its centenary one of its most distinguished and devoted former superintendents has written what John Wesley would have called 'A Plain Account' of the work of the Mission during its

xi

first century. It is a fascinating story of Christian enterprise and of devotion often bordering on the heroic. It is a significant piece of social history. It is a gallery of portraits. It is a mine of anecdotes, some humorous, some deeply moving. It is a tribute, modestly paid by one who led the enterprise through some of its most demanding years, to an army of Christian workers, clerical and lay, paid and voluntary, who have sustained through all its vicissitudes the work centred on the Grosvenor Hall.

A. STANLEY WORRALL
MARCH 1989

# SUPERINTENDENT'S NOTE

No new superintendent could ask for a better introduction to his work in a Methodist mission than to be able to read of its one hundred years of history. That has been my unique privilege.

It has made me aware of the great debt of courage, commitment and vision which we owe to the past. It has inspired me to dream dreams for the future of the Mission's work. It has invoked in me a spirit of thanksgiving and commitment.

For this and so much more I am indebted to its author, and I warmly commend his book to the friends, old and new, of the Grosvenor Hall. I would wish in addition to express the profound gratitude of the Belfast Central Mission Committee to the Northern Ireland Bankers' Association whose generosity has made this publication possible.

DAVID J. KERR
BELFAST CENTRAL MISSION
MARCH 1989

# PREFACE

I am grateful to the Belfast Central Mission Committee for its request that I should write this book. It has been a privilege and a pleasure to respond. That response would have been impossible without the help of many people and circumstances. Twenty-two years of active service in the Mission, and ten more connected with it in retirement, have provided me with a fund of oral information and an awareness of tradition that nothing else could have done. In particular I learned a great deal in conversation – some of it formal, some casual – with Mrs Margaret Anderson, Mr Robin H. Anderson, Miss Agnes Barr, Messrs Joseph Culbert, Hal Dixon and W. Evans, the late Reverend S.D. Ferguson, Mr and Mrs Samuel Hanna, Mr and Mrs Edward Howard, Mrs Mary James, Mr Dermot P. Johnson, Mrs Moira Kelly (née Spence), Miss Hazel Ker, Messrs Edmund McGibben and William Matier, Mr and Mrs George Megahey, the late Mr William T. Millington, Mrs Sadie Nicholson, Mr Walter Smyth, the late Mrs Mary Thompson, Mrs Pearl Thompson, Messrs John Watson, John H. Weir, Wesley Weir, the Reverend John W. Young, and my daughter Ruth.

Valuable written information came my way from the pens of the late Mr Frank M. Anderson, the late Miss Elizabeth Allen, Mrs May Coey, the Reverend Robert A. Nelson (who drew my attention to de Lacey Ferguson's article, 'Woman of Ulster', mentioned in chapter 6), and Mrs Winifred O. Spence.

Most valuable of all were the Mission's archives – a veritable Aladdin's cave – which provided a wealth of photographs, the minutes of every Mission Committee meeting and leaders' meeting since their inception, a complete set of all published accounts and reports, the records and reports of Craigmore Home, details of the Whitehead Home, numerous copies of the *Grosvenor Hall Herald*, and amazingly, a set of desk diaries covering the most of thirty years following 1895. These last carried post-mortems on many of the big events, details of preaching plans, attendances and collections, plus tickets, leaflets and programmes over many years of Happy Evenings, press cuttings and invaluable memorabilia. They gave a colour to the narrative that otherwise would have been lost for ever. The variety of outstanding photographs from the camera of the late A.R. Hogg, the Mission's photographer and projectionist for many years, was augmented by many others put at our disposal by Mrs Margaret Anderson, Mr Hal Dixon, Miss Marjorie Gill, Mrs Nellie Holland, the Reverend David Houston, Messrs John and Wesley Weir, from my own family collection, and many others. I had recourse to many reports in the *Belfast News-Letter*, *Belfast Telegraph*, *Northern Whig*, *Irish Times* and the *Irish Christian Advocate*.

To many others I am grateful. They include Messrs D.H. Montgomery, W.H. Patterson and John Weir for comments on initial drafts; my successors Dr Norman Taggart and the Reverend David Kerr for their encouragement and co-operation; Dr A. Stanley Worrall for his generous Foreword; Mr Dereck Jamieson, who ferried photographs backwards and forwards to Larne, Co. Antrim, where Mr Tommy Ewing gave countless hours of painstaking expertise to their reproduction; the Northern Ireland Bankers' Association for its generous subsidy; my brother, Mr Herbert W. Gallagher FRCS, for reading and correcting proofs. Finally, appreciation must go to the Mission secretary, Miss Esther Fyffe, who for many years kept my records and looked after my correspondence and who has often since come to the rescue when I needed help in recollecting details of incidents and in finding documents; to Mrs Mandy Higgins for her interest and accuracy in the typing of the manuscript; to Mr Wesley Weir, without whom there would have been no book — week in, week out he has encouraged, researched and made possible the preparation of the photographs and manuscript; and to Barbara, whose support, understanding and patience over all the years and in many difficulties have continued, even to the extent of tolerating the noise in our caravan as I hammered out on the typewriter the concluding sections of this book.

ERIC GALLAGHER
MARCH 1989

# PART ONE

# THE STORY SO FAR

# I
## AT POINTS OF NEED

Belfast grew more rapidly than any other city in the United Kingdom during the second half of the nineteenth century. The 1830 population of 50,000 had almost doubled by 1850; by 1900 it had multiplied seven times to 350,000. The Great Famine of 1845–9 and the emerging mills and factories combined to depopulate the countryside, and the movement was intensified by the development of the railway system. In 1839 what was to become the Great Northern Railway stopped at Lisburn, Co. Antrim. Progressively it reached Lurgan in 1841, Portadown a year later, Armagh in 1848, all in Co. Armagh, and Dublin in 1853. Over the same years the Co. Down system was spreading and by 1848 the northern lines had reached the Co. Antrim towns of Ballymena and Carrickfergus. In succeeding years all of Ulster was opened up. Belfast was easily reached.

Not only easily reached, Belfast had much to offer. By 1860 the western hill streams had encouraged the siting of nearly forty flax mills in the Shankill ward and there were, it is estimated, thirteen flour and corn mills, half a dozen breweries or distilleries, four ropeworks, several sawmills, tobacco factories, soap and starch works in different parts of the city. Even then, the 'Mulholland' mill in York Street was employing six hundred workers. Contemporaneous with all this was the amazing growth of the ship-building industry, eventually to be controlled by two firms of world repute, Harland and Wolff, and Workman Clark.

Increase of population necessarily meant growth in size. Between 1820 and 1850 new thoroughfares like Lisburn Road and Crumlin Road had appeared. Many of the incomers from the rural areas settled near the railway stations where they had arrived. Sandy Row, the York Road area and Ballymacarrett were quickly to become well-known placenames, evocative of local

3

loyalties. The handing over of the impoverished Donegall estate to the Commission of Encumbered Estates made longer leases possible and so encouraged long-term investment. The movement from the prestigious residential houses in Donegall Place, College Square and Wellington Place to the south side of the city had begun. It all led in the second half of the nineteenth century to the erection of new public buildings and spacious houses on the grand scale. By the end of the 1860s, Bedford Street had the Ulster Hall and buildings like Bryson House, and Dublin Road had its terraces of large gracious residential properties. Beyond Bradbury Place was University Road and the development in the strip farms between the top of the Malone Ridge and the Bog Meadows. Such trends were matched to some extent in north Belfast between the Antrim Road and the Shore Road on the shores of Belfast Lough. By 1880 Hercules Street, famous homeland of the butchery trade, was giving way to the wider and commanding Royal Avenue. Belfast had emerged as a very attractive place to any tourist looking for gracious buildings, busy and expanding business life, and an almost unrivalled setting between hills and sea.

However, tucked away from the main arteries was another Belfast. The thousands of houses built around the mills, factories and railway stations stood in stark contrast to the residential and commercial areas of the city. Although thatch had been forbidden for new houses in 1840, it was to be more than 140 years before the last thatched house in the city had disappeared. New regulations were to demand a minimum street width of thirty feet (nine metres) but by 1850 the majority of the streets were still less than twenty feet (six metres) wide and nearly two thousand houses were in squalid entries and closes with many of them literally back to back. Approximately three thousand had no back yard of any kind. In 1852 between seven and ten thousand houses had no water supply. They had to depend on public water fountains, pumps and water carts. In 1878 the city fathers demanded that there should be a water closet and ash pit provided for every new house and a back entry at least ten feet (three metres) wide. However, it would be well into the twentieth century before Belfast could begin to claim acceptable public housing.

It was no wonder that the health of the city's teeming population

4

left much to be desired: 'In 1851 average expectancy of life from birth was nine years, and half the population was under twenty years of age.' (Quoted in *A Social Geography of Belfast*, Emrys Jones, Oxford University Press, 1980.) There was improvement of a kind over the next half-century. Nevertheless, by 1900 Belfast's health committee was concerned that pigs were still being kept in back yards. Consumption, or pulmonary tuberculosis, was rife, and in 1906 the health committee was to report:

> For the last twenty-five years at least the mean mortality from typhoid fever has been so great in Belfast that no other town or city in the United Kingdom equals or even approaches it in this respect.

Other factors such as child neglect, unemployment, alcoholism and immorality are devastating evidence that all was far from well in many areas of the city's life during this period.

Today it is fashionable to decry and criticise the claim the Churches make for themselves in the educational field. Whatever the merit of those claims at the end of the twentieth century (and they are not to be completely written off), at the end of the nineteenth century they could hold their heads high with justification. Norman McNeilly, in his meticulous history of the Belfast Education Authority, *Exactly Fifty Years*, paints a graphic picture of the chaotic and run-down educational system inherited by the Northern Ireland Ministry of Education in 1922. Had it not been for the work and crippling self-sacrifice of many of Belfast's parish churches and congregations, there would have been an even more inferior system in the city. Belfast Education Authority was eventually to take over a total of seventy-five Church schools. Almost all of them were situated in the densely populated industrial areas. What the situation would have been like without their contribution, however inadequate many of the buildings were, can only be left to the imagination. Education came low on the list of the city's priorities.

Adding to these difficulties was also Belfast's age-old and continuing problem of sectarianism. The participation of Ulster Presbyterians in the United Irishmen rising of 1798 is well documented. So too is the Protestant contribution to the building of St Mary's, Belfast's first Roman Catholic church, which was completed in

1784, with Protestants attending its opening, but that happy state of affairs was not to continue. In 1756 the 556 Catholics in the city were 6.5 per cent of the total population of 8,549. By 1834 their total of 19,712 was 32.4 per cent out of 60,803 and in 1861 they formed 34.1 per cent – 41,237 as compared with a total population of 119,444. As population proportions changed, rivalries emerged and sectarian tension and bigotry arrived. In 1857 a commission of inquiry stated:

> Since the commencement of the late riots the districts have become exclusive and by regular systematized movement on both sides the few Catholic inhabitants of the Sandy Row district have been obliged to leave that district.

By 1886 the sharp segregation into tribal areas that is all too prevalent today was well under way and Belfast's leading Christian Churches were increasingly concerned about the moral, physical and spiritual condition of the city's population. Into that situation the Methodist Church was about to make its own historic and dramatic entry.

# 2

# IN AN UNCHURCHED CITY
## 1850–89

The Churches could not ignore the challenge of the burgeoning Belfast which received its charter as a city in 1888. Methodist, Presbyterian, Roman Catholic and Church of Ireland communities engaged in attempts to tackle the problems created by the expanding population.

In 1800 there were five Presbyterian churches in Belfast. By 1850 the number had grown to seventeen — an increase of twelve in fifty years and in the next thirty-three years there would be twenty-one new churches in the city. During the same period, the Church of Ireland also tried to keep up with the population explosion: prior to 1850 there would seem to have been some half-dozen parish churches in Belfast; by 1888 there were twenty-three. As for the Catholic Church, in 1850 there were only three churches and three priests to serve their growing population. In 1865, when Dr Patrick Dorrian became Bishop of Down and Connor, it was not in any better shape. When he died in 1886, the situation had been revolutionised: Dr Ambrose Macauley states that there were then 'six fine spacious churches, a temporary one at Ardoyne and an eighth being built, two male religious orders, five orders of nuns, a flourishing seminary, handsome convents, homes for orphans and a hospital'.

Methodism's response was as courageous as it was dramatic. Mission halls sprang up in several areas of the expanding city. They were to be found in Laganview, Mitchell Street, Jennymount, Hutchinson Street, Agnes Street, Wilton Street and Hurst Street. Large churches with for the most part ancillary premises were erected in remarkable succession: Falls Road, 1854; University Road, 1864; Eliza Street, 1869; Jennymount, 1871; Carlisle Memorial, 1876; Knock, 1883; Crumlin Road and Sydenham, 1884; Mountpottinger and Agnes Street, 1887. For good measure,

Methodist College was opened in 1868.

That this huge programme placed a strain on central and local funds is unquestionable. That strain was amply demonstrated in a major debate in the Irish Methodist Conference of 1887. The Agnes Street congregation was finding difficulty in paying for its new premises and the Belfast District Meeting (later Belfast District Synod) had advocated the sale of the nearby Wilton Street Mission Hall in order to help reduce the debt. One of the most outspoken advocates of the sale was the senior assistant secretary of the Conference, the Reverend R. Crawford Johnson, then stationed in Enniskillen, Co. Fermanagh. He indicated his conviction that all the halls should be worked on 'mission' lines. He himself had (at a time he did not disclose) tried to do this in Wilton Street. He recalled marching down the street at the head of a band followed by only a handful of children. They were singing 'Hold the fort for I am coming'. When they got to the verse 'See the mighty host advancing,/Satan leading on. . .', he realised how utterly ludicrous the situation was and he told the Conference to its evident amusement that he could never sing the hymn again. The Church needed, he said, a broad statesmanlike approach to the whole question. He concluded: 'All such chapels as Wilton Street should be "feeders", not "suckers". Wilton Street has only been a sucker – a source of embarrassment and weakness.' He had amused the Conference but had failed to persuade it: Wilton Street was to survive for several years to come. Little did he know in 1887 that within two years he was to be intimately associated with the preservation and development of the same Wilton Street hall.

The Conference debate, however, had stimulated interest in the working of the mission halls. Gradually there was a realisation that a new approach was necessary. Leading ministers and laymen organised a house-to-house canvass, which indicated that thousands in Belfast had literally no Church connection whatever. They requested the Conference of 1888 to appoint 'a minister for special mission work in Belfast'. Instead the Conference appointed the Town Mission Committee. That year, however, it also appointed a 'general missioner' for the areas of counties Antrim and Down, which were part of the Belfast Methodist District.

8

(General missioners were common in British Methodism for work over wide areas.) The minister appointed was the Reverend R. Crawford Johnson and he was also made a member of the committee.

Crawford Johnson was then forty-seven years of age. Born on 15 June 1841, he had already made his mark on the Church's work. From his native Antrim, where his father ran a family grocery business, he had been sent to the Wesleyan Connexional School (now Wesley College) in Dublin. On the completion of his school days he gained employment in the Shillington firm in Portadown, Co. Armagh, where he learned many of the business methods and principles that were to stand him well in later years.

The year 1858 had been a turning point for Crawford Johnson. It was the year of his conscious decision to commit his life to Christ. A year later the prairie fire of the '59 Revival broke out across the province. It found the young man ready to 'devote all his spare hours to Christian work'. Soon his thoughts turned to full-time service. After a three-year course of training in one of British Methodism's theological colleges, Didsbury in Manchester, he was appointed in 1867 as a probationer for the ministry. In June 1870 he was married in Donegall Square Methodist Church to Miss Nannie Rosamund Johnston, daughter of Mr John Moore Johnston, a leading layman in Glenavy, Co. Antrim, whose gener-osity had made the erection of his local church possible. By 1885 Crawford Johnson was chairman of the Enniskillen District, a remarkable appointment for one of his 'juniority'.

In the summer of 1888, with his wife and five teenage sons, Crawford Johnson arrived in Belfast to take up his new work. Within a matter of weeks he was involved in the planning and work of the Town Mission Committee. It met in August when 'the need for more evangelistic work in the densely-crowded districts, where there were thousands of non-churchgoers, was carefully considered'. The committee decided to appoint two lay mission-aries or workers, Messrs John Coulter and John Adams. They were to visit homes, street by street, recording the church affiliation, if any, and they were to be responsible for Sunday evening services, respectively in Mitchell Street (off Brown Square in Peter's Hill) and Wilton Street on the Shankill Road. They were

9

employed at thirty shillings (£1.50) per week. Between 1 October 1888 and the beginning of February 1889, they had made over seven thousand calls and had been appalled at the irreligion and poverty they found – street after street in which there were scores and scores of homes with no Church connection and where no minister of religion had ever called. In one street alone 55 homes out of 110 were completely unchurched.

On Monday, 11 February the two men told their story to a largely-attended meeting in Donegall Square church. The great and good of Belfast Methodism were there and they were concerned at what they heard. They had no doubt about what was needed and they resolved as follows:

> That this meeting pledges itself to give both work and money and also hopes that the executive committee will be able to make the necessary arrangements to secure the appointment of a minister to superintend the work of a Methodist City Mission.

The honorary treasurer of the Town Mission Committee, Mr T. Foulkes Shillington, who was later to occupy the same position in the contemplated mission, was a prominent Belfast businessman and a principal of Musgrave and Company. He was a native of the Aghalee district in Co. Antrim, where his forebears, a Plantation family, had settled in 1658. An *Irish Christian Advocate* report on 8 December 1920 stated that the Shillingtons were thought to have come from the village of Shillington in Hertfordshire. When he addressed the February meeting in Donegall Square church, he spoke about the prospects and the challenge facing his committee. He would like to see a city-centre headquarters for the emerging mission but realised the financial implications. His suggestion that perhaps Donegall Square church might see its way to becoming the headquarters of the new work was not taken up.

Between February and June, Messrs Coulter and Adams intensified their efforts. The work was already taking on a new dimension. They were no longer simply knocking at doors: they recognised the necessity of doing something about the poverty that they were encountering. From time to time they appealed in the pages of the *Irish Christian Advocate* and elsewhere for 'old clothing, boots, shawls, bread, butter and eggs'. They had quickly come to terms with the relationship between faith and practice.

Meanwhile Crawford Johnson had been pursuing his work as general missioner. Early in 1889 the committee had decided to request the Conference to appoint him as superintendent, the minister responsible for the contemplated work, should he be willing to undertake it. He took some time to make up his mind. Eventually he acceded to the committee's request, but on the understanding that it would accept the inevitable financial burdens that would lie ahead. With Belfast Methodism pledging a guarantee fund of some £275 per annum for three years, all was set for approval by the Conference in June 1889. When the matter came before the Conference, there was much discussion but little argument. The report of the debate, such as it was, makes pointed reading: 'Members listened with considerable impatience not only to the few shadowy objections which were raised but also to everyone who tried to express his sympathies with the project.' 'Belfast City Mission' appeared on the list of stations and appointments under the Knock circuit. It was a kind of semi-independence.

On 28 June 1889, reporting on the decision, the *Irish Christian Advocate*'s leader-writer welcomed the new mission, 'which had been launched with all the éclat of Connexional authority, support and sympathy'. Crawford Johnson was appointed 'city missionary' to lead the new advance and 'No better appointment could have been made.' He was the best-known minister in the Connexion. The article concluded: 'Let not circuit selfishness so "boycott" the Mission that young men and women who are really wanting to find something to do shall be kept idle in religious indolence.' The Mission was, in the mind of its progenitors, intended to be a mission of the whole Methodist Church to the city.

# 3

## AT NO FIXED ABODE
### 1889–95

Government by committee can be a nightmare. Not so the Town Mission Committee appointed by the Conference to develop the work it had authorised. Composed of Crawford Johnson, ministers of the city and a number of the best-known and active laymen in Belfast, it quickly demonstrated a capacity for hard work and decisive action. The secretaries were the Reverend James Harpur and the Reverend George R. Wedgwood and the honorary treasurer, Mr T. Foulkes Shillington. Between September 1889 and the end of the year, the committee met eleven times, and met on fifty-eight occasions up to the end of April 1895, by which time the new Grosvenor Hall had become a fact of life.

Members of the committee met officially for the first time before the end of July 1889. They were in good heart but there was no euphoria. They discussed the expectations of the Conference and the realities of their finances.

We saw that the work proposed embraced the following objects:

To commence operations in different centres.
Arrangements to be made to begin with Duncairn Gardens.

To secure new sites.

To revive and extend the work in connection with some of the older Mission Halls.

It was an ambitious programme but the realities were against them. There was a debt of £85 on the account of the previous year and there was no fund for the employment of lay agents: the guarantee fund of £275 had sole reference to the 'support of a Methodist Minister as a City Missionary in Belfast'. Also there was no money in hand to proceed immediately with a proposed building at Duncairn Gardens.

There was disappointment but no defeatism. Work in the small hall in Wilton Street would continue. No temporary hall was available for Duncairn Gardens and there was no money with which to commence building operations, so it was decided to defer the Duncairn project pro tem. The decision did not stick. A site at Duncairn had been acquired on the understanding that building would commence forthwith, otherwise it would revert to the vendor. By October 1889 more money and support seemed to be in the offing and acting in good faith, the committee accepted a tender for £1,295 and work began on a school and hall.

The committee turned its attention to the mission at Laganview, just over the Queen's Bridge. It had been sustained for nearly twenty years in very inferior accommodation. It had been kept going only because of the support of the Donegall Square congregation. At the end of August 1889 the committee had offered, in spite of its liabilities, to relieve 'the Square' of the burden and to build a hall. The offer was accepted and by mid-October plans were ready for a hall and school. However, a decision to proceed was deferred and by December the Donegall Square quarterly meeting 'offered to accept a grant from the committee and to undertake the building of the hall at Laganview'. The committee's grant of £150 was given to Donegall Square church on the understanding that the Mission would not canvass financial support from Donegall Square members, who in turn would not seek subscriptions from Mission contributors. In the event a hall at Laganview was erected and furnished at a cost of £450.

As there was no fund for the support of the lay missionaries, to its regret, the committee had to dispense with the services of one of them. He was the younger and he was unmarried. He went into business and eventually became the head of the successful Belfast printing firm of John Adams and Company.

The most significant decision taken was that the city missionary should conduct special services throughout the city in the 'different districts where the working classes reside'. Sandy Row was singled out as Crawford Johnson's first priority. For several weeks the lay missionary, John Coulter, visited street after street. He reported: 'In many streets the overwhelming majority of the people go to no place of worship and here and there those trained in our churches and schools are found in a state of rank and absolute heathenism.' Ample preparation was made and the local minister, the Reverend W.H. Quarry, and his leaders did all that was humanly possible to ensure a successful mission. For two weeks, from 1 to 15 September, services were held every evening in Sandy Row church. Crawford Johnson reported some weeks later: 'In fact, as an effort to reach the lapsed masses, the mission was a total failure, as night after night hardly any but the regular church-goers attended the services conducted in the church.'

As defeat stared them in the face a new possibility presented itself. They learned that one of the large tents belonging to the General Mission of the Methodist Church, used for summer evangelistic services, was about to be dismantled for the winter months. The tent was borrowed and erected on empty ground in Hunter Street. Children watching its erection encouraged their parents to attend; services commenced on 18 September. The result was as immediate as it was dramatic: night after night the crowds poured into the tent. There were also afternoon meetings for women and children. Almost at a stroke the Town Mission was reaching the very people who never crossed a church door, many of them becoming the workers and leaders on whom the Mission was to depend. However, winter was at hand. It was clear that tent services could not continue indefinitely, and equally clear that the field that had so unexpectedly opened up should not be deserted.

In the crisis Crawford Johnson demonstrated his preparedness to attempt the unusual and unorthodox. In Great Victoria Street, on the site of today's Grand Opera House, stood Ginnet's Circus, otherwise known as Hermon Hall. It was one of a chain of music halls found in a number of towns throughout the United Kingdom and owned by a man named Ginnet, resident in the south of England. The building, which seated up to two thousand people, lay empty for weeks at a time when Mr Ginnet's company was playing elsewhere. After negotiations, Mr Ginnet was willing to

Between 1889 and 1905 Dr R. Crawford Johnson led his people from place to place in Belfast: Sandy Row church (top left); the tent (top right); Ginnet's Circus (bottom left); and finally, Grosvenor Hall (bottom right). St George's Hall and the Ulster Hall were other stopping places.

A Sunday afternoon meeting in 1901 at the Custom House, Belfast. The Steps were on the Mission's outreach programme until the 1970s.

A food depot in 1901; from the beginning the Mission fed the hungry.

Tea and buns for the 1902 children's Christmas party in Grosvenor Hall. Among the helpers are John Young (seated centre); James Smyth and Richard Addis (fourth and fifth from left, front row); and John N. Spence (third from right)

Dr Crawford Johnson (front row, centre) and his wife to his left, with Mission staff and committee members at the Palm House, Botanic Gardens, Belfast, 1903. T. Foulkes Shillington is immediately behind Dr and Mrs Johnson.

James Dixon, the Soldier Evangelist, (standing, third from right) says grace in

There was a nightly run with food and tea for men and boys sleeping rough on the warm Springfield brick fields, c. 1905.

A.R. Hogg's screen and
gas projector at action
stations in Grosvenor
Hall, c. 1906. The
Happy Evenings
brought colour to
drab lives.

let the premises, when available, on two conditions: the religion propagated by the prospective tenants must be of a 'respectable nature', and the rent had to be paid before each weekend, otherwise the doors would remain locked. He was satisfied that these conditions would be met and the tent services were transferred to Ginnet's Circus.

There was doubt as to whether the people would respond to this novel arrangement. On 10 November 1889, the first Sunday evening in the new venue, the Reverend W.H. Quarry and his Sandy Row congregation marched round as a body to Great Victoria Street with the intention of swelling the crowd. When they reached the hall it was already full and they could not gain access. They held an open-air meeting on the street outside. The crowds kept packing the building every Sunday and on weeknights as well. It soon became a case of 'adults only'. As a 'recompense', meetings for young men, boys and girls were arranged for Friday evenings. However, by the end of January Mr Ginnet required repossession of the hall. So started a process that was to go on for a number of years – a move from one location to another. The Mission went this time to St George's Hall in High Street. In some ways it was a good move: the rent was cheaper – £50 for six months against the £5.5s.0d. (£5.25) per week to Mr Ginnet.

Meanwhile, the Mission had been publicly and ceremonially launched on 8 and 9 October 1889. The expanding work and prospects demanded more help for Crawford Johnson. He was dispatched to England to negotiate the services of James Grubb, a young theological student at Richmond College, London, who was to become almost a legend in his lifetime as an outstanding and captivating preacher. Crawford Johnson also secured the services of one who was to be on the Mission staff for several years: Miss M. Munro was seconded by Mr George Clegg, founder of a home for female evangelists in Halifax. Initially her services were provided free of charge to the Mission. (She remained until 1897 when she went to Bolton.) Shortly afterwards, Mr James Dixon, a colourful character who became known as the 'Soldier Evangelist', joined the staff. His salary was raised independently by Crawford Johnson. An ex-serviceman, his moral and physical courage had stood him in good stead throughout his army career, which ended when he lost one arm in battle. Crawford Johnson had a great admiration for him, writing:

> Physique accounts for something in a preacher and his massive figure gives you the idea of manliness and strength. If Brother Dixon has not the rhetoric of the schools, he has the tongue of fire, the very eloquence of God.

James Dixon was a loyal member of the staff until he went to Canada after World War 1.

The work was mushrooming. The first traditional Methodist class meeting was held on 1 December 1889. It was the seed from which the strength of the congregation was to come. A large room was rented for weeknight meetings and fellowship classes in Linenhall Street. A hall was secured free of charge in Dock Street to be used during the course of building in Duncairn Gardens and as a 'feeder' for it. The services also continued in Wilton Street. By the end of May 1890 a principal had been appointed for the school soon to be opened in Duncairn, and two other lay workers were in post.

The first annual report in 1890, printed by John Adams, concluded with a 'Wanted' page in bold lettering. Among the people and items required were:

> Young men and women, who can support themselves and Candidates for the ministry of independent means who would desire to graduate in the school of active service for a year or two. £5000 for the erection of Churches at Duncairn etc. Cast-off clothes for the poor.

One may smile at the hopes, but some of the optimism was well founded. In any case the Mission's role and *modus operandi* had been established at least in embryo within a year. Underlying all those items mentioned were the matters that were to be the Mission's concern for the next hundred years: evangelism, children, the outcasts of society, prostitutes, drunkards, old people, the poor and the underprivileged, and even the healthy and the well-to-do. Crawford Johnson's gospel was to the whole human condition – soul, mind and body.

The conditions in which the work was carried on almost defy

belief. The superintendent had every reason for referring to his congregation and himself as 'ecclesiastical gypsies'. From one month to the next they hardly knew when or how the tenancy of any premises they were occupying would terminate. They moved with an almost incredible lack of fuss or complaint from one hall to another. At different times and for short periods they found themselves in St George's Hall, the Ulster Hall and the Circus. The weeknight operations were still more scattered and uncertain – the Linenhall Street room and Carlisle Memorial lecture hall were added to the list. An excursion to Lisburn, as early as Easter Monday in 1890, helped to band workers and leaders together. On that day one of the Mission's early stalwarts, Billy Spence, took part in his first public meeting. Committee minutes, annual reports and press coverage are studded with references to the variety and quality of the work attempted and accomplished.

First and foremost, reference must be made to the congregations. The momentum of the initial move to the Circus was sustained irrespective of where the services took place. The congregations were large and were described as 'nondescript' for the services attracted a wide spectrum of the community. Crawford Johnson and his young colleague, James Grubb, drew the crowds. They were an admirable combination; each was a convinced evangelist, each was his own man and able in his own way to relate the gospel to the issues and social evils of the day. Of the two, the superintendent was the philosopher–evangelist; James Grubb, the more dramatic. The intensity with which the latter preached made great demands on his physical and nervous energy. Alcohol, gambling and sexual immorality were regular targets. On 10 January 1890 the *Irish Christian Advocate* reported that on New Year Sunday they 'endeavoured to deal a deadly blow to the great poisonous upas-tree'. However, they adopted no mere negative approach. In December 1891 Crawford Johnson, ahead of his time, was preaching on 'The Christian and politics'. He stressed that Christians should be concerned about social and political issues. Another widely-noticed sermon concerned the working conditions of the city's young shop assistants. He was still more blunt in the spring of 1904; 'the vote is the only thing a candidate fears. A vote

17

is a sacred trust which you must use for the good of society and in this way you put a conscience into politics and make Jesus King.' Conversions took place in remarkable numbers. They were no flash in the pan for the records reveal how many of them became full members of the Church.

Thousands of leaflets printed every week, paid for by the advertisements each leaflet carried, had full details for the following Saturday and Sunday, complete with arresting sermon titles. They were distributed on the streets to workers going home, in the city centre and house to house. The building up of the congregation was the priority. It was here that the organisational flair of the first two superintendents, Crawford Johnson and Robert M. Ker, was crucial. They planned their work and worked their plan. Class or fellowship meetings were held every week. The meetings were not all 'religious' – sewing, reading and writing classes and gymnasium sessions all helped to knit people into a coherent unity. There was work as well for them to do. There were as many volunteer workers as would form many a large congregation eighty years later. The dimensions of the programme required massive numbers. No wonder that the first chief steward, Mr Richard Addis, converted during the 1889 tent services, needed between forty and fifty stewards and sometimes more every Saturday and Sunday evening.

Life in the new Mission was far from being a dull affair. The West London Mission had commenced 'Happy Sunday Evening' gospel services. Crawford Johnson went one better – he launched Saturday evening entertainment, including what the modern broadcaster would call a 'God slot'. 'Happy Evenings for the People' commenced as early as 30 November 1889. They were novel and their entertainment content was controversial. The superintendent and his colleagues had to defend them from time to time. The weekly diet of good family entertainment, combined with a popular input of religious song, readings and homilies, drew the crowds in. Visiting singers included people like W.H. Jude, Madame Jessie Strathearn, Madame Annie Gray – they were all names to conjure with. Miss Lorraine Johnston, principal contralto from the Royal Choral Society in London, and the Fisk Jubilee Singers, with their roots in the struggle for the abolition of slavery in the United States, were always a draw. Regimental bands from British Army units stationed in or near Belfast were regulars and were big attractions. There was always the local talent, including some committee members, who could keep the show on the road: Mrs Herbert Nixon at the organ and piano, Miss Annie Coulter's choirs, band entertainment, elocutionists and many others. There were also Irish and Gaelic nights (more popular then with the Protestants than they might be in today's sectarian generation), and Scottish nights.

There was education as well as entertainment. Lectures on scientific, historical and geographical subjects were arranged for working men. What is more, they were well attended even with an entrance charge. The lecture programmes also came in for their share of criticism. Robert M. Ker, an early colleague who was to succeed to the superintendency in 1905, was challenged about them. Scientific lectures, he was told, had nothing to do with religion. He had his answer: 'It is a candid belief with the staff that when a man becomes a Christian, he should sound new depths of feeling, reach to nobler heights and understand better the world in which he lives.'

The great public occasions never went without notice. There were memorial services for Queen Victoria and other well-known persons in Church and state. Such seemingly uncontroversial occasions could be criticised as well. In November 1902 a memorial service was held for one of British Methodism's outstanding ministers, the Reverend Hugh Price Hughes. This innocuous event prompted a Church of Ireland clergyman, the Reverend George Gardner Parkinson Cumine, to send a letter of protest to the *Fermanagh Times*. It was headed 'Memorial Service FOR the Dead'. He said the advertisement for the service was such as grated on the ears of all sound Protestants. (However, it might suit 'Ritualists or Romanists'.) He went on: 'What are we coming to? "A Memorial Service FOR the Dead" to-day: prayers for them, probably, to-morrow, and not a word of protest allowed to appear!' The rector, a 'sound Protestant', was clearly suspicious that the Mission was adopting the Roman Catholic practice of praying for the dead. Even in 1902 there were those who suspected the ecclesiastical equivalent of 'reds under the bed'.

Very soon staff and committee were convinced that it was not enough simply to preach about and against social evils. Many photographs survive of the street children so often referred to as 'street Arabs'. They became an agonising and continuous problem which was to lead eventually to the children's homes so well known today. The pictures of barefooted and ill-clad youngsters are emotive but 'for real'. Food, clothing and shelter were sought and provided for these waifs, all of them needy and many of them homeless, sleeping out in the brick fields, factory engine rooms and elsewhere. Another by-product was the hungry men who began to appear at the afternoon Sunday school when food was on the agenda. Very soon they had their own meeting. Almost ninety years later the Brother Man service is still on the weekly programme. Rescue work also among the prostitutes was an early exercise. The records make repeated reference to the 'moral scavenging' in the Academy Street and Green Street area. Dr Ambrose Macauley in *Patrick Dorrian, Bishop of Down and Connor* refers to a mixed school in Academy Street, managed by the redoubtable Dr (Roaring) Hugh Hanna, attended by both Protestant and Catholic children. Between one third and one half of the pupils were illegitimate and the assistant teacher was stated to be a prostitute. Attempts were being made as early as December 1891 to acquire a rescue home in Queen Street. The dangers and risks, both physical and health, in some of Belfast's slums, described in one report as 'debased and debauched to the last degree', led to the introduction of a uniform for the Mission's women workers in order to ensure their protection.

Open-air meetings several times a week, special services in tents (Mulhouse Street was a favourite venue) and different mission halls, and grappling with the challenge of the ever-present Wilton Street hall were part of the weekly programme. From the beginning, the Sunday afternoon open-air meeting at the Custom House, Belfast's 'Hyde Park Corner' of the period, was priority number one: 'thousands of artisans in their best serge suits crowded round the Custom House steps to hear the Methodist choir, the sectarian sermons of the Belfast Protestant Association, or the propaganda of the socialists' (*Edwardian Belfast: A Social Profile,* Sybil Gribbon). Many years before Mr T.A. Fullerton, a prominent member of the committee, supported by his wife, and the Reverend John White of the Congregational Church, had fought and won the battle for freedom of speech at the Custom House. He joined forces with Crawford Johnson and the meeting became the Mission's. It was a very successful meeting and was to continue into the 1970s. An article in the *Irish Christian Advocate* of 30 May 1890 dealt with the recipe for popular open-air meetings. Items on the programme, it said, 'must be brief and varied. Protracted prayers, dull singing, long addresses will not keep the people together.' It was desirable 'to invite the listeners to a later indoor meeting about to begin in some nearby hall'. Clearly the article referred to the Mission's successful meeting at the Custom House which was immediately followed by a service in St George's Hall. Every Sunday afternoon, just prior to the evening service, Mrs Johnson and a band of ladies provided tea for the meeting's workers in 'Mr Greenhill's boardroom', adjacent to St George's Hall.

Billy Spence, a tough bargee working on the River Lagan, was one of the triumphs of the Custom House service. One of the Shankill Road's most notorious characters and known as 'the bull dog', the police were wary of Billy: when he was drunk, he was a match for three or four of them. One Sunday, after a heavy night's drinking, he made his way to the Custom House. He saw James Grubb and thought the preacher was a doctor. Making his way into the crowd, Billy was convinced that he himself was the target for what James Grubb was saying: 'If I could only get men to spend ten minutes in thinking where they would spend eternity. . .' Billy Spence went home and went to his work the next day and spent a good deal more than ten minutes thinking. Finally some days later, in the hold of an old mud lighter, near the Twin Islands on Belfast Lough, his struggle ended and he became one of the Mission's most ardent workers and remained so for many years. At his funeral his coffin was carried by a bearer party of Shankill Road-based policemen.

Something too had to be done – and was done – about what the *Irish Christian Advocate* called on 1 May 1891 'the rock of offence and stone of stumbling. (When will the debt take wings and fly?)' Crawford Johnson could not get Wilton Street out of his system but he had a remedy and it was a novel one. A worker was employed to conduct services there at a remuneration of ten shillings (50p) per week – that amount to be paid for a reasonable trial period and thereafter to be reduced to nine shillings (45p) per week. Presumably the idea was to encourage local generosity and thereby increase local support of the missioner – or alternatively to demonstrate the hall's inability to survive. It was 'mend or end'.

Contemporaneous with the need to get the city-centre effort off the ground, there was the major obligation at Duncairn Gardens. The school was completed in August 1890 and was opened the following month. It had a ground-floor classroom fifteen metres by eleven metres and four metres high. It had a gallery and hat and cloak rooms, and there was an upper-storey hall seventeen metres by eleven metres. In addition, a 'sanitary yard was provided with suitable apparatus for boys and girls'. The growth of the school was dramatic. Two-hundred-and-seventy-two pupils were enrolled by October and 330 by the end of November, by which time it had been recognised by the Commissioners of Education. Within a year or so it could boast of over one thousand pupils and a staff of twenty-eight. The strain on the physical accommodation was certainly eased but not removed by the difference between average attendance and enrolment – the school probably never had any more than 650 in one day. School attendance figures for the period suggest an average day's attendance of about two-thirds of the total enrolled. Sunday services in the upstairs hall were well attended from the beginning. An enlargement of the site with a main-road frontage was negotiated in December 1890. By 1892 plans were commissioned for a church building and additional classrooms. They were approved and a tender accepted in the sum of £3,093 in April with the help of a loan from the Star Life Assurance Company at 4½ per cent interest. Successful opening services were held in December 1894 and for almost half a century this beautiful and imposing church housed one of Irish Methodism's largest and most generous congregations. Tragically it was burned to the ground in the April air raid of 1941.

Finances were rarely absent from the committee's agenda. The circuits had promised their guarantee fund of £275 per year but there was regrettable and serious delay in fulfilling the promises. Early on the superintendent was compelled to record in the 1890 report: 'We have received the mites of the poor: we await the munificence of the rich.' In August 1890 they were appealing urgently for gifts, and on 29 August 1890 the *Irish Christian Advocate* carried the sad news: 'In response to last week's urgent request we have received – nothing.' It was considered essential in that month to appoint a strong deputation to wait on the quarterly meetings of Carlisle Memorial, Knock and University Road circuits to persuade them to fulfil their promises. At the end of 1893 there was almost a sigh of relief when the committee realised the Ulster Hall collections were producing £6 per week. The tide had turned.

Success underlined the need for a permanent large 'central' hall with ancillary premises. Early in 1894 Crawford Johnson had said that they were 'ecclesiastical gypsies'. He was sure that their nomadic religious life should not continue any longer. A year before, the honorary treasurer, Mr Shillington, had spoken publicly about the need for a 'central' hall and by September of that year the committee also was convinced. At a cost of £5,000 they purchased the greater part of the site on which the present Grosvenor Hall stands. They mortgaged the premises to the Star Life Assurance Company to secure the sum of £4,000 at 4¼ per cent interest per annum, and borrowed the remainder from the bank at 5 per cent. Tenders were received from several firms in England as well as Belfast; in the event the contract was placed with Mr T. Foulkes Shillington's firm, Musgrave and Company, whose tender for £2,800 had been 'easily the cheapest'. On 1 August 1894 building operations commenced. Work proceeded rapidly and by the end of September one passer-by had written to the *Irish Christian Advocate* that 'the shape is happily heterodox being almost square'. His comment is borne out by the dimensions thirty metres by twenty-seven metres. There was a gallery all round with tiered seating beneath and the hall seated twenty-five hundred people. There were five accesses to the gallery and five entrances to the building – four on the Grosvenor Road frontage and one on Glengall Street. The outside walls were of red brick with moulded string courses. The structural work was of rolled steel and the roofing, galvanised corrugated iron. The opening ceremony took place before a crowded congregation on 25 October just three months after work had commenced.

Crawford Johnson and T. Foulkes Shillington had a pragmatic

eye to the future. They secured the premises on deeds of trust dated 29 March 1894 and 21 December 1896. The trusts declared that 'the said premises shall be used and occupied in connection with the City Mission. . . in such manner as the said Trustees may determine' and further that

> a power of sale of the sd premises or any part thereof shall be vested in the sd Trustees and may be exercised by them at any time hereafter and the proceeds of such sale or sales made in exercise of the aforesaid power shall be applied in or towards the discharge of the incumbrance and liabilities whether personal or otherwise lawfully contracted or occasioned in the exercise of the Trusts hereof and subject thereto for or towards such purpose or purposes in connection with the sd Mission or should it no longer exist in such manner as the sd Trustees may determine.

There was also power for the trustees to lease any part of the trust premises at any time out of use or not required for the purposes of the Mission. The deeds have since been renewed twice.

Thus by the beginning of 1895 the Mission had established its role and it had acquired a reasonably long-term and adequate local habitation. The new hall was one of the largest and most sought-after buildings in the city. What about the Mission's name? It had started off in the minds of its planners as 'The Belfast Town Mission'. 'Town' quickly gave way to 'City' and then in order to avoid confusion with the Presbyterian-based Belfast City Mission, the name was changed to 'The Belfast Methodist Mission'. However, by 1895 it had become and has remained ever since 'The Belfast Central Mission'. That was not the end of the story. Fronting on the lower part of the Grosvenor Road (identified on the trust deed and until then recently known as College Street South), the name of the new hall was obvious. From the outset it was called, as its successor has been, 'The Grosvenor Hall'.

# 4

## IN POVERTY AND HUNGER
### 1895–1905

There were years of controversy and tension following William Ewart Gladstone's Home Rule Bills of 1886 and 1893. The period 1895–1905 was marked as well by the death of the seemingly immortal Queen Victoria, and the Second Boer War in faraway South Africa. Belfast took less notice of the last event than it did of the lurking possibility of Home Rule and the passing of the monarch. The queen's death was, however, the occasion of only temporary emotion and though the Home Rule issue was never very far below the surface, Belfast was content enough to go about its affairs without undue concern. There were other matters affecting the city's life with which the Mission quickly had to grapple.

It was a decade of continuing poverty and disease. Infant mortality was at an intolerable level. At the end of December 1897 the Belfast coroner disclosed that twenty-five out of every hundred burials in Belfast were of children under one year of age. He went on to make the controversial assertion that the majority were due to the neglect of parents. There were labour troubles in 1895 and 1896 and sectarian riots in 1899, all of this exacerbating the poverty. There were other distresses – a disastrous fire in the shipyard in 1896, and a calamity at Smithfield Mill in January 1902 in which some Mission members lost their lives. The human fallout in terms of unemployment, malnutrition, hunger, starvation and sexual immorality can hardly be quantified. The Mission had ample justification for its 1902 leaflet setting out its aims, which read as follows:

1 To rescue non-churchgoers
2 To feed the poor and clothe the naked
3 To rescue and uplift the down-trodden children of the slums

4 To rescue from the haunts of vice and sin

5 To rescue drunkards from the public house

6 To help the working man when out of employment

7 To make Belfast like unto the City of God

Such was the agenda. How did the Mission face the challenge during the period 1895 to 1905?

The church and ancillary buildings at Duncairn Gardens had been completed. The success of that project was dramatic and in July 1894 Duncairn was granted its independence; it resulted in the transfer of the Reverend James Grubb to this new circuit. Crawford Johnson had no ministerial colleague for the ensuing year and then there were two appointments – the Reverend George W. Thompson (1895–7), who worked particularly in Woodvale, and the Reverend Louis W. Crooks (1897–8), later to join the Church of Ireland. In 1898 the Reverend Robert M. Ker, then beginning his third year of probation, was appointed to the Mission. No one could have foretold the long-term significance of that appointment or of the one to be made four years later when the Reverend John N. Spence joined the staff.

Wilton Street was still on the agenda. A day school had been started in 1893 and it had been recognised by the Commissioners of Education. In 1900 it finally reverted to the Agnes Street congregation which had been relieved of responsibility for it after the Conference of 1889. There was responsibility for another hall where the going was difficult. It was at Andersonstown in west Belfast and the work was time consuming and often unrewarding. It would eventually be transferred to the Balmoral (Osborne Park) circuit but not until after 1905.

The main thrust of the effort to reach the unchurched was concentrated in and from the Grosvenor Hall. In October 1905, during one weekend, the staff reckoned that over nine thousand seats had been occupied. There were regular congregations or audiences of over two thousand. One intriguing diary entry in 1905 refers to an audience as being an '£8 house'; reckoning on the usual one (old) penny per person, a collection of £8 meant eight times 240 – as near two thousand as did not matter. Assuming that a single coin in the offering represented one person, the following figures were recorded in the year 1894–5:

| | |
|---|---|
| Sunday | |
| 11 a.m. | 13,128 |
| 4 p.m. | 39,295 |
| 7 p.m. | 94,670 |
| Saturday | 45,303 |
| Classes | 7,943 |
| | |
| Total | 200,339 |

Therefore the average attendance per week was 3,853; the Sunday 4 p.m. meeting was held over six months of the year, the Saturday meeting over five months. It was a rough-and-ready calculation but probably far more accurate than the congregation headcounts claimed by many preachers. Congregations came from many parts of the city. Indeed right up to the end of the large Sunday evening congregations, professional and business people and students attended, some on special occasions, others more regularly. However, the vast majority came from the streets on the lower Grosvenor Road, from in and around Sandy Row and Donegall Pass, the lower part of the Donegall Road, the lower Shankill Road and Newtownards Road.

The Hall was a base from which the Mission reached out and sought for those for whom the Church had ceased to have, or never had, any attraction. Summer after summer, services were held in large marquees pitched in different parts of the city – Hilland Street, Brown Square and Mulhouse Street were some of the more popular venues. Frequently on a summer evening there would be a second session; it was to be known as 'the midnight meeting for drunkards'. Without exception each of these attracted hundreds who would never have crossed the doorway of any church. To use the recurring language of the records, 'the working classes' were being reached. (Indeed Crawford Johnson saw no difficulty in putting the premises at the disposal of strike meetings. Given what he had said about the relationship between Christians and social issues, it was the natural thing for him to do.) Many of the men and women attracted to the services were to become energetic and loyal workers in the Mission. From the beginning a conscious attempt was made to gather them into a purposeful

27

community. Classes, choirs, youth organisations and outings and excursions for the workers all played a part in the grand design.

The open-air meetings demanded and received major and continuing dedication and sacrifice. There was the regular Sunday afternoon effort at the Custom House with all its rival meetings and side shows. It was there that three of the 'greats' in the Mission's history of that decade were regularly to be seen and heard. They were Billy Spence, already a legend, James Dixon, a valued member of the full-time staff and T.A. Fullerton, not so charismatic perhaps but ever dependable and loyal. In addition there were other open-air meetings during the week – at Queen's Bridge, Newtownards Road, Grosvenor Road, Shankill Road and other locations.

Because of sectarian unrest in the city in the spring of 1899 the lord mayor and city council called for the abandonment of outdoor gatherings. In so doing they sparked off a spate of letter-writing by Crawford Johnson. He considered their action an unwarranted intrusion on religious liberty and he wrote personal letters to a host of public figures including Prime Minister Arthur J. Balfour, Foreign Secretary Lord Salisbury, Chief Secretary for Ireland Gerald Balfour, Mr Campbell Bannerman MP, and two local members of parliament, Mr J.H. Haslett and Mr William Johnston. The handwritten replies of these worthies or their private secretaries are still to be found in the Mission's strong room.

Before the autumn had arrived, however, the restoration of quiet in the city had resolved the matter. Opposition had not only come from civic quarters: by the end of the year the superintendent felt obliged to defend his participation in open-air evangelism against critics within the Churches and he defended it again in 1904. Following correspondence in the local newspapers, he put himself on record in the *Irish Christian Advocate*, 7 January 1898, as follows:

> Let me define my position regarding open-air preaching. There are several kinds of preaching I neither admire nor defend. (1) The controversial. Controversial preaching in Ireland is very injurious. Roman Catholics in Ireland may be opposed to Protestantism but they are not opposed to Christianity. Therefore I bring a gospel without offence. (2) I do not believe in the preaching of fads and

ecclesiastical hobbies. (3) Mendicants. I do not believe in passing round the hat at the end of a meeting. (4) Mountebanks who let their tongues rage like a fire among the noblest names defaming and defacing. We have a few street preachers who simply preach a gospel of abuse.

He then posed three questions:

(1) Is open-air preaching scriptural? (2) Is it rational? Is it not true that many will not go into a building? We therefore go to them. The church needs more oxygen. (3) Is it justified by results?

He left no doubt about the answer to the last question.

There were the regular evangelistic missions held in the Grosvenor Hall itself. Some of the great preachers and missioners of the day were invited to conduct such missions – their names included Gypsy Smith, and 'Father Connellan' was to conduct services on more than one occasion. He was a controversial figure. Crawford Johnson was no sectarian preacher; there is no evidence that he practised proselytism. On the contrary, he and his successor, Robert M. Ker, frequently took action to avoid offence either to Roman Catholic leaders or others. However, he believed that there were signs of welcome new life and freedom in the Catholic Church and so there was no hesitation in bringing this former priest to conduct services. Crawford Johnson told the story to an American audience of Father Connellan's decision to leave the 'Church of Rome'. He had been asked to write an article or pamphlet on the subject of transubstantiation. The more he considered his subject the more unhappy he became with the teaching of his Church. He finally decided to disappear and gave the impression that he had been drowned by leaving his clothes on the bank of the River Shannon. His parishioners were heart-broken at the loss of their priest and memorial services were held. Meanwhile in London he went to hear the famous C.H. Spurgeon and underwent a profound religious experience which eventually brought him back to Ireland as a freelance evangelist. Father Connellan preached about the necessity of a personal relationship with Jesus Christ. His strictures on the Catholic Church and its system never failed to attract large numbers from Belfast's Protestant heartlands. He had a facility for allusion that amused his listeners and played to the prejudices of many of them. A report in the *Belfast News-Letter*, 26 November 1907, deals with a lecture entitled 'Ireland on the dissecting table' in which he said Ireland was bleeding at every pore: 'The surgeon on the seven hills relieves the patient to the tune of £5,000,000 and Surgeon John Redmond bled Ireland to the tune of £30,000 annually.' He continued with thrust after thrust, criticising the leading British and Irish politicians who were in any way involved in the Irish Question. It would be tempting to ignore or refrain from making comment on the controversial Father Connellan, but that would be at the cost of the integrity of the whole story.

One other matter must be mentioned before leaving the outreach to the unchurched. In March 1896 the Mission was asked to take under its wing the work of a small hall in Cambrai Street, off the Woodvale Road. Superintendent and treasurer alike were all too aware of their straitened resources so they agreed that the hall should be part of the Mission's outreach, that it should receive all the help possible but that it should be worked independently. Plans were commissioned and by September of that year Woodvale Hall was opened. However, it was a sad unfortunate episode and the records are reticent about what happened next. The minutes simply state that in June 1897 'the Woodvale situation was left in the hands of the superintendent and treasurer'. In September 'the painful situation' had necessitated the closing of the hall. In December it was still closed because 'it is impossible for the staff to work it'. The Reverend William Maguire, superintendent of the North Belfast Mission in Frederick Street and, together with other Belfast superintendent ministers, a member of the Mission Committee, offered to accept responsibility for it and in March 1898 it was reopened under his guidance.

The second item on the Mission's declared agenda was 'To feed the poor and clothe the naked'. The deaconesses from the beginning were asking for clothing and were distributing what was offered where it was needed most. By the spring of 1899 a cheap-food depot was underway (a bun and a mug of tea for a halfpenny) and a second depot was opened in December 1903. Incidentally, the sale rather than the gift of food, albeit at nominal charges, demonstrated the conviction of staff and committee that some kind of payment helped to preserve a measure of human dignity. In 1904 the diary records that a soup kitchen was opened; in November of that year weather and poverty combined to lead to the publication of a leaflet indicating that 'Nourishing soup can be had daily at 12 o'clock: applicants to bring their own jugs: ½d. minimum charge per jug.' In addition, during the same month, 130 meals per day were being served.

Children were listed as a third area of concern. The slum children were gathered weekly into a Sunday afternoon school. One of the highlights every summer was the 'Arab excursion' and each Christmas had its 'waif festival'. The logistics of these operations were formidable. The Reverend John W. Young (whose late and respected father, Mr John Young, a convert in the 1889 tent services, was from an early date and for many years responsible for the Sunday school as a voluntary worker) recalls the precise arrangements which operated Sunday by Sunday for the serving of the meal. To control a Sunday school of between eight and nine hundred unruly children required careful preparation. The printed instructions given to every teacher and worker tell their own story:

## BELFAST CENTRAL MISSION.

# School for Waifs & Strays.

### RULES FOR TEACHERS.

I. –All teachers to be in their classes at 2-15 or earlier. This is necessary for the control of the school.

II.– –Teachers to strictly remain with their classes during school hours. By this means order will be maintained, and the children kept from mischief.

III.–Teachers will please insist on the scholars continuing in whatever classes their names are enrolled. If they are allowed to continually change, the Roll can never be properly marked.

IV.—A certain number of teachers will be named for the distribution of mugs, buns, and tea. These teachers will please go as soon as called, and their duty being performed they are expected to return to their classes as soon as possible.

V.—Those who distribute the mugs will be responsible for collecting them, and returning them to kitchen. It will help greatly if the other teachers will gather the mugs and have them in a convenient place for those whose duty it is to remove them.

VI.—During the tea time there is a tendency for the children to become noisy, so the teachers are earnestly requested to do their utmost to maintain order at this time, especially taking care to prevent any throwing of bread.

VII.—It will be easily understood how the absence of teachers causes disarrangement and trouble. Hence, teachers are urged to be regular in their attendance, but if they cannot be present they are expected to let the Superintendent know of their intended absence, and if possible to provide a substitute.

VIII.—As one object of the school is to reach the parents through the children, it is highly desirable that the teachers visit the children in their homes.

IX.—Whenever the children are asked to attend on a week-night the teachers are expected to assemble with them.

It was a more mammoth task still at Christmas and in the summer. There were regularly from twenty-five hundred to three thousand participants at Christmastime. For the summer excursion to Glenavy, Co. Antrim, or Bangor or Newcastle in Co. Down two trains and a number of bands were regularly required. Before the excursion, the colossal job of preparing food for twenty-five hundred children and two hundred workers was carried out. The children, preceded by the Grosvenor Hall band and a banner with the motif 'Save the Children' emblazoned on it, were escorted to the station and on to the train. Every one of them (and the workers) had two meals; all of them were cared for throughout the day, and at its end every child was taken back to Belfast and accounted for. Organisation of an incredibly high standard was required throughout; so too was the work of people willing to undertake, without complaint, the tasks allotted to them. Some tickets, issued to both children and workers on these excursions, survive. On each child's ticket was the rather optimistic condition of issue: 'This ticket is granted on the express understanding that the receiver will gladly obey orders during the day.' A deep commitment was expected from the workers or helpers: their duty was clear: 'In accepting this ticket, workers signify their intention of devoting the day to the interests of the children.' There was no question of leaving the children unattended and just having a free day at the sea. The diaries of several years contain, in the impeccable handwriting of the Reverend John N. Spence, the details of the food, minerals and milk required. The catering end was generally in the hands of another member, Mr James Smyth, whose son, a leading Belfast businessman, Mr Walter Smyth, is a trustee and was for many years a member of the Mission Committee.

'To rescue from the haunts of vice and sin': that too was part of the aim. Even before the Grosvenor Hall had been built, the 1893 report had referred to 'work in slumdom' among those who were 'debased and debauched to the last degree'. Academy Street was not the only street regarded as a 'place of ill fame'. An *Irish Christian Advocate* report on 7 December 1894 tells of the voluntary workers 'who descend into hell every Saturday afternoon'. The Mission's workers were never off duty. They did not regard Saturday as their only obligation; the factory and the work place were their mission field as well. They were to have no greater success than that which happened to one man in May 1905. His name was Ned Howard, a shipyard worker when he was fit enough to make his way to the Queen's Island. In his own words his story was published in the *Grosvenor Hall Herald*. Dissolute, a blasphemer and an atheist, he was the despair of his wife and family: they were neglected and the children were without clothes or comfort. Weekends were spent drinking and if he was fit to go to work on Monday, the men in the yard gave him the cold shoulder. His name was a byword. He was at his lowest throughout April 1905; his blasphemy and drunken habits had caught up with him. One morning in early May he plucked up courage to speak to another workman about the state he was in. The man he spoke to was a member of the Grosvenor Hall, who was equal to the challenge. Life changed that day for Ned Howard and to the end of his years he was one of the Mission's most respected members and workers. His son Ted, with his wife and their daughters, are among the devoted members of the Hall today, and his great granddaughter and her daughters are frequently in their place on Sunday mornings.

Alcohol and drink trafficking were constant targets. They were recognised as a social evil and denounced as such. Full-time staff and voluntary workers stood shoulder to shoulder in the fight. Pledge-signing was consistently advocated and 'temperance' missions and meetings were no unusual occurrences. The work was not without its disappointments; the 1907 report posed the despairing question: 'Can a female drunkard ever be saved?' The plain answer is that many were. As early as December 1894, Crawford Johnson was contemplating the benefits of providing a 'coffee bar' as an alternative to the public house. 'There is no point,' he said, 'in declaring and denouncing evil if we as Christian men do not move forward.' So the Happy Evenings on Saturday nights were provided. Lantern slides and cinematograph shows became a routine part of the menu. The appointment of the well-known A.R. Hogg as the Mission's photographer and projectionist ensured good-quality production. Before long Mr Hogg was to be found providing promotional shows in provincial centres in aid of the Mission.

The ravages and degradation caused by unemployment were faced as well. In the 1898 report the superintendent declared: 'Sooner or later those engaged in Mission work on a wide scale will be confronted with the social question.' In the 1902 report he said:

> To plead with a man concerning his soul while his body is starving is to go near to making him a sceptic: but at the same time to give alms for the body without asking concerning the welfare of the soul is ceasing to follow in the footsteps of Christ.

A house-cleaning-and-repair squad was formed and a labour yard started in 1903. The latter gave steady employment to many over several years and was a stepping stone to more satisfying work; at one stage it was employing as many as forty men. For a period it operated under the management of James Dixon. There was no starry-eyed attitude to what they were doing, as a minute of one committee meeting in 1904 makes clear: 'It helps to sift the deserving from the impostures [sic].'

In the 1901 declaration Crawford Johnson had concluded with the hopeful aim: 'To make Belfast like unto the City of God'. In the closing years of the Victorian era his vision was a not unnatural dream, not dissimilar to the dream of the great missionary, C.T. Studd: 'To win the world for Christ in one generation'. It was not to be: the dreams of both men remain unfulfilled, but it was important that the attempt was made and made in all good faith.

During these years, a large building in Glengall Street, owned by Messrs May and now the headquarters of the Ulster Unionist Party, was pressed into use and named Glengall House. As it was costing £275 per year to rent, it was relinquished, and a new purpose-built annexe was erected at the rear of the new Grosvenor Hall at a cost of £5,000. Electric light, heating and ventilation for the Hall were also provided in 1900.

Grosvenor Hall was quickly in great demand by outside bodies as well as by larger Methodism. The lettings provided useful income but even before it was opened the foresight of Crawford Johnson was evident. He had his own political convictions – he has been described as liberal unionist with socialist leanings; there is no trace, however, of any party-political allegiance in his public utterances. Whatever his politics, he was convinced that the Hall was no place for party-political activity. But he was ready to use it and did so for strike meetings – like several of his successors, he believed that if people had a grievance, or thought they had, it was better to talk and reason it out. He even spoke on occasion to strikers in the Hall. On 27 September 1894 the trustees reached a 'definite understanding that the Hall should not be used for any political purpose as generally understood'. It was a decision to stand the trustees, and their successors, in good stead on more than one occasion.

As early as 1891 Crawford Johnson had written about the 'Four Ds'. Three of them were all too well known: dirt, drink and the devil. He added a fourth – DEBT – and in terms of the Mission's finances, it was destroying him. Throughout the period he appealed again and again for help to liquidate it. The general public of many denominations gave well but from time to time he felt that his ministerial brethren and their circuits in Belfast could do more. The income generated by the literature department, with its 'penny hopefuls', supported the wage of one deaconess, and the Happy Evenings were a regular and valuable source of revenue. However, it was not until 1902 that a grant of £2,000 from the Twentieth-Century Fund of Methodism, a challenge offer of £1,000 from another source, and the giving of the congregation enabled him to rejoice in the *Irish Christian Advocate* on 24 October at the 'lifting of the cloud'.

There were other worries as well as debt. There was hostility with whispering criticism and innuendo about 'sheep stealing'. Crawford Johnson rebutted the charge. He claimed that not a single one of his converts had been a member of any other Church. He continued: 'We want to hear no more of the unnecessary and unworthy gossip from other Churches of which we catch rumours from time to time.'

He had other tasks as well. There were invitations to civic functions and to serve on civic committees. Senior assistant secretary of the Conference when he was appointed to the Mission, he had been elected as a delegate to the Oecumenical Methodist Conference (now the World Methodist Conference) in 1891 and to the General Conference of the American Methodist Episcopal Church in 1896. The *Irish Christian Advocate* of 19 June 1896 disclosed the award two months earlier of an honorary doctorate of divinity by the Victoria University, Toronto. At a welcome-home party on his return from the American Conference the news was made known. In his response to the greetings he disclosed that he had on a number of previous occasions declined the award of honorary doctorates and would have done the same again had it not been for the fact that he had first learned of the Victoria award in a newspaper report and was not willing to offend the university. He had become the Irish Home Missions secretary in 1892 and a year later he was elected secretary of the Irish Methodist Conference and secretary of the Methodist Church in Ireland. Four of his successors in the Mission superintendency were also to be secretaries of the Conference. They and other secretaries would smile and perhaps be jealous at a contemporary's assessment of his secretaryship which appeared in the *Irish Christian Advocate* on 18 June 1897:

> Crawford Johnson is far away the astutest organiser we have. He has all the business of the Conference cut and dried and pigeon holed, ready for discussion and resolution and will leave nothing undone to facilitate despatch.

The Conference of 1898 did him the unusual honour of electing him secretary and vice-president in the same year. (It should be noted that the vice-presidency is the highest honour the Irish Conference can confer on any of its ministers. Today it carries with it, as a by-product, the presidency of the Church.) The Conference was ready to see him occupy both positions, but on his election to the position of vice-president, he withdrew from the secretaryship. (As a matter of interest, the documents of the Mission and the minutes contain no reference to any of these extramural honours that came his way.)

From 1901 Crawford Johnson's health deteriorated. In that year he was away from his duties for several months and then came back again. Nonetheless, he had to request permission from the 1902 Conference to retire for one year. After a lengthy holiday in South Africa, he returned at the Mission's invitation to the superintendency in 1902 but his energy had gone. He carried on for two more years and finally sought permanent retirement in 1905, offering to preach from time to time as and when he was able to do so.

# 5

## IN BRICK FIELDS AND BEYOND
### 1905–14

R obert Moubray Ker succeeded Crawford Johnson in 1905
when he was just beginning his tenth year in the ministry.
He was born in 1872 in Newtownbutler, Co. Fermanagh,
the fifth son of the Reverend and Mrs Robert Ker. His father had
dropped the second 'r' in the family name so as to avoid confusion
with another Robert Kerr also in the Methodist ministry. 'RM' had
been sent to Methodist College, Belfast, and gained his place on
the 1st XV rugby team. In October 1888 a severe wetting resulted
in an illness which brought him to the point of death. He was
never allowed to play rugby again but he retained his love for the
game. Thankful that he had been spared, life for him took on a
new meaning. In a published tribute to his father, Ernest Ker
describes what happened:

> He now resolved to dedicate himself to the discipleship of Christ. I
> am sure that none will deem it inappropriate to write of this turning
> point. To overlook it would be to leave unexplained the rest of my
> father's career. . . In June 1894 he was accepted as a candidate for
> the ministry.

The years 1905–14 were traumatic in Ulster's history. Belfast was
to be rocked by massive labour troubles: eighty years on, in trade-
union circles the carters' strike of 1907 is still vividly referred to.
The Home Rule cloud returned with a dramatic persistence. The
thousands living in the crowded streets and alleys near the north
Belfast waterfront and the thousands in Ballymacarrett on the other
side of Belfast Lough must almost have been deafened by the
staccato hammering of the rivets being driven home in the new
ships that were making the two firms of Harland and Wolff and
Workman Clark the envy of the shipbuilding world. In the morning

and evening rush hours the convoys of tramcars, with their 'Workmen Only' signs, trundled backwards and forwards to the Queen's Island loaded and overloaded with their 'dunchered' Islandmen, some of them precariously hanging on to whatever they could grasp on the staircases or open platforms. Twice a day the Queen's Bridge could be a veritable sea of capped and overalled humanity sweeping all before it, walking, running or being pushed along either to or from the shipyard. That swirling mass is well described in Ulster poet Richard Rowley's lines:

> Terrible as an army with banners,
> Through the dusk of the winter evening,
> Over the bridge
> The thousands tramp. . .

It was the same with the linen mills and ropeworks. In Belfast there was work in plenty for many, but not for all, throughout those history-packed years.

There was, however, another side to the story. On 24 August 1913 the *Irish Christian Advocate* reported the city's medical superintendent officer Dr W.H. Bailie's findings that in the previous year 802 citizens had died from tuberculosis and that there were at the time of his report another 741 persons in hospital suffering from this disease. According to the 1912 census, approximately 450 families in Belfast were each living in one room despite the fact that in the city there were over ten thousand empty houses. Tuberculosis and poverty went hand in hand, and poverty also had other agonising companions.

The Grosvenor Hall was not then and never has been an ivory tower. It was affected by the kaleidoscope of the changing scene. Besides the appalling conditions of the poor, it had other challenges to face. The new building was not without its deficiencies and the annexe had to be replanned and considerably enlarged. Further borrowing was necessary. Flooding on the Grosvenor Road in 1907 (which was to be a recurring problem) caused major damage and led to protracted correspondence and threatened litigation with the city surveyor and Belfast Corporation. Adjoining property developments made for difficulties as well. Warden Brothers had acquired Ginnet's Circus and had opened

Belfast's Grand Opera House. It was a significant acquisition for the city but in its early days it was to be a source of major irritation and concern to the Mission. To provide the Grand Opera House with light and power, the owners erected a large generator on the Grosvenor Hall side of the building. For the next five or six years the noise it created gave rise to almost constant legal negotiation between Warden Brothers and the trustees. The committee minutes of the period bear eloquent testimony to the time, energy and effort required before what was a technical problem rather than one of a lack of good will was sorted out. Another property problem was a large four-storey warehouse, erected immediately beside the Grosvenor Hall on its western side. Its weight caused major cracking in the fabric of the Hall. Again there were long and difficult negotiations before a satisfactory settlement was reached. There was also trouble over the rating of the Hall itself. Its unorthodox outreach in the Saturday Happy Evenings led the Belfast Corporation to insist that it did not merit relief from rates. The trustees did not agree and the result was a legal war of attrition which finished in the High Court with a case heard by the Lord Chief Baron in October 1912. The result was that the Mission was exempted from the Police Rate but was held liable for the Poor and General Purposes Rate.

There was also the question of the Falls Road church in Divis Street which had been erected in 1854. Situated on the edge of the Pound and not too far from Sandy Row, it was perilously near the community interface. In August 1864 it had been damaged in intercommunity violence. Its work had become more and more difficult and in March 1904 the Mission Committee was asked to undertake responsibility for it together with its school and church at Andersonstown. For the next two years the Reverend John N. Spence and a deaconess gave it their concentrated attention but the results were disappointing. Eventually in March 1906, with great reluctance, the committee decided to seek relief of the burden on two main grounds: the impossibility of carrying out the type of work associated with the Hall and expected by the Conference; and the questionable stewardship of resources. In June it formally requested the Conference to relieve it of a responsibility which 'kept two of our best workers there while so many fields are white unto harvest. Had the same amount of concentration been available in Avenue Hall last winter the nucleus of a new congregation would have been easily formed.' At the 1906 Conference Falls Road became part of the Agnes Street circuit and remained so until its demolition in the mid-1960s to make way for the Divis complex, following acquisition by the Northern Ireland Housing Trust.

The time given to electricity generators, bricks and mortar, or litigation with the rating authorities was not allowed to stand in the way of the work of evangelism, which was pursued with fervour and success. Conversions took place regularly at Sunday worship. An intriguing minute of a committee meeting in 1906 refers to the conversion of one unnamed person 'who is now filling an honourable position in Methodist College, Belfast'. R.M. Ker and his colleagues had every reason to write in the 1912 report that 'The influence of the Grosvenor Hall Mission has spread further and gone deeper into the lives of the poor of the city than one would think possible.' A year later the report talked about the Hall, 'tightly wedged in between temples of pleasure and houses of industry, surrounded on all sides by the world, the flesh and the devil'. The gospel preached by R.M. Ker and his colleagues was a practical gospel. As with Crawford Johnson, they believed in challenging their converts to relate their faith to everyday life and civic and social duty. The title of one sermon in January 1907 was by no means unusual: 'The citizen in the polling booth'.

The weekly programme went on irrespective of other concerns. The Happy Evenings had become a popular feature of Belfast life but they were not without their ups and downs. It was difficult to sustain a high quality of programme and there were occasions when the standard fell. One correspondent wrote indignantly to the *Belfast Telegraph* in November 1913 that

> Handel would have turned in his grave if he had heard how one of his well-known works had been performed the previous Saturday evening in one of Belfast's best known halls. The performance had been an exhibition of incompetence and cheek.

Nonetheless, it was no longer possible to accommodate the

numbers wishing to be present and it had also become necessary to provide a children's afternoon session as well.

On the first Saturday of the 1906 season R.M. Ker said expense would not be spared and the cinematograph would play a large part in the programmes. New films would be procured and it was the intention of the promoters to have them as pure and healthy in tone as possible. Mr Ker went on to say of the cinematograph: 'It is evident that the little instrument has come to stay.' They had no hesitation in making use of it. Of itself it was neutral; it would be and was used to the glory of God. The advertising leaflets often carried the claim: 'A thousand feet of living pictures will draw a thousand spectators.' Year by year the footage was increased but there was a limit beyond which capacity audiences could not be increased. A random leaflet for a Happy Evening in 1912 included such masterpieces as *Bunny and the Twins, Max and the Donkey, Wild Duck Shooting, Those Eyes,* and *A Husband's Awakening.*

Then there were the lectures for working men – a kind of Grosvenor Hall 'Workers' Educational Association'. Hundreds often booked for a season of lectures by some of the most distinguished scientists and scholars of the time. Sir Robert Ball FRS lectured on 'Recent discoveries about the sun'. He was followed by Professor L.C. Miale FRS, FGS, on 'Gnats and mosquitoes'. There were lectures on 'British spiders', 'Flying machines', 'Experiences in Russian Polish jails' and one by the president of the British Association, Sir David Gill KCB, LL D, on 'Stars and nebulae'.

There was work in the shipyards and linen mills by day but there were poverty and degradation in the city's brick fields by night. There are still people in Belfast who remember these well-known features of the outward spread of the city. In the early years of the twentieth century they were for the Mission a new field of practical Christian caring. Stories began to reach the Hall that poverty could be seen as nowhere else in the Springfield brick fields. Extant documents refer again and again to a story of stark human misery. R.M. Ker left a vivid pen-picture of what the Mission did. Night after night, Mission workers accompanied him and the young Reverend John N. Spence, bringing warm tea and food into a shadowy world of grown men and boys shivering and huddling together against the warm walls of the brick kilns. One night they found in one group alone sixty-five men, their average age was about twenty. The demands on the staff could never have been met had it not been for, to quote the superintendent from minutes of a March 1906 meeting, the 'most harmonious working among the hundreds of volunteers. The worries have been few and the inspirations very numerous.' He also paid tribute to those who had been involved as stewards for the large audiences on Saturdays and Sundays. These were led by Richard Addis, the first of a line of dependable chief stewards. He said that the stewards 'so wisely controlled the audiences that he had a minimum of trouble'. The pattern set then was to last right down to the 1970s when the film services, which had taken the place of the Happy Evenings, came to an end.

Richard Addis had his successors – John Stewart, John Allen, who died suddenly, Robert Ferris sen., for a few months, to be succeeded by his son Robert Ferris jun., and finally William T. Millington, all of them were supported by their cohorts. They were powers in the land. One superintendent at an industrial service had agreed to receive the banners of the trade unions at the Communion rail. The stewards said 'No': there would be no suggestions of 'red or any other form of unacceptable politics'; but in many ways they were a very liberal and tolerant group of men. The big moment in the halcyon days of large attendances was the reception of the offering on Sunday evenings. At a pre-arranged signal two lines of fifteen men entered from opposite doors led by the chief steward and his deputy. It was always a 'high' moment, provided the entry was synchronised. One Sunday night the signal was given on one side and mischievously hidden on the other with the result that one line arrived and the other did not.

Large numbers of waif children continued to roam the streets uncared for. Even as late as 1913 the Belfast School Attendance Committee reported that in 1912 school attendance averaged 76 per cent; a year before compulsory schooling in 1892 was introduced it was 66 per cent. In other words thirty-four children out of every hundred were on 'the loose' in one way or another. Again and again the deaconesses were unearthing extreme misery and degradation. There was the report that came one morning to the

Hall: a man had booked himself and his infant son into a lodging house. His wife, he said, had left him and he needed a roof above their heads and some care and attention. After settling in, he went out 'to do some shopping'. He never returned. The landlady was left with the infant and she cared for him as long as she could. Eventually she sent to the Grosvenor Hall for assistance and advice. She clearly had neither right nor ability to keep the child. The Mission Sister brought the infant back to the Hall; enquiries were of no avail. The Mission's lack of a children's home was all too apparent. Arrangements were made with Dr Barnardo's to take the boy – but what was he to be called? There was no information about his birth or parentage. The Baptismal Register of the year tells the story. It would be invidious to record the full name; however, it can be said that the words 'Grosvenor Hall' appear among the names given to him. The following note was entered on the register by Mr Ker: 'This child was found deserted in a lodging-house by Miss Spence. She took charge of him. . . No particulars can of course be given of birth, age or parentage.' He was only one of many children who were to owe their start in life to the caring work of the Hall in those early days.

The routine programme went on year in, year out. The summer excursion continued to be an annual highlight. Some of the diary comments between 1907 and 1909 are fascinating. In 1907 the Reverend John N. Spence recorded: 'Mrs Hudson Shepherd kindly provided a brake for the smallest children. Whilst the kindness of this act is much appreciated, it caused a great deal of trouble separating the eligible.' On the excursion to Bangor the same year they brought fifty gallons (227 litres) of skim milk. 'This proved a positive nuisance, the children drinking for drinking's sake.' In 1908 the excursion, again to Bangor, was 'a disaster'. They had more than their share of July rain and the Reverend John N. Spence complained of 'listless workers'. A year later he noted: 'We could have done with more Paris buns, the sugar buns being a sticky commodity.'

By 1908 the deaconesses, officially referred to as the Sisters of the Mission, had established a reputation for caring that brought them into the field of probation work. Increasingly the city magistrates were glad to hand over Probation of Offender Act cases to them. Repeatedly it was reported to the Mission Committee that 'the police court work was progressing or developing very satisfactorily'. On 13 June 1911 the *Belfast News-Letter* reported that at the Recorder's Court on 12 June 1911 Judge Craig observed: 'If Miss Curran's work is an example, the Central Mission is doing excellent work in the city.' It was an example to be repeated and two other colleagues, Miss Elliott and Mr James Dixon, were to spend most of their time before that year was out as probation officers. Like most of the Mission's work, the results in this field were incalculable. On 31 March 1911 the *Irish Christian Advocate* reported Mr Ker's claim that 'many of the waifs and strays had become noble men and women, citizens of whom Belfast could be proud'.

Shortly after his appointment as superintendent, Mr Ker had written about three urgent needs. They were:

1  A social wing at Grosvenor Hall
2  A Home for fallen women
3  Proper accommodation for a 'man down on his luck'.

The first of these needs had been met fairly quickly. The replanning and enlargement of the annexe had made the day-to-day social work much easier.

What was to be done regarding the work among women? How heavy the challenge was can be gauged from a report made to one committee meeting in 1910. During that year, it was stated that 'sixteen women and girls had been placed in the Salvation Army Home, eleven in Edgar Home, four restored to parents and twenty-eight children have been placed in other homes'. In late 1908 and early 1909 an opportunity had arisen to do something practical for young women. A large house in Whitehead, Co. Antrim, had come on the market. It was drawn to the attention of the superintendent and committee almost certainly by the late Mr John Young, who, though he had recently gone to live in Whitehead, still made the journey every Sunday to Belfast in order to attend the services and take care of the afternoon school. The house was acquired and in October 1909 Mr Ker informed the committee that over five hundred underpaid factory girls had had a holiday that would otherwise have been impossible. By the summer of 1913 it was necessary to purchase 'a new and more suitable home', again in Whitehead. This also made possible the commencement of children's holidays and on 20 October of the same year the committee learned that 'one hundred and fifty puny children had been sent for a week to the sea in September'. So started the holiday programmes that have gone on for over seventy years, catering for the old, the young and underprivileged without reference to class or creed.

The outbreak of war in 1914 effectively put an end – though Mr Ker may not have realised it – to his dream of proper accommodation for the man 'down on his luck'. He discovered, as his predecessor had done, and as his successors would find, that with available resources there were limits to the amount of work that could be undertaken at any one time.

Meanwhile the political temperature had risen inexorably after 1906: storm clouds were on the horizon and Ulster Protestants did not like what they saw. Church life all over the country was affected and Methodism was not immune. As in other denominations, those who favoured Home Rule and some concessions to the nationalists were no more popular with their fellow-religionists than were supporters of the Anglo-Irish Agreement in 1985. Amazingly, the minutes of the Mission Committee make only two passing references to the controversy. Mr Ker, however, in a *Grosvenor Hall Herald* issue of 1910, made an appeal to the congregation that in the coming election members with differing political views should continue in fellowship, as they had done in the past. Also of interest is an undated letter which reads as follows:

Dear Mr Reid,

After your deputation left, the Trustees had a long and earnest conversation on the matter which had been put before them. The majority of them are still of the opinion that the Hall should not be used for the purpose suggested by your committee and they are all the more sorry to have to take this view as they realise that they are seeming to go against the wishes of many of the members of the Methodist Church. The legal difficulty I mentioned to you before still seem [sic] to them extremely great, and moreover they are persuaded that the policy of keeping all meetings, which might be

The gospel was preached at many places; this meeting is at Commercial Court, Belfast, c. 1913.

Summer excursions to the seaside helped the children to widen horizons, dream dreams and revel in new experiences. This trip in 1913 was to Newcastle.

Miss Annie Coulter (second row, third from right) and one of her prize-winning Sunshine Choirs in 1915; next to her is R.M. Ker.

# For God, and Home, and Little Children!

SOLDIERS' MOTHERLESS CHILDREN IN GROSVENOR HALL HOLIDAY HOME.

A publicity leaflet
depicting the first
group of the wartime
'family' at
Whitehead Home,
c. 1916.

The Grosvenor Hall band at Methodist College, Belfast, c. 1919. The band still makes a significant contribution to the Mission's work.

Throughout the 1920s the 'railway carriage' at Orlock served as a holiday home. It was purchased in 1931 by Edward Howard (far right), seen here with members of his family.

Two of the early 'greats' getting the 1922 summer excursion underway – Ned Howard (left) and Johnny Allen (front right); Dr W.L. Northridge is standing in front of the banner.

City-centre traffic
came to a standstill
on 29 October 1926
for the funeral of

considered by even a section as political, outside the Hall, and which they have carried out successfully for years is that which they should still adopt considering the divergent views of those interested in the work of the Mission.

As to welcoming the ladies, who would like to rest in the rooms of the Hall on the night of the Demonstration, there is only one mind about that, and I can assure you the Sisters of the Mission will be happy to entertain them.

There was no indication whatever as to the exact occasion referred to in the letter, though it is fairly obvious that it had probably something to do with the Home Rule controversy. Some considerable time later recourse was had to the first minute book of the trustees of Grosvenor Hall and the mystery was unravelled. On 5 February 1912 the trustees had before them a request from the lord mayor of Belfast for the use of the Grosvenor Hall as a military barracks, should there be a need for such use on the occasion of Winston Churchill's controversial visit to Belfast planned for that month in support of Home Rule. The request was unanimously refused on the grounds that 'the work associated with the Grosvenor Hall left them no option in the matter'. At the conclusion of the meeting Mr Ker intimated that on the previous evening he had had an 'approach from the Methodist Anti-Home Rule Committee who wanted the use of the Hall for a Methodist demonstration on 14 March'. The trustees considered the request 'inappropriate'. The background to the approach was a preliminary anti-Home Rule meeting held in the Ulster Minor Hall in early February. It was reported that there was 'no bombast, no boasting, no bitterness but only the resolution of a quiet determination not to have Home Rule'. This committee wrote to the *Irish Christian Advocate* announcing their decision to hold a monster Methodist demonstration. They had concluded: 'Let all Methodists, who are Unionists from whatever standpoint, see to it that they do not compromise themselves and their friends by any promise to refrain from active support of our movement.' The letter was signed 'the Reverend T.W. Davidson, the Reverend H.G. Collier, Messrs John B. Aicken, R.W. Charlesson, A.T. Farrell, William Fulton, John B. McCutcheon (Hon. Secs.) and Joseph Reid (Secretary, 105 Royal Avenue, 7 February 1912)'. All of them were men of standing or substance or both.

Although their request had been declined, they were not to be put off so easily. They requested the trustees to receive a deputation. This request could not be refused, and so on 1 March a deputation of six influential members of the Anti-Home Rule Committee pressed strongly for the decision to be rescinded. The case was made at length and eventually they withdrew. The minute of the meeting records:

> A long and earnest conversation took place, the matter being regarded both from the legal and also from the standpoint of the influence such a demonstration might have upon the work of the Mission itself. Mr Shaw moved and Mr Bigger seconded that the request of the Committee be granted. This on being put to the meeting was lost – two voting for and four against.

Why there was not an outcry among the Methodist and Protestant people of the city is at first sight hard to understand. The decision was clearly, and on the admission of the trustees themselves, controversial. Irish Methodism was unquestionably and by a large majority against Home Rule. In the event the demonstration was held on 14 March 1912. It took more than one sitting of the Ulster Hall to house the Methodists who wished to protest their loyalty and on that day two Methodist demonstrations were held within it. There were also two demonstrations in the Exhibition Hall and an overflow in the People's Hall of the North Belfast Mission. How then, in the face of all the excitement and controversy, did the Grosvenor Hall trustees escape criticism? One of the signatories of the letter from the Methodist Anti-Home Rule Committee was John B. McCutcheon. A well-known Belfast solicitor, he was also legal advisor to the Grosvenor Hall trustees and though he was one of the strongest Methodist opponents of Home Rule, he did not allow his political convictions to run away with his legal good sense. He advised the trustees that to grant the Hall could well prejudice their case in the rating litigation. Almost certainly he must also have persuaded his anti-Home Rule colleagues that the Hall and its trustees should not be sucked into a potentially damaging controversy. The trustees' responses to the requests leave no doubt that the Mission had its friends far outside the ranks of unionism and the trustees were not prepared to offend them or to compromise on their policy regarding the use of the Hall for party-political purposes. So it is still.

The decade concluded with the Conference of 1914. As far as the Mission was concerned, two events occurring within days of each other in April of that year brought great sadness. On 10 April the *Irish Christian Advocate* reported the deaths of Dr Crawford Johnson on 5 April, and of Mr T. Foulkes Shillington on 8 April. For many years they had worked together in the closest harmony and in death they were not divided.

T. Foulkes Shillington's contribution to the development and consolidation of the Mission's work cannot be overestimated. His supervision of the finances had been meticulous. He had put his considerable business expertise and reputation at the disposal of Crawford Johnson and his successor R.M. Ker. On top of his considerable business commitments, he was also a member of the senate of Queen's University Belfast and a life governor of the Royal Victoria Hospital. In 1902 he had presented Craigmore, his family home in Aghalee, Co. Antrim, to the Methodist Church for use as a boys' home, which was eventually amalgamated with the Mission's children's home at Childhaven in Millisle, Co. Down.

As for Crawford Johnson, his death was widely reported and reference made to it in the Churches of other denominations as well as in his own Methodism. The leading newspapers, including the nationalist *Irish News*, carried long obituary notices. The 1914 Conference paid its last tribute to its outstanding son. It did so at considerably greater length than those usually accorded to deceased ministers. Fittingly, the tribute said:

> The Belfast Central Mission must ever be regarded as Dr Johnson's chief and lasting monument. . . His pity for the sinful, his compassion for the waif child, his advocacy of civic righteousness and his great success in reaching the careless and outcast, soon secured the attention and won the respect and esteem of the citizens.

It also, most unusually, made a point of mentioning the sons of Crawford Johnson. It had good reason to do so. The Mission may have lost its founder but it still had the Johnson family very much in its thoughts and among its supporters. One son, Philip, had died in 1907. It had been his intention to make a gift to the Hall to help with the acquisition of a worthy pipe organ. After his son's death his father gave a substantial sum which encouraged the purchase of an organ dedicated to Philip's memory. Another son, Alfred, was the first to preside over it and a third son, Henry, was later to be the devoted and efficient honorary treasurer of the Mission for many years. The Johnson name lived on.

# 6

# IN WAR AND ITS AFTERMATH
## 1914–26

The omens in the early summer of 1914 were not good. The secular and religious press alike were increasingly concerned with the build up of armies and armaments and the ever-growing probability of war with Germany. Despite these fears, however, Ulster was preoccupied with the Home Rule Crisis. Throughout these turbulent months the Mission continued to be optimistic about its work. By mid-summer R.M. Ker's long-established superintendency was in its eleventh successful year. All seemed set for a lively expansion of the outreach programme, when, on 4 August 1914, war was declared.

Like Crawford Johnson, R.M. Ker had around him a magnificent band of workers, committee members and advisors. Mr Henry M. Anderson, later the legal advisor of the Ulster Bank, had succeeded his brother Hugh as honorary secretary, when Hugh, the first layman to hold the office (1898–1902), had been transferred to a bank outside Belfast. Henry remained as honorary secretary until 1939 when he became honorary treasurer until his retirement in 1947. Hugh's departure had been a loss to the Mission. His son Frank was for many years a devoted honorary secretary and two members of the family are still associated with the Mission's work – Henry's son, Mr Robin H. Anderson, a trustee and committee member, and Mrs Margaret Anderson, Frank's widow, an indefatigable supporter. At the closing services in the old Hall in 1926, after paying tribute to the late Mr T. Foulkes Shillington, Mr Ker went on to say:

There has been with me today the memories of the men who saw this day by faith. . . Charles Young, Joe Bustard, Joe Montgomery, Thomas Fullerton, George Whitten, Richard Addis, Philip Johnson,

51

Jack Daly and scores of others. I want to put for the last time in the old Grosvenor Hall a wreath of memory upon their graves.

At the 1914 Conference the Reverend John N. Spence was transferred to Dublin as superintendent of the Dublin Central Mission. His departure was a loss. He was succeeded by the Reverend W. Johnstone Hunter, a good appointment which was interrupted very suddenly by his work with the Young Men's Christian Association on the battlefields of France and still later in 1917 as a chaplain to the armed forces. His successor, the Reverend John J. Daly, was not appointed until 1919. In June 1914 the most immediate concern was to find someone to take the honorary treasurership. Mr A.C. Marshall, the head of a milling firm, was approached. He agreed to act but later found himself under so much pressure that he was reluctantly compelled to decline the appointment. It was June 1915 before his place was taken by Mr David J. Lindsay, who was to give almost a decade of interested and valuable service in that position. After Mr Lindsay's death, Mr Henry M. Johnson, a son of the founder, succeeded him in May 1925.

The 1914 summer programme had gone ahead normally. The waifs' excursion to Newcastle, Co. Down, had catered for twenty-six hundred children. The customary tent mission had been held and the Sunday congregations had been good. However, by October the situation was transformed out of all recognition. A committee minute of October 1914 tells the story:

> The appeal of Lord Kitchener for recruits was loyally responded to by the workers of the Mission. About forty men of all departments including Mr John Young, a member of the Committee and Superintendent of the Arab Sunday School, joined the new armies. Besides, a considerable number of reservists were called up from families under the care of the Mission. Some departments of the work had to be reorganised.

For the next four years and long afterwards the effects of World War I were evident in the Mission's work and above all else in the agony and heartbreak of Mission families. Issue after issue of the congregational magazine, the *Grosvenor Hall Herald*, contained references to members reported as missing or wounded, and all too frequently 'killed in action'. In 1916 the Easter Rising in Dublin went without reference in the records: not so the Battle of the Somme. The Grosvenor Hall congregation was not exempt from the appalling carnage: the losses were irreparable. The committee regularly sent messages of greeting to two of its members, Mr Alfred W. Johnson, Crawford Johnson's son and an early volunteer, and to Mr John Young, who was called up with the Young Citizen Volunteers, was wounded at the Somme and who, though offered a commission, was content to serve as Sergeant Young in the Royal Irish Rifles for the remainder of the war.

On top of the war effort, high emigration also accounted for disruption within the Mission. A revealing reference to this development appeared in an article written by Mr Ker for the *Irish Christian Advocate* in December 1916:

> The Mission has given hundreds of its best and most promising lives for the enrichment of the Colonies... In some large towns and cities of Canada can be found enough ex-Mission members to form by themselves a small congregation.

Mr Young's place in the afternoon school was taken by Mr James Smyth. Along with the chief steward, Mr Richard Addis, Mr Smyth ensured the successful continuation of the school and of the big events at Christmas and in the summer, catering for crowds as large as ever. At Christmas, for feeding purposes, the children were divided into seventy-four groups and spread all over the Grosvenor Hall with two or three workers assigned to each group so that each child was adequately and fairly provided for.

The social work of the Mission was still called for. On 1 January 1915 the *Irish Christian Advocate* stated that fifty thousand free meals had been given in 1914. On 6 August 1915 its account of a summer excursion that month said: 'The usual large number was brought to the Donard field in Newcastle.' The report noted that:

> a good few were pallid and anaemic, while sores on heads, arms and legs, undressed and unattended, were all too numerous...

Many girls of eleven or twelve were carrying the latest baby in the household in their arms.

Today social workers and paediatricians might have diagnosed child abuse as well as poverty. Either way there was a need.

From 1915 a major social problem of dramatic and unexpected proportions became apparent in Belfast. A committee minute of October 1915 sets the scene:

> For some time it had been urged upon the Superintendent of the Mission by the Police Court Magistrates, the Society for the Prevention of Cruelty to Children and by the Soldiers' and Sailors' Families Association that the Mission would be doing a good work if it would undertake the care of those children of soldiers and sailors whose mothers or other remaining guardians were incapable through drinking, vicious habits, or broken health of attending to the little ones.

After careful consideration it was decided to allow Miss Harrison to remain in charge of the holiday home in Whitehead and to accept children as far as accommodation would allow, provided that the children's allowance, payable by the Government, should be paid to the superintendent of the Mission. So started the home for which there was soon so much demand that it was necessary to acquire larger property in Whitehead. Mr Ker reported to the 1919 Conference that during the four previous years, 370 children had been committed to his care. The work among these children meant greater financial problems as well as greater effort.

However, nothing was allowed to interfere with the Mission's outreach. Sunday congregations continued to be good in spite of the absence of servicemen. On 12 December 1916 the committee could be told: 'There are no empty seats on Sunday evenings.' The open-air services at the Custom House were never stopped. The Grosvenor Hall band provided an attraction at this venue from time to time, though by mid-1916 it was reported that 'attendances were less because of men at the war'. The Saturday Happy Evenings continued to be a popular and helpful morale booster and a valuable factor in the work of the Mission. The programme frequently featured film reports from battlefields and other news about the war effort. Sunday sermons had their references and comments as well — not always in the most charitable of New Testament tradition. On 31 March 1916 the *Irish Christian Advocate* quoted one chaplain to the forces, addressing the Mission's anniversary meeting and winning applause with the declaration: 'The way the Germans are fighting the war proves to everybody they are barbarians, not human beings.'

One social problem which called for repeated attention was the simple use of alcohol, not merely its abuse. Mr Ker and his colleagues regarded it as not only something which hampered the war effort but as a moral menace and home-breaker. From a sermon delivered in the Hall in December 1916, the *Grosvenor Hall Herald* quoted the eminent Reverend R. Lee Cole when he categorically stated: 'If peace came today, Belfast would have the same disgraceful scenes as it had on Mafeking night.' (It is interesting to note that in the same sermon he warned that the 'country should beware lest Pope Benedict [rides] to power in the [peace] negotiations'.) Dr William Temple, at that time rector of St James's, Piccadilly, and later to become Archbishop of Canterbury, regarded strong drink as a moral and national danger. There were many who shared Dr Temple's views, not least among them George V. Mr Ker was in good company.

The death took place in 1921 of the Reverend John J. Daly after a protracted and distressing illness which had resulted in a complete loss of sight. The courage and faith with which he faced death left a profound mark on the congregation. The Reverend Dr William L. Northridge, the biblical scholar, who had joined the staff a year previously as third minister, replaced him.

Trade depression and unemployment followed the cessation of hostilities in 1918 and these were accompanied by communal unrest. All made the Mission's work harder. Nonetheless, there was a steady consolidation. There was no lessening in demand for places in the Whitehead home. Other provision was needed to enable the holiday programme to proceed uninterrupted. Accommodation for sick and needy children was secured at Orlock and Portavogie in Co. Down. New families were added to the congregational rolls in large numbers. There was also, most surprisingly, an upturn in finances. Thus it was possible, early in 1923, for the Mission Committee to refer formally to something which had been talked about for a long time. That was the need for new buildings as Crawford Johnson's hall had outlived its usefulness; the committee responded positively and set about the planning process.

However, later that year unexpected difficulties confronted the committee and a special meeting was called on 2 November 1923 to discuss two items of special business. One was to approve the secondment of Dr Northridge for deputation work in America in connection with the appeal being made to American Methodists for financial support of the Forward Movement – the campaign to raise money to build new churches especially in Belfast. That request was approved willingly. The second matter was of far greater long-term import. It was to consider information that the trustees of Donegall Square church were proposing to erect a large hall and suite of central church offices and committee rooms on their city-centre site. The news had a traumatic effect. The Mission's superintendent and members alike realised that the plans they were already discussing for permanent and adequate buildings could well be duplicated if Donegall Square church were to go ahead. They asked for further details of what was proposed. During the same month, they received a deputation from the Donegall Square trustees. The Reverend F.E. Harte was the spokesman. He said that the Donegall Square building had been declared unsafe; there was a need to hurry so that the site could be preserved for the future. He added that no social work was contemplated and no opposition or rivalry intended – the proposed large hall being thought of was for local purposes.

There the matter lay until April 1924 when the Donegall Square trustees formally requested the Mission not to proceed with its plans until they (the Square trustees) had come to firm decisions as to what they were going to do. The Mission Committee agreed to defer action but indicated its reluctance to face a prolonged period of indecision; it would appreciate firm information one way or the other by 1 September. In the event, by December, no information had been received from either the Forward Movement, whose interest had been invoked, or from the Donegall Square trustees, and so on 15 December the Mission

Committee's unanimous decision was taken to commission plans for a new suite of buildings and to seek what help might be forthcoming from the Forward Movement. Incidentally this was to be the second and last occasion in all its history that the Mission was to seek help from the Methodist body as such.

During the period of these deliberations and uncertainties, Mrs Ker had been visiting America. She was travelling with Dr and Mrs Northridge. Dr Northridge's place for the year was taken by the young Reverend Robert A. Nelson, later to be spoken of as 'the best theologian the West has sent to Ceylon'. Throughout the visit, Mr Ker sent two letters a week to his wife. Those letters are in the possession of their daughter, Miss Hazel M. Ker. They give a fascinating picture of life in the superintendent's Rugby Road manse and of work in the Mission. There were the regular visits to the home in Whitehead and concern about the burdens carried by the matron, Miss Harrison, and her senior colleague, Miss Johnston. There are insights into the running of this and that organisation. He begrudged the time and nervous energy involved in entertaining visiting lecturers and artistes. He could not face the prospect of giving hour after hour humouring one well-known and somewhat difficult prima donna and he commandeered the inimitable help of Mrs Fullerton, the widow of Mr T.A. Fullerton, whose name appears on page after page of the Mission's early records. Mr Ker's next letter to America revealed that Mrs Fullerton had been too much for the guest singer. One evening she had kept her in conversation until 10.30 p.m. by which time the visitor had had enough.

In his day T.A. Fullerton had been in charge of York Street post office and on his death a quarter of century previously he had been succeeded by his widow. She has been immortalised by her late husband's distant relative, de Lacey Ferguson, an American academic who came to Ulster in the 1920s to seek out more of his roots. He can have written few more readable articles than his 'Woman of Ulster', a pen picture of the redoubtable Mrs Fullerton. He had made his way to the home of this remarkable woman. The pictures in her living room were the first things that caught his attention. In addition to photographs of her late husband, there were pictures of John Wesley, Benjamin Disraeli, the royal family and Edward Carson. She had two main interests in life – Ulster unionism and the Grosvenor Hall. She spoke of three great eras in Irish life. They were the pagan era, the Christian era, and the 'de Valera' (the devil era). But for all her strong opinions, when a loyalist mob came to burn out her Roman Catholic neighbours, she donned her coat and hat, went out into the street and having drawn herself up to her full height of four feet eleven, she told the leader of the mob to go: 'They are my neighbours and my friends. You don't touch them' – and they didn't, they went home. Mrs Fullerton reflected the Grosvenor Hall tradition of 'live and let live', a tradition that has existed up to the present day.

Mr Ker's letters to America kept his wife up to date with other events. There was information about the harvest services: flowers that year were in short supply but they had had one novelty – a canary in its cage. (In conformity with the accepted practice, decorations were auctioned at the conclusion of the weekend's services. That year, Ned Howard, who was acting as auctioneer, was open for bids for all that had been on show – including the canary.) There was also an unexpected piece of news about a neighbour who had 'got a new hat costing £10 and a new dress at £25 and even the handkerchief matched the dress'. One reference to the contemporary religious scene must be mentioned; it was about the famous Ulster-born American evangelist, W.P. Nicholson: 'I am glad that Nicholson has finished in Belfast. Whatever he does or does not do, he makes it harder for other people to do their work.'

By 1925 the plans to rebuild Grosvenor Hall were progressing satisfactorily. For some time Mr Hugh Turtle of Messrs McLaughlin and Harvey had been interested in what the Grosvenor Hall was doing. He volunteered to visit and inspect some recently-built Methodist mission premises in England. Accompanied by Mr Ker, he visited eleven English centres, and on their return they presented information and comments to Messrs Young and Mackenzie, the appointed architects for the work in Belfast. By 21 October plans for the new building were finally approved.

The estimated cost worked out at £50,000. The sum total of

cash in hand and promised donations was £10,000. There was a hope that the eminent Methodist benefactor, Mr Joseph Rank, might be persuaded to help an Irish mission just as he had helped many in England. A legendary name in the milling world, Mr Rank generously offered the gift of £10,000. The Forward Movement eventually consented to contribute a maximum of £10,000, 'if it became available'. Application was made to the Ministry of Labour for grant aid under unemployment relief regulations. The application was refused on the grounds that 'the building would be used for denominational purposes'. Mr Ker was no more easily deterred than Crawford Johnson would have been. Sir Samuel Kelly, Major D. Graham Shillington and Mr Hugh Turtle were appointed to accompany the superintendent on a deputation to the minister. By 4 November the superintendent was able to report to the committee that the minister had eventually consented to a grant of 60 per cent of the wages involved, provided that certain conditions were observed and that work commenced before 25 December. By 23 November a firm tender in the sum of £45,968 had been received and accepted from McLaughlin and Harvey and work began almost immediately afterwards. Temporary premises were acquired from the Barbour linen and thread company in Glengall Street. In addition, the use of the Wellington Hall and accommodation in Great Victoria Street was negotiated. Closing services in Grosvenor Hall were held on the first Sunday of January 1926 and the first pile was driven into the ground on 26 January. So the work went ahead, though not without its problems.

Mr Ker, who had been secretary of the Methodist Conference for some time, was elected vice-president of the Conference and president of the Church in July 1926. He reported to the July meeting of the Mission Committee that he had acquired additional accommodation for children's holidays at Groomsport, Co. Down. Earlier that month he and Mrs Ker had attended the graduation of their son Ernest at Queen's University Belfast and Mr Ker had then gone to attend the meetings of the British Methodist Conference being held that year in York. August allowed them a short but broken holiday in Portstewart, Co. Londonderry, and at the beginning of September an already overcrowded schedule became even more hectic. In addition to routine work, there was the pressure of preparation for the approaching stone-laying ceremony of the new hall planned for October. On top of all this was the unpredictable duty associated with the presidency. On successive days during the month he attended and spoke at meetings of the Belfast, Enniskillen and Derry District Synods and all of course before the days of car ownership by Methodist ministers.

On Thursday, 7 October Mr Ker paid a presidential visit to his old school, Methodist College. The headmaster, the late John Watson Henderson, asked him to address the pupils in full assembly. Mr Ker voiced his pride in the school's good name, its academic successes and the hope that it might have a long overdue win in the Ulster Schools' Rugby Cup that season. The hope was fulfilled the following St Patrick's Day – a day he did not see. The following week his duties brought him to Dublin for central Church committee meetings. On Saturday, 16 October he travelled to Cork where he was to preach on the Sunday and then on Monday he was to proceed on the traditional presidential visit to the circuits and congregations in west Cork. While in Dublin he had been affected by a severe drop in the temperature and he was still feeling its effects when he reached Cork. On Monday before leaving Cork he wrote to Mrs Ker: 'I was very tired on Saturday night but felt much better yesterday morning.' Tragically the improvement was short-lived. He insisted, however, on keeping his appointments each day but by the end of the week he was seriously ill. He managed to get back to Cork and to the home of his friend Mr John Musgrave, where he had stayed the previous weekend. Mrs Ker joined him and it soon became clear that there was no possibility whatever of his getting back to Belfast for the stone-laying ceremony the following week and he dictated a message which he wanted read at the ceremony. That was his last public action. In spite of the best medical advice and attention possible, he died in Cork on 27 October. His passing stunned the congregation; the community at large was shocked. Messages of sympathy from far and wide crowded in on Mrs Ker, among them, those from the Duke of Abercorn, the Governor of Northern Ireland, Lord Craigavon, Northern Ireland prime minister, and Mr W.T. Cosgrave, premier of the Irish Free State.

His funeral took place in Belfast on the day the foundation stones were to have been laid. It is still remembered and talked about over sixty years later by older members of the congregation. It had been his wish that the ceremony should go ahead but that was out of the question. The funeral service was held in Donegall Square church with the moderator of the Presbyterian General Assembly in the pulpit and in the presence of a capacity congregation which included the lord mayor and city chamberlain. The doors of the church were shut an hour before the service commenced. The crowds lining the funeral route and following the hearse left no doubt that R.M. Ker's funeral was one of the largest ever seen in the city. The moderator was one of the hundreds who walked to the city cemetery. Daily papers carried long tributes and the 1927 Conference recognised the Church's loss. One sentence said everything: 'Solicitous for all in need, the care of the destitute and orphan children was his chief delight.' He died in his fifty-fourth year. He had achieved much and had walked with ease among ordinary people and the great of Church and state.

# 7

# IN THE HUNGRY YEARS
## 1926—39

John Nettleton Spence was a product of country Methodism. The Spence family had been resident in Magheralin, Co. Down, for many generations and had a long and distinguished connection with the Church in that area. Their roots and history have been graphically described by Winifred O. Spence in her unpublished biography of her late husband, the Reverend Robert Hull Spence, John's younger half-brother. John and Robert both entered the ministry and each was to make his own contribution to the life of the Church. During his earlier years in the Mission, John had been publicly criticised for his 'socialist' views when he had attempted to relate the implications of the gospel to the world around him. He had been transferred as superintendent to the Dublin Central Mission in 1914 and had later volunteered for chaplaincy work. After the war, he had served as superintendent in Bangor, Co. Down (Hamilton Road), and Lisburn, Co. Antrim, both important appointments. Surprisingly, in April 1925 the Mission invited him to return as 'Junior Minister'. Equally surprising was his acceptance of the invitation and what can only be called a demotion. He can have accepted only because of his conviction regarding the significance of the Mission itself and his affection for R.M. Ker, who, without warning, had been taken from his people in the zenith of his powers and influence. Now called to follow him, John N. Spence was confronted with the heavy responsibilities associated with the Mission, having had only a year in which to familiarise himself with the lighter routine work. With the assistance of the Reverend Hugh Allen for some months, and of the Reverend Albert W. Gamble and the Reverend R. Ernest Ker the following year, Mr Spence set about his enormous task.

All was ready for the opening of the new hall
on 22 September 1927.

The opening ceremony of the new Grosvenor Hall on 22 September 1927; among the dignitaries on the platform are Lord Mayor Sir William Turner, and Joseph Rank, the industrialist and Methodist benefactor.

Mr and Mrs Hugh Turtle on either side of the president, the Reverend Randall C. Phillips (front centre), in a photograph taken to mark their gift of Templepatrick House to the Mission on 4 August 1928.

Hungry men, women and children queue for food outside the Ker Hall in Glengall Street, Belfast, during the 1932 Outdoor Relief crisis.

Warden John Young (left) shepherds a party of happy children into the holiday home at Childhaven (previously Templepatrick House) in Millisle.

Mission staff in 1940. Left to right, seated: Robert R. Cunningham, John N. Spence and Alfred Collins; standing: Miss H.M. Cathcart, Miss N. Meechan (later, wife of the Reverend Dr Albert Holland), Mrs E. McCann, Miss E. Allen and Miss Wilson.

Christmas dinner for homeless men at Grosvenor Hall, 1942.

A missionary play
produced in 1942 by
the Christian
Endeavour Society at

On 19 November 1926 he made his first major public appearance as superintendent at the new hall's postponed stone-laying ceremony. Stones were laid by the Duchess of Abercorn, Lady Kelly, Mrs T. Foulkes Shillington, Mrs H.M. Johnson, Lady Whitla, Mrs Hugh Turtle, Mrs F.C. Cowdy, Mrs Ker, Mrs E.B. Cullen, and a child from the Whitehead home (in memory of service personnel). The president of the Church, the Reverend E.B. Cullen, presided. (As immediate ex-president, he had automatically succeeded to the presidency on Mr Ker's death.) Among the main speakers was Sir William Turner, lord mayor of Belfast, who reminded the audience that over five million people had attended Sunday services in the old Hall. It had been decided that the Glengall Street wing of the new complex should be named after R.M. Ker and the committee hoped that the wing would be operational by the New Year, 1928, if not before it. In fact, it was used for a children's party before the old year was out.

Work went on apace on the main building. A demarcation dispute arose between two of the trade unions representing men working on the site and work came to a standstill. A minute of the Mission Committee meeting held on 8 March 1927 records the superintendent's report that 'The building dispute had been brought to an end by not proceeding with the work which gave rise to the dispute between the two Trade Unions concerned.' It is not clear what amenity the Mission had lost because of this Draconian decision.

On 2 April the official opening of the Ker Wing took place with Mrs Harold Barbour presiding, and the ceremony was performed by Miss Paul, a member of a family to whose benefactions over the years the Mission owes much. Opportunity was taken to thank publicly Mr (later Sir) J. Milne Barbour for the free use of premises in Glengall Street during the building period. The new hall was officially opened on 22 September by Mrs T. Foulkes Shillington and dedicated by the president of the day, the Reverend William H. Smyth. The auditorium, with its two bronze Praeger medallions at the entrance doors commemorating Crawford Johnson and R.M. Ker, was and still is the finest of its kind in Northern Ireland. Its acoustics are second to none. It was packed to its capacity of over two thousand seats for the ceremony chaired by the lord mayor, Sir William Turner. Methodist College had run a massive two-day bazaar to raise the funds to pay for the oak-panelled platform. (It was rumoured that some of the money came from a ballot or raffle for a sheep. This led to some controversy which came to an end only after emergency meetings and correspondence between the headmaster, Mr J.W. Henderson, and Mr Spence, with the former putting himself on record that no money so raised had gone towards the platform.)

The Hall was crowded again for an evening service when the chair was taken by Mr Joseph Rank. To mark his coming, the *Belfast Telegraph* carried a profile of him. It described him as a self-made man whose interest in Methodism and its city missions was well known. His munificent gift of £10,000 to the Hall's building fund had already been well-publicised. His business acumen and practical approach to life were quickly obvious when he suggested that the Mission should immediately look to its publicity programme and indicated that an electric sign over the main door was essential. The address was given by the Reverend T.A. Smyth of Great Victoria Street Presbyterian Church and later moderator of the General Assembly. The treasurer, Mr Johnson, spoke of the need for £22,000 (£32,000 having been already given or promised towards the estimated total outlay). Before the offering could be taken, Mr Rank rose to his feet and went to the rostrum. Mr R.H. Anderson, son of Mr H.M. Anderson, recalls the audible gasp when he announced that, if the opening ceremonies produced £10,000, he would donate a further £5,000. Before long the superintendent was able to avail himself of Mr Rank's generous challenge. A committee minute for 6 October, just over two weeks later, reveals the result:

> £10,000 had been asked for and had been practically raised. This was due first to the generosity of the builders who, finding their contract had worked out favourably through the assistance of sub-contractors, some fall in wages and the earnest support of every worker concerned, remitted to the Committee £3,000 of their charges.

The committee was grateful but the minute regarding the fall in workers' wages is an indication of the emerging social crises in the city.

As well as new buildings, 1928 saw new faces at the Mission: the Reverend Robert J.J. Teasey and the Reverend Albert Holland joined the staff that year. The former was succeeded three years later by the Reverend William J. Oliver; the latter stayed until 1938 when he completed a decade of most successful ministry.

The new buildings naturally gave fresh impetus to the work. They enabled the resumption in adequate premises of the Happy Evenings and the lecture programme which from the beginning had been so popular. The Happy Evenings, however, had to contend with increasing competition from the advent of the sound cinema. Successive committees heard about decreasing attendances. By September 1932 the superintendent said they would soon have to face the installation of a 'talking machine'. In December he had altered the phrase to 'a voice production installation'. By the following June 'sound apparatus' had been installed and nine months later income generated by increased audiences had resulted in the entire liquidation of the installation cost of £1,195.

The lecture programme was eventually to fade out but not before some further lectures had been given. One delivered by the late Mr Randolph Churchill on Thursday 21 January 1932 was the most controversial of them all. For the Grosvenor Hall it must have been a bizarre occasion. The lecture was entitled 'Young England looks at America'. The chair was taken by J.M. Andrews MP and the charge for admission ranged from sixpence (2½p) to two shillings and sixpence (12½p). The Churchill name had guaranteed a good audience and the lecture was well reported. He spoke of his visit to America and his arrival in Kansas city, then, like every other American city, subject to the prohibition laws. The manager of his hotel, he said, 'to the everlasting credit of the American people presented me with the usual bottle of whisky'. He went on to talk about prohibition, 'that grotesque, fantastic and amazing piece of legislation'. It was the brainchild of the wives of wealthy American businessmen who liked 'hearing preachers of the evangelical Puritan denominations. The women are rich and pay good money to the preachers.' He went on in the same vein, having a shot at Lady Astor, an American-born and notable figure in British political life, saying:

> I often think how lucky it is that we have Lady Astor in these islands to preach prohibition. It is the one thing that ensures the fact that we shall not have prohibition. I don't know if you have ever listened to a speech by Lady Astor: if you have, you will know that it is the first thing that will drive you to drink.

He then went on to talk about British and American co-operation.

In the tradition of Crawford Johnson and R.M. Ker, John N. Spence sternly opposed the drink trade and all that went with it. The papers next day gave full coverage to Mr Churchill's comments on the prohibition issue and had little to say about the main thrust of the lecture. As far as Mr Spence and the reputation of the Mission were concerned, the damage had been done. The long *Northern Whig* report on 22 January 1932 and its concluding paragraph certainly did not catch the mood of what happened. It tersely stated that the Reverend J.N. Spence in 'thanking Mr Churchill for his brilliant lecture ventured to suggest that with the years that brought wisdom Mr Churchill might unsay some of the things he had said'. The report had been detailed but it did not refer to the drama of Mr Spence's intervention. He had not been on the programme to speak. Indeed it would seem that he had made his way from the back of the Hall at the end of the lecture to voice his concern and to distance himself and the Mission from what had been said. Later, in the *Irish Christian Advocate* he made it clear that Mr Churchill's agent had sought the opportunity for his client to give the lecture and he had been engaged on the distinct understanding that he would refrain from any reference to prohibition and the drink trade that could be considered inimical to the position on the issue taken up by the Mission and its superintendent.

In 1925 Hugh Turtle had become a member of the Mission Committee. His interest in its work had increased considerably since then with his greater knowledge of what was being done. A minute of an extraordinary meeting of the committee held on 4 August 1928 reveals how deep that interest had become:

The object of the meeting was to receive formal possession of Templepatrick House and grounds [Millisle], which Mr and Mrs Hugh Turtle had purchased and were most generously giving to the Mission for the purposes of work among the poor children. In handing over the property, Mr Turtle indicated that the property was given without any condition whatsoever and with the hope that it might be a blessing to many.

So started one of the most far-reaching projects the Mission has ever undertaken and which still brings credit to it after sixty years. Within weeks Mr Spence was on record as referring to the new property as 'Childhaven'. It was a title that at the time and for many years afterwards seemed particularly fitting. It lasted until the 1980s when work among senior adolescents called for a more apt name. Within two years, the Childhaven complex, sited on one of the finest vantage points on the Co. Down coast, was completed at a cost of nearly £11,000. It comprised what was for many years called 'The Orphanage', 'Childhaven Holiday Home' and 'Mother's House of Rest'.

The Mission's work during the years 1926–39 went on against the background of deteriorating social conditions. Stanley Herron and Brian Caul in their *A Service for People: Origins and Developments of the Personal Social Services in Belfast*, published privately in 1980, deal at length with social conditions in Northern Ireland. By the year 1925 there was an unemployment figure of 25 per cent in Northern Ireland compared with 11 per cent in Great Britain. Illness among children of parents on the lower income groups was rife. Between the years 1925–9 an average of over 460 children, maximum age fifteen years, died each year in Northern Ireland workhouses, with the vast majority of deaths in the under-five bracket. People whose unemployment benefit entitlement had come to an end were dependent on what they could get from the Poor Law Relief schemes. These schemes were financed from local rates and as there was pressure on the Poor Law guardians to keep demands on rates as low as possible, the relief payments were kept correspondingly low.

Almost from the day John N. Spence became superintendent, the committee minutes carry repeated references to 'abject poverty among people formerly in comfortable circumstances' and his fear of a 'time of general distress'. By September 1932 a point of no return had been reached. Indignation in the unemployed matched their poverty. Herron and Caul report the functioning of an Outdoor Relief Workers' Committee earlier in the summer. It is not widely known that the same committee had approached Mr Spence for the use of the Grosvenor Hall for a protest meeting. The Mission Committee, which to its credit had some time earlier agreed to the use of the Hall premises for the annual conference of the British Trades Union Congress, came face to face with the city's distress and discontent on 10 September. At that meeting they gave a positive response to a written request 'from Mr Barnes on behalf of the Outdoor Relief Workers' Committee asking for the use of the Hall for a public meeting to consider their present position and needs'. The response then was the same as it has been over the years – before and since. If men have a grievance, it is better that they should talk about it. Permission was granted 'if the Superintendent was satisfied with the resolutions to be put before the meeting and the names of the committee in charge'.

The sequel is a turbulent part of Belfast's history: mass protest marches of Roman Catholic and Protestant workers were arranged in early October (Mr Spence took part in at least one of them). Some of them were broken up by the police and rioting ensued. In the event the Poor Law guardians, with Government prompting, agreed to raise the relief rates. They had been standing at:

married couple with no children, eight shillings (40p) per week

married couple with one child, twelve shillings (60p) per week, with four shillings (20p) for each subsequent child up to a maximum of twenty-four shillings (£1.20) per week

The new scale, eventually arrived at with great difficulty, was much increased but still pitiably far from what was needed:

married couple with no children, twenty shillings (£1) per week

married couple with one or two children, twenty-four shillings (£1.20) per week

married couple with three or four children, twenty-eight shillings (£1.40) per week

married couple with more than four children, thirty-two shillings (£1.60) per week

Nearly sixty years have passed since the 1932 Outdoor Relief riots and sadly the contribution of the Churches to awakening the conscience of the community regarding the plight of the unemployed has been practically forgotten. The Presbyterian voice was clearly sounded and so was that of the Church of Ireland. In 1932 the *Irish Christian Advocate* reported a meeting of the Belfast Methodist Council, which was held in early October, when one well-known Methodist trade-union official referred to the Poor Law guardians as 'the most heartless, cruel, callous and relentless Board that had ever been in the city'. The Mission itself was involved in the Outdoor Relief Movement at three levels – practically, 'politically', and before long there was to be joint ecclesiastical involvement as well in which it would participate. Its own response had started long before the discontent had reached the level of mass street demonstrations and riots and continued during the actual period of maximum unrest and well into the 1930s. For instance, the March 1933 committee meeting was told that 'five tons [4,536 kilograms] of potatoes were distributed in one stone [6 kilogram] lots – none were bought'. The programme of free meals was continued not only in the Glengall Street premises but in other centres – the hall of Newtownards Road church being one of them; it was its first introduction to Mission work now being actively pursued under its own banner as the East Belfast Mission. The new holiday home at Childhaven, Millisle, was to prove a godsend. Large numbers of children from impoverished and beleaguered families benefited from the holiday programme – there were over seven hundred of them in 1933. Mr John Young, who by that time had transferred to Millisle, reported to the committee in June of that year that he had noticed signs 'of great physical deterioration in the children owing to the poverty'. A year later, 730 children had a fortnight's holiday, many of them showing all the indications of malnutrition. Even in December 1934 250–300 dinners were being given daily to adults and children – either free or at a charge of one penny each. Throughout, the Mission's traditional criterion applied: 'Need not creed'.

The Mission's involvement was not confined to its own practical programme of relief. There was a 'political' side that has not been fully appreciated. Mr Spence was already well known and respected in the city by the time the crisis broke. More significantly he had won the confidence of the trade-union movement. His willingness to put the Hall's premises at the disposal of the British Trades Union Congress had not gone unnoticed and he had conducted the religious service associated with its meetings. Angela Clifford in her *Poor Law in Ireland*, published by Athol Books in 1983, states:

> The Reverend Spence, attached to the Central Methodist Mission (Grosvenor Hall) was particularly active for the unemployed and was. . . closely involved with the labour movement. . . The Methodists were involved in the relief workers' struggle for better conditions from an early stage. They helped the relief workers formulate demands and continued to support them even when the decision to strike, with which they disagreed, had been taken.

Her reference to the formulation of demands is an interesting corroboration of Mr Spence's drafting abilities which were before long to be recognised by many others.

There have been those who have completely ignored the involvement of the Churches in this chapter of the age-old struggle for justice. Others have grudgingly admitted that the Churches did something but that it was a case of 'too little, too late', even though it is clear from the Mission Committee minutes that Mr Spence was involved long before the beginning of October 1932. He was soon to be joined by the Reverend John W. Stutt, superintendent of the North Belfast Mission. Each of them went public in letters to the press. When the Poor Law guardians were digging their heels in against any increased payment and the Government was not seen to be overconcerned, both Mr Spence and Mr Stutt stated publicly that the state had a responsibility that could not be evaded. Mr Spence particularly called for agreement between the Poor Law guardians and the Government. Before the end of September 1932 the North Belfast Mission People's Hall and the Grosvenor Hall hosted protest meetings of the workers. Both superintendents attended a crucial meeting held in the People's Hall on 29 September, when the decision was taken by the relief workers to call a strike. The Belfast papers of 30 September covered the meeting and reported that both superintendents spoke strongly against the proposal to strike. Mr

Spence believed a strike would jeopardise the workers' case and Mr Stutt argued that such a decision should be taken only after more adequate notice. They had a 'rough ride' and in spite of their reasoned protests they were ruled 'out of order'. As it happened, before the meeting Mr Spence had already written a letter to the press in support of the campaign for improvement in Poor Law relief. To his credit he made no attempt to withdraw the letter after the decision had been taken. However, in an addendum he did make clear his disapproval of the strike but he also expressed the hope that the decision 'will not be allowed to prejudice what are just claims on the part of the suffering men'. The whole episode is a classic case of justified political (as distinct from party-political) action on the part of the Churches.

The third level of involvement was in the joint Churches' 'Relief Programme'. On 21 October 1932 a meeting of clergy and laymen of the Protestant Churches was held in the Church of Ireland Clarence Place Hall. That meeting gave birth to the United Churches' Relief Fund Committee. Three honorary secretaries were appointed: the Reverend Dr Robert Corkey (later Minister of Education in the Northern Ireland Government and moderator of the Presbyterian General Assembly); the Reverend R.C.H. Elliott (later Bishop of Connor); and the Reverend John N. Spence. The committee organised an appeal to the Protestant people of the city for money and commodities. That appeal was signed by five people: Dr Charles Grierson, Bishop of Down; James Little, moderator of the Belfast Presbytery; John A. Duke, president of the Methodist Church; Alexander Cairns, chairman of the Congregational Union; and Samuel Ruddock, secretary of the Belfast Baptist Council. Wherever the fault lies, tragically today there is no participation of the Congregational and Baptist Churches in joint initiatives of this kind.

Over the next two and a half years thirty-four meetings were held of the full committee or its executive. The minute book tells a story that reflects considerable credit on all concerned and of which too little is known. Of those thirty-four meetings, twenty-seven were held in Grosvenor Hall and the minutes of thirty-two of them are in the handwriting of Mr Spence. He was by common consent one of the main driving forces behind what was to

become a remarkable piece of inter-Church co-operation. By the
time the committee went out of existence, it had raised
£6,463.9s.11d. (£6,463.50) and it had disbursed £6,442.5s.7d.
(£6,442.28), and an unquantified amount of food and clothing to
3,961 individual families in the city. There was a mastery of
detailed arrangement in the whole operation that still evokes
admiration. While it is clear that the fund was Protestant-based
and that the Catholic Church had its own arrangements, there
would seem to have been no sectarian bar in the distribution of
help. Mr Spence's part in the operation was recognised by Bishop
Grierson, who wrote to him on 27 September 1934, 'in my long
ministry I never felt it easier to recognize true loyalty or brother-
hood than with your good self. You really helped me personally
much.' A year later Mr Spence wrote to Dr Mageean, Catholic
Bishop of Down and Connor, in an initiative suggesting a joint
Church leaders' appeal for an end to the sectarian riots in Belfast.
In his reply dated 20 July 1935 the bishop, though not acceding to
the request, assured Mr Spence that the efforts, which he appreciated, of the Protestant clergy 'will have the help and co-operation
of the whole Catholic community'. A pastoral read the following
Sunday at all Masses in Belfast sought that co-operation. Almost
thirty years later cyclical violence again involved a superintendent
of the Mission in a similar and this time successful request for a
joint appeal.

Amazingly, in spite of the poverty in the community, the
Mission's finances gave little cause for major concern. Considerable redecoration of the Large Hall was required within a
short time of its opening. The Childhaven building programme
had been pushed through, and the 'talking machine' had been
installed in the Hall. All was paid for and by 1936 the debt on the
Grosvenor Hall itself had been eliminated – thanks eventually to
the grant from the Forward Movement, which worked out at
£10,000, and a further gift of £500 from Mr Joseph Rank.

The new buildings attracted larger congregations. Long before
the days of sensitivity to the needs of the physically handicapped,
a building was provided where there was not a single step, from
the ramp on the Grosvenor Road entrance right through to the
exit on Glengall Street. The staff could refer in December 1930 to

'greater spiritual fervour in the services'. In 1933 the superintendent was looking for a small hall in which to encourage young people in evangelistic work. The Sunday Brother Man service, with its accompanying meal, was at full strength throughout the 1930s, with as many as five hundred men attending frequently. In 1935 it was reported that the open-air work at three centres had been very successful – especially at the Custom House steps. In the autumn of 1935 the seating in the Large Hall was reduced by some three hundred places and this 'resulted in better conduct on the part of the audience'. There was music for all tastes provided by the large Sunday evening choir with its professional lead singers, young people's choirs under Miss Annie Coulter and Mrs M. Coey, the Grosvenor Hall band and the newly-formed male voice choir, which initially auditioned well over one hundred men, of whom only forty were chosen – a tribute to both interest and quality. It was a period during which considerable numbers of conversions took place at Sunday services, and in 1936 a sub-committee was appointed to consider 'new enterprises in evangelistic work'.

Youth work benefited from the new accommodation. The 35th Boys' Brigade Company, Christian Endeavour Societies, choirs and other organisations continued to develop. All of them made their mark in their respective areas of activity. Indeed in 1934 four of the five initiators of the Irish Churches Football League, the nursery of the Blanchflower brothers, George Best and other talented Northern Ireland players, came from a Grosvenor Hall organisation, the 35th Boys' Brigade Old Boys' Association. Eddie Barry in the league's official history states: 'The prime movers in getting the League off the ground were Tom Speers (35th OB), Charles McCabe, who played a leading role, William Millington, Stafford Young and Bob McNulty, who represented Sandy Row Methodist.' Tom Speers was the first chairman of the league and Stafford Young the first secretary.

In 1937 the trustees of the Craigmore Home, which had been opened in 1903, approached the Mission Committee and asked it to accept responsibility for the children there and to agree to the amalgamation of the home with Childhaven in Millisle.

These years saw the passing of more of the Mission's early

members, including the first chief steward, Mr Richard Addis, the ex-bargee Billy Spence, and the redoubtable Mrs T.A. Fullerton, who died on 24 September 1936 in her ninety-third year. The *Irish Christian Advocate*, in its obituary notice, recalled that in the days before the Mission she had regularly supported her husband and the Reverend John White at the Custom House steps, and with them had helped to win the battle for free speech. It mentioned her quick practical mind, her ability to sum people up in crisp sentences, her rigid stances, her high ideals for preachers and her quickness to detect any deviation from strict orthodoxy. R.M. Ker had made no mistake when he had left the prima donna in her care.

# 8

# IN BLITZ AND BLACKOUT
## 1939–50

Ministerial head-counters have argued that 1939 saw the Hall reach its zenith and that everything since has been the descent down 'the western slopes'. Unquestionably the Grosvenor Hall congregations never again reached the totals of the halcyon days. But who is certain that 'mission' means seat-filling and big collections? Assisting the poor and needy still demanded most of the Mission's energies. By 1939 conditions had improved but the relatively full wartime employment and all that it entailed were still to come – so too were the air raids and the evacuations of 1941.

In spite of the looming war clouds, the summer programme of 1939 went through smoothly and normally. The Reverend Alfred Collins had joined the staff a year previously. He and his wife quickly found their feet. The Reverend Alan R. Booth had come the same year as third minister to commence what was to be a most unusual and distinguished ministry. He was later to be general secretary of the Student Christian Movement and then in succession director of the Churches' Commission on International Affairs and director of Christian Aid, emerging as an internationally-recognised leading Christian thinker. His ministry, as far as the Hall was concerned, was of short duration. He was in post for the 1938 summer programme and he took part in the massive Sunday-school excursion. Alan Booth was a born storyteller and was not averse to describing, with just that suggestion of frill, some of the things that had caught his attention. One of his vivid verbal pictures was of John N. Spence pleading eloquently in heart-rending language for the wherewithal to send away 'a couple of thousand children to the sea-side for a day of undiluted happiness and escape from the city streets'. Then he described the sequel on the day of days with Mr Spence distraught and frustrated because the helpers were not where he wanted at the time he wanted, highlighting him rushing up and down the train and the station platform, threatening to send this boy and that packing back home immediately in disgrace if he did not toe the line and above all else keep quiet. Alan Booth's place was taken in 1939 by the Reverend Robert R. Cunningham – all six feet and a good deal more of him. He had been born in the west of Ireland and brought up in Co. Fermanagh. Popular with both sexes, he was essentially a man's man whose reputation with trade unionists was to grow with the years.

Thus supported by Alfred Collins and Robert Cunningham and the Sisters of the Mission, John N. Spence embarked on the war years and what was to be the last decade of his active ministry. Within weeks some major issues had to be faced. Childhaven had no recourse to Northern Ireland's electricity system. Its elevated site lent itself to the erection of a wind-charger, which would generate some electricity, and one was installed. Then there was a request from the Deaf and Dumb Institute on Belfast's Lisburn Road for the use of the holiday home as an evacuation centre in the event of air raids. The response was positive, though it took some agonising. The home would be made available willingly, if, at the time the call was made upon it, it was not needed for the Mission's holiday programme.

Before 1939 had ended, the death took place of Mr Henry M. Johnson. He had been superintendent of the morning Sunday school for many years and had been honorary treasurer for fifteen. In paying tribute to him, the 1939 Mission report described him as 'Loving, generous, wise in counsel, straight as a die and faithful in all things'. He was succeeded as honorary treasurer by Mr Henry Anderson and Mr Johnson's son, Dermot, followed Mr Anderson as secretary.

The year 1939–40 was the year of the 'phoney war': Germany's onslaught on the Low Countries was still to come. Nevertheless, many of the Mission's men and some of its women were already in the forces. The years of depression were over: men who had not worked for several years found themselves in Short and Harland's aircraft factory or Harland and Wolff's shipyard. All this meant employment but for the Churches it created special difficulties. Aircraft and shipyard work meant Sunday work. Then there was the blackout: that was bad enough for local and suburban churches, but for downtown congregations it was a catastrophe as far as winter evening congregations were concerned.

Nonetheless, the resilience of the congregations was considerable. They steadied after the initial alert, and right up to the spring of 1941 the evening attendance was holding its own reasonably well. However, the Easter and May air raids of that year were a body-blow. Within days 25 per cent of the Mission's women and children had been evacuated and it was the autumn of that year before even a slight increase in congregational strength could be reported. In December 1941 the committee was told that two-thirds of the children who normally attended the afternoon Sunday school had been evacuated and had not returned. The afternoon Sunday school never really recovered fully from the evacuation. The pattern had been broken and in any case a chronic shortage of good teachers went hand in hand with the advent of Sunday work. The Children's Church (surely one of the first of the kind) had been discontinued. (This was an arrangement, then in its infancy, which enabled younger children in the congregation to leave worship before the sermon. Teachers or leaders provided suitable instruction or opportunities for relevant play or other activities.) There is no mention in the records of any members of the Grosvenor Hall congregation having been killed in the raids though 'many homes had been destroyed'.

Pastoral work during the war brought new challenges and problems for all the Churches. There was support to be given to families whose husbands and fathers and sons and daughters were on active service. Information restrictions meant infrequent letters and when they did come, often in their photocopied mimeographs, they conveyed little news and certainly none about the whereabouts of loved ones. There was the comforting of wives and children, or sweethearts, when the dreaded message of 'missing' or 'killed in action' arrived. There was the strain and anxiety of the blackout and the early occasional air-raid warnings. And then there were the blitzes in 1941. I recall vividly what they meant for ministers and clergy: the regular visits through the night to crowded air-raid shelters, searching for families whose homes had been destroyed, or finding some old deaf person cowering under a staircase long after the all-clear had sounded. I remember too a visit that Easter Tuesday evening to a home belonging to a family in my Woodvale congregation, talking to husband and wife, and playing with their little boy and his toys. Next day I helped to dig all three lifeless bodies from the rubble of their home. Inside one twenty-four-hour period I buried them and eleven others of my congregation killed that night. That was the kind of work Belfast Churches faced in 1941 and the Grosvenor Hall was no exception.

With difficulty most of the congregational work was continued and one new venture was attempted. In co-operation with the teaching staff of Edgehill College, the Methodist theological training institution, and others, evening classes were held weekly in English language and literature, Old and New Testaments and Christian doctrine. This initiative was arranged for those who were willing to enrol, whether they were connected or not with the Mission. The open-air work continued but there were initial problems. As the days grew shorter people were reluctant to leave the 'safety' of their homes and in any case it was difficult to gather and hold a crowd in the blackout. One committee meeting discussed the matter and the secretary recorded Mr Cunningham's observation verbatim: 'If a man has something to say, he can gather a crowd and hold it.' Robert Cunningham was never short of listeners. In the spring of 1940 George VI had called for a National Day of Prayer. The Belfast Central Mission and the North Belfast Mission observed it with a joint open-air meeting at the Custom House steps. Eventually the two missions were to co-operate each week in this way.

Mr Cunningham was called to Mountpottinger church in 1940. He was succeeded by the Reverend Samuel D. Ferguson. Equally at home in the open air, he welcomed questions and heckling. One Sunday afternoon he had a rough ride from a persistent interrupter, who was of vehemently-expressed left-wing views. Eventually Sam Ferguson stopped him in his tracks. He asked him if he had read Karl Marx's *Das Kapital* or anything written by Engels. The heckler was evasive but Sam Ferguson repeated the

78

question and asked for a yes or no. When at last the reply was no, Sam told him to go home, read them, come back and only then would they pursue the argument. After the meeting, a colleague enquired from the speaker if he had read the books himself. 'Not at all,' was Sam's answer, 'but *he* doesn't know I haven't read them.' One unchanging feature of these meetings was the numbers of Catholics who attended. The audiences were by no means composed of Mission members and camp followers. All sorts were there – latter-day 'political Protestants', atheists, agnostics and 'pickers-up of unconsidered trifles'.

The 1941 air raids left a major portion of High Street devastated. It became known as 'Blitz Square' and was a 'natural' for open-air work. Long before the war was over, a meeting was held there every Saturday morning and it continued until rebuilding operations made that no longer possible. Among the speakers there was a camaraderie about open-air work in those years – the Communists, for instance, proclaimed their faith on Blitz Square, but they were happy to wait until the Grosvenor Hall meeting had concluded. And there was a mutual respect among denominations that was to disappear regrettably in Northern Ireland's neo-orthodoxy and political fundamentalism of later years.

Up until 1941 the Deaf and Dumb Institute had not had the need to avail itself of the facilities at Childhaven. And even immediately after the raids, it looked as if the institute would be able to carry on without evacuation. However, accommodation for refugees was in seriously short supply and the superintendent felt duty bound to offer the holiday home as an evacuation centre. He reported to the committee on 5 June 1941:

> After the raid the Home was offered to the Ministry of Public Security for sixty children but the Ministry's officials had treated the offer in a very cavalier fashion and did not take it up.

As it turned out, what the ministry disdained, the Deaf and Dumb Institute was glad to have. By the end of 1941 the institute's premises were needed for other purposes and its request to the Hall was renewed; in early 1942 it had taken over the home. This of course could have meant a serious blow to the Mission's holiday programmes but the challenge was met with amazing resilience. There were wooden sheds and a gymnasium on site, and a summertime conversion each year provided a kitchen, games room, storage area and a large dormitory.

Wartime Belfast was alive with men and women in uniform. Particularly at weekends, service personnel gravitated to the city in huge numbers. The pressure for sleeping accommodation grew by the week, especially after Dunkirk in 1940 and in the years before the D-day invasion of Europe in 1944. In the summer of 1942 the front wing of the Grosvenor Hall property was thrown open as a hostel for servicemen. It was intended to house forty persons but weekend after weekend over eighty men sought shelter. It was gladly given – at least the air and floor space was given but the provision of beds and bedding was another matter. The army wanted shelter provided and was grateful for it but it seemed either unable or unwilling to go beyond forty palliasses and blankets. Eventually the American Red Cross was approached and came to the rescue.

Every building, shop, factory and household had to cope with the continuing blackout regulations. It was bad enough for households but for those who were responsible for large buildings used at night it was a nightmare. The Grosvenor Hall comprises what are really three separate wings – the Ker Wing in Glengall Street, the huge central block and ancillary rooms of the Large Hall and the front wing on Grosvenor Road. Fire-watching at that time was no child's game. After 1941 a team of at least three able-bodied persons was required seven nights a week. With many of the men on night work, it was necessary to have paid fire-watchers, who would be on duty whether or not volunteers were able to turn up. Money that was hard come by was required to pay them.

By 1942 the Mission staff was very conscious that the greater supply and 'greater circulation of money had lessened claims' on social-relief funds. However, if money was in greater supply, it brought problems with it as well. As early as December 1941 Mr Spence was sharing his concerns with the Mission Committee regarding the numbers of children in the city born out of wedlock. He was as much concerned with the 'gross injustice of branding babies for life with such a term' as he was with problems of sexual promiscuity. The moral problem did not go away and before long he was seeking the co-operation of the appropriate officials in the Church of Ireland and the Presbyterian Church. In the early months of 1942 he took part, with the Dean of Belfast and the clerk of the Presbyterian General Assembly, in a deputation to the city commissioner of the Royal Ulster Constabulary, which raised the issue of street prostitution. It is not evident that the visit resulted in any great moral reformation but it is added evidence of Mr Spence's lifelong conviction that 'the spiritual and social gospels cannot be dissociated'.

An important development in 1943 was the linking of the Springfield Road congregation with the Mission circuit. It was a challenge gladly accepted and it has been a happy arrangement. Over the years the relationship has continued to be warm. Springfield Road members have been among the most loyal and generous of the Mission's workers. Childhaven especially has reason to be grateful for what they have done and given. Initially the work at Springfield Road was the immediate responsibility of a greatly-loved retired minister, the Reverend Robert Maxwell. He was succeeded by another retired minister, the Reverend John A. Duke, who died suddenly and who was replaced by a young candidate for the ministry, now the Reverend Dr John Turner. In 1945 the Reverend George A. McIlwrath, also retired, took over and continued until 1947 to be succeeded by the Reverend Wilfred A. Agnew, 1947–8.

In 1944 an opportunity presented itself in a very needy and demanding situation. The social and religious conditions in one of Protestantism's heartlands just off the Shankill Road and Old Lodge Road were 'crying out' for attention. A small hall in Conlon Street was acquired on a rental basis. So began one of the most challenging of all the Mission's ventures. With the enthusiastic support of one family named Midgley, Mr Spence and his colleagues soon had an impressive work programme launched. By September 1945, Billy Boyd, one of the Conlon Street members, later to be Alderman William R. Boyd MP, was recognised as a 'Local Preacher on Trial'. He was soon to be known as an able and acceptable open-air and indoor speaker and eventually to be one of Northern Ireland's Labour members of the Stormont parliament.

A leaders' meeting was constituted and by the end of 1945 there was a Sunday school of over one hundred pupils and a congregation of approximately seventy on Sunday evenings. A busy youth programme, which included two football teams, was promoted and by 1946 there was active discussion regarding the need for a new and permanent building.

The end of the war in 1945 did not provide a land of plenty. Six years of wartime rationing were followed by a period of continued shortages. Once more the Mission found itself in the familiar role of social relief. It engaged in a large-scale distribution of blankets and bedding which came its way from the Women's Voluntary Service organisation and the Young Men's Christian Association for whom such items were then surplus to requirement. Food, also in large quantities, came to war-weary Britain and Northern Ireland from the dominions and colonies, particularly from Australia and from South Africa. The Mission was asked by the Ministry of Food to co-operate in its distribution; on 7 March 1947 the *Irish Christian Advocate* quoted Mr Spence: 'Last week over 300 families were recipients.' He could have repeated that assertion for every week.

The advent of the welfare state in 1948 saw the disappearance of much of the abject poverty but the basic needs remained. By July 1949 Mr Spence saw clearly that the state was going to take over much of the work that the Mission had been doing over the years. He welcomed the new social provisions: he had argued for years that the Mission must be something more than a social agency. Nonetheless, he could not bear to think that Childhaven would disappear, it was dear to his heart. Those who remember him speak frequently of his love for children. On 5 March 1948 the *Irish Christian Advocate* quoted him: 'To close Childhaven would be unthinkable.'

The war years and immediate post-war period brought their inevitable changes. The air raids had made the first significant dent in the Mission's geographical area of pastoral concern. It was a dramatic beginning to a population shift that reached its devastating climax in urban redevelopment and the Troubles of the 1970s and 1980s. By the summer of 1942, however, the evening congregation had fought its way back to about 1,300 people; by the end of 1944, with improved streetlighting, attendances were estimated at over 1,400; and by September 1947, it was claimed, perhaps optimistically, that it was at pre-war strength.

In June 1942 the death had taken place of the superintendent's wife, Mrs Jane Lyons Spence. She was a niece of the late Mr Andrew Bonar Law, former British prime minister. Many of John N. Spence's schemes and projects had been hammered out on the anvil of her keen and penetrating mind. Her social concern and her deep interest in the work at Childhaven were common knowledge. She was greatly missed and by none more than her husband. Typically, he carried on for the remainder of the war years alone and without complaint. In the autumn of 1945 he found comfort in the love and companionship of Frances Ludlow, matron of the children's home at Childhaven, whom he married before a large and approving congregation in his beloved Grosvenor Hall. Another of the early stalwarts, Mr James Dixon, died in February 1943.

There were changes also in the ministerial staff. The Reverend Alan R. Booth had served in the year 1938–9, the Reverend S.D. Ferguson, 1940–7, the Reverend W.A. Agnew, 1947–8 and the Reverend R.G. Bagnall, 1948–50. The Reverend Alfred Collins left in 1943 when the Reverend R.R. Cunningham returned from Mountpottinger by invitation, this time as second minister. During these years the retirement took place in 1948 of Miss Wilson, one of the band of deaconesses. She had served for over thirty years. Shortly after, Mr Spence called Miss Mary Gihon to take her place; in his whole career he made no more far-seeing or important appointment. Mr John Young retired from the superintendency of a depleted Sunday school in 1944. His place was taken by the unique Tom Pakenham – later Councillor Thomas Pakenham JP and doyen of the Boys' Brigade movement. He left his special and indelible mark on successive generations of boys in the 35th Boys' Brigade Company. In retirement he continued in active life until his sudden death on holiday in November 1988.

The year 1947 saw the retirement of Mr Henry Anderson from the honorary treasurership. He had been secretary from 1902 to 1940 and had accepted the treasurership on the death of Mr

Henry Johnson. The 'family firm' arrangement, however, was carried on with Dermot Johnson, Henry's son, becoming treasurer, and Francis (Frank) Moran Anderson, Hugh's son, being appointed secretary.

By 1948 John N. Spence had entered the forty-eighth year of his active ministry. Like both of his predecessors and two of his successors, he had been elected to that most strategic of all appointments in the gift of the Irish Methodist Conference – the secretaryship. He was vice-president of the Conference and president of the Church during the year 1940–1. His advice and counsel were sought inside and outside Methodism. In September 1948 he told his committee of his wish to retire. The months from Easter to June 1949 were taken up with farewells and presentations. When Conference came, the stationing committee announced a major crisis in the supply of ministerial manpower. Mr Spence was pressed strongly from all sides to remain in post. He hesitated and asked for time to consider what he should do. On the last morning of the Conference he indicated his willingness to remain for one more year. A year later he had no second thoughts.

With the award of the MBE, the state belatedly had taken notice in 1949 of what he had done not only for Methodism but for thousands of his fellow men and women. No one connected with the Mission had seen more changes in the social life of Northern Ireland. At the time of his retirement he reminisced that when he originally joined the staff in 1902, the working day had started at 6 a.m., butter was eight pence (4p) a pound, eggs seven pence (3p) a dozen, and a good journeyman's wage was eighteen shillings (90p) a week.

Like Crawford Johnson, he retained his connection with the Mission. His work with the Mission extended over thirty-seven years in active ministry and eleven in retirement. He died on 24 September 1961 in his eighty-eighth year. The 1962 Conference recalled how the Mission had 'deepened his native passion for justice and developed in him an implacable opposition to social impurity and wrongdoing'. John N. Spence had always good reasons for the decisions he had taken, no matter how controversial they might have been. His successors learned that there should be better reasons before they contemplated altering anything he had done.

# 9

# IN YEARS OF CHANGE
## 1950–7

The Mission had completed over six decades in 1950. In all those years it had known only three superintendents. Inside the next six years three more were to be appointed and a fourth at the end of the seventh. They were dramatic years not only because of unexpected breaks in continuity which a Mission cannot easily afford, but because other forces were operating in the life of the community which the Churches could not ignore. The 1950s brought vast improvements in social conditions. Everyone benefited from the welfare state, rationing came to an end, employment figures increased and the standard of living rose. New housing estates in the suburbs appeared – Turf Lodge, New Barnsley, Taughmonagh, Braniel, Garnerville, Rathcoole, the 'White City' below Bellevue and others as well. The morning rush hour in Belfast saw the virtual disappearance of the bicycle and the 'Workmen Only' tramcars. They were replaced by trolley buses and tradesmen's cars. New streets and highways were needed to cope with the increased traffic. Custom House Square was only one of many places to see its age-old seclusion being destroyed by the town planners. And of course there was the advent to Northern Ireland of television with its consequent effect on church attendances.

Against this background, Robert R. Cunningham succeeded to the superintendency in 1950. He had entered the ministry in 1933 and had been invited to succeed Mr Spence in 1949. However, the 1949 Conference's pressure on Mr Spence to remain resulted in Robert Cunningham's having to wait another year. The delay unquestionably unsettled him. Nonetheless, he had been back in the Hall for seven years and he was well known and liked. He quickly settled into his new responsibilities without any detectable sign of disappointment.

The new Northern Ireland Education Act 1949 was a major revolution. It brought with it a new generation, and a very different one, of young people in the Hall's area of influence. There were grammar-school children beginning to avail themselves of their results in the eleven-plus examination with all its terrors and pressures. Those who did not go to the grammar schools made their way to the new intermediate schools and had opportunities and successes that had been denied to their parents. Youth work took on a new dimension: in all the Churches it had to fight for its survival. The proliferating extramural societies in schools and secular youth clubs became serious rivals. In the Hall Tom Pakenham had taken on the captaincy of the 35th Boys' Brigade Company, and for many years he and his fellow officers exerted a quite remarkable influence on succeeding generations of recruits, especially from the Sandy Row, Grosvenor Road and Lower Shankill districts. In March 1952 a Girls' Life Brigade Company was formed under the energetic and determined captaincy of Sister Mary Gihon, assisted by her lieutenants Marjorie Gill and Alice Hutchinson.

The education act also brought with it adult night classes in the 'Tech' and the intermediate schools. Any revival of the Grosvenor Hall lecture programme was out of the question. The pressure for places in grammar schools was such that the already established institutions could not cope. Dr Stuart Hawnt, Belfast's director of education, initiated and presided over a programme of educational expansion such as the city had never dreamed of. In quick succession he launched three new grammar schools – Grosvenor High, Carolan and Annadale. Until permanent and purpose-built accommodation could be provided on the Orangefield campus, Grosvenor High School was located in Roden Street in what became the home of Kelvin Intermediate School. The headmaster of Grosvenor High, Mr William Moles, was sensitive to the claims of religious education and his school became one of Robert Cunningham's top priorities. A telling and credible witness for the Christian faith, Robert Cunningham made full use of this opportunity, as he also did with the chaplaincy at the Royal Victoria Group of Hospitals.

By the mid-1950s traffic for east Belfast via the Queen's Bridge had been rerouted into Custom House Square and eventually a new road was engineered diagonally across the square. With the dramatic increase in noise and physical danger, open-air work at the Custom House steps was becoming more difficult. In any case the welfare state had dealt a mortal blow to the trade of the quack and ready-medicine purveyors, who provided novelty and excitement for the crowds that used to frequent the place on Sunday afternoons. The North Belfast Mission and the Hall meetings at the Steps were amalgamated under the leadership of both ministerial staffs and supported by lay-stalwarts such as the Mission's Alderman William Boyd and John Blair, and North Belfast's John Bryans. Mr Blair is now well into his nineties and the centenarian John Bryans JP, doyen of the Orange Order, was still mentally alert up till his death in the spring of 1988. The Steps still drew a reasonably regular attendance but 'there had passed away a glory from the earth'. If the Steps were proving more difficult, there was still opportunity at Blitz Square, which was seized with enthusiasm, and the Saturday morning meeting there drew the crowds, Robert Cunningham revelling in the heckling. Perhaps the most celebrated of all the meetings was the one on 10 April 1954 when Donald (now Lord) Soper was the speaker. He had come to Belfast for Sunday services at Donegall Square church. Robert Cunningham prevailed on him – not that Donald Soper needed much persuasion – to speak on Saturday morning. His controversial views were well known and the audience was large, the relatively young Ian Paisley among it. The scenario that became so frequent in later years quickly unfolded itself. It was a battle of wits between the two men but Donald Soper's final thrust was devastating. That might have been the end of the story in Hyde Park or Tower Hill but not so in Belfast. On 16 April 1954 the *Irish Christian Advocate* reported the meeting and it commented in conclusion:

> We have to record with shame that the most abusive heckling came from another branch of the Christian Church. Dr Soper, scorning a microphone, came out triumphant and completely in control.

Nonetheless, even though it was a victory, it was a costly one. His future visits to Northern Ireland were assured of noisy opposition and he himself, the target of virulent denunciation.

The Happy Evenings were showing signs that they had run their course by 1950. However, the superintendent's rapport with the late Mr George Lodge of the Grand Opera House led to the free gift of valuable cinema equipment and furnishings and in early October of that year, with his colleague the Reverend (now Dr) Hedley Plunkett, Robert Cunningham initiated what was for Belfast a new kind of evangelism in the form of a 'cinema mission'. The crowds responded and there was a nightly audience of never less than twelve hundred people. Its success led almost immediately to the commencement of the Saturday evening film service which became for the next twenty years or so one of Belfast's major Saturday evening attractions.

By any standards these events were extraordinary occasions. In the 1950s it was customary to see crowds queuing from the front doors of the Hall, right round the block, down Glengall Mews and along Glengall Street almost as far as the Boyne Bridge. A normal programme commenced with community hymn-singing, the words being thrown on the screen, followed by a musical contribution from an individual or group of singers. Each week a major feature film was shown and at its conclusion the minister on the rota had to use all the agility of which he was capable to get to the rostrum to deliver a short address before the crowd on the gallery made their rush for the exits. The address attempted to take up some point of significance from the film.

The service undoubtedly had a religious and evangelistic motivation. Earlier in the week much work was done by ministerial staff, helped by the chief projectionist, John Watson and his assistant Billy Gourley or the ever-dependable Hal Dixon, ensuring the selection of a suitable film. The man-hours spent previewing and eliminating, often on cold winter nights in the darkened and unheated Hall, are beyond computation. Sadly however, as with other Mission initiatives, the film service was not free of criticism and opposition. There were pamphlets and pickets to warn and dissuade all and sundry from attending such 'evil' services. Nonetheless, to this day there are those in leading positions of Northern Ireland's social and religious life who readily admit to challenges faced and decisions reached because of what they heard or saw at a Mission film service. Many who came for reasons best known to themselves discovered more about themselves and the important things in life than they had thought of.

Welfare state or not, there was no let up in the early 1950s in the requests for assistance or the need for holidays. On 12 January 1951 the *Irish Christian Advocate* reported the superintendent's observation: 'More cases were found of real hardship and necessity in 1950 than for many years past.' There were still perennial cases of genuine poverty or social inadequacy that the regulations of the state can never cover satisfactorily. Mr Norman Thompson assumed responsibility for the Brother Man service in 1953 and even at that date found no lessening of need and poverty among the men who came week by week.

Since John N. Spence's initiative in 1944, work at Conlon Street had continued to develop. In September 1950 a flourishing youth club was established in the premises of Hemsworth Square School. A leaders' meeting was constituted in March 1952. The records frequently refer to the embarrassment caused by the inadequate accommodation provided by the small hall. An alternative site was acquired in December 1950 in the adjacent Fortingale Street and plans were commissioned for a new building. Over the next three years, delay, difficulty and frustration set in. Robert Cunningham found himself facing problems on two fronts. Although the war was over, materials were still in short supply. More ominously, he found himself at odds with Methodism's officialdom. Questions were raised regarding the nearness of Conlon and Fortingale Streets to the churches at Carlisle Memorial and Agnes Street. There was clearly increasing opposition to the emerging building scheme. The superintendent could have understood the objections had they been voiced when the Conlon Street venture was getting off the ground. More than once he shared his disquiet with friends: he had been unsettled at the postponement of his appointment in 1949, and like Crawford Johnson before him, he thought he should have more support from his ministerial brethren than seemed to be coming his way.

These uncertainties and stresses coincided with an approach to him from the prestigious St Andrew's-Wesley congregation in Vancouver of the United Church of Canada. He responded positively to an invitation to fulfil a preaching engagement in St Andrew's-Wesley and taking his officials into his confidence, he made the return journey over a long weekend. The following Sunday evening as usual he welcomed worshippers at the front door of the Grosvenor Hall. One member met with a different greeting. He told her he had not seen her for some weeks. She replied that he had seen her more recently than that and he was amazed when she told him that it had been in Vancouver the previous Sunday. Robert Cunningham's world had become a village.

The preaching engagement was soon followed by a formal call to St Andrew's-Wesley and the Cunninghams left the Hall at the beginning of June 1954. There was a long tradition in the Hall of members 'going to the boat' to say farewell to one of their number who might be emigrating. It was never more movingly in evidence than on that June night. The choir, his men's Bible class of almost one hundred, and nearly three thousand others were there to say farewell to a superintendent greatly loved and whose departure they found hard to understand. He himself marched at the head of the Grosvenor Hall band to the dockside. In Canada he exercised an outstandingly successful ministry at St Andrew's-Wesley until his sudden death in February 1975. He was elected president of the Vancouver Conference and awarded an honorary doctorate of divinity.

Robert Cunningham left the Mission with its standing high in the estimation of the general public. A measure of that esteem is evidenced by the fact that in successive years the chair at the Mission's anniversary meeting had been taken in succession by the Lord Chief Justice of Northern Ireland, Lord MacDermott, the vice-chancellor of Queen's University Belfast, Dr (later Lord) Ashby and the Governor of Northern Ireland, Lord Wakehurst. At the 1954 anniversary meeting Lord Wakehurst stressed that, irrespective of the changes, 'The Mission would supply a personal touch which we could not expect from a Government Department.'

The Mission officials, Mr W.T. Bambrick, who succeeded Mr Dermot Johnson as honorary treasurer in September 1953, and secretary Mr Frank Anderson, along with the Mission Committee, had given long and anxious thought to the question of who should be the new superintendent. They finally submitted the names of two ministers, either of whom, if appointed, would have the confidence and support of the committee. They were the Reverend Joseph B. Jameson and the Reverend John W. Young, the latter an old boy of the Hall. In the event Joseph Jameson was appointed and transferred from the neighbouring Donegall Square church, thus becoming the fourth superintendent of the Mission to carry the dual responsibility of superintendency and secretaryship of the Conference. He came with a well-attested reputation for wisdom and efficiency in administration. The 1954 Conference appointed the Reverend (later Dr) Samuel H. Baxter as his senior colleague in the place of the Reverend Aelfryn Jones, who had succeeded the Reverend Hedley Plunkett in 1952, and who also went to Canada in 1954 in response to a call from the United Church.

The Jameson–Baxter combination augured well. Mr Baxter, a convinced evangelist, revelled in the Saturday evening film service and the large Sunday evening service. He was happy to be free from the worries of administration and to know that they were being efficiently looked after by the superintendent. The Conference had done well for the Mission in the two appointments.

Within weeks of his appointment, Mr Jameson was able to announce a benefaction of some thousands of pounds from Hugh Turtle in memory of his wife. The terms of the gift enabled substantial sums to be available at later dates for badly needed work in the children's home, and the building fund for the home for the elderly, started in 1962, and also for a continued investment which has enabled successive superintendents to make modest grants to deserving cases at their sole discretion.

In quick succession the committee was alerted to the necessity of providing more basic essentials at the children's and holiday homes at Childhaven. However, it was the work at Conlon Street that engaged the concentrated attention of the new superintendent. He had been the minister at Carlisle Memorial prior to his appointment at Donegall Square church and was well aware of what was happening in Conlon Street, almost on the door steps of the Carlisle Memorial and Agnes Street churches. He knew that although it was supported by considerable local enthusiasm, there were questions regarding the desirability of erecting a new building, and therefore it was essential to be circumspect and sensitive. He reported in detail to the Mission Committee at its March meeting. He indicated that it would cost at least £10,000 to erect a reasonably suitable building on a none-too-attractive site and that it would cost at least £1,000 per year to maintain the work. What was to be done? On his advice the matter was referred to the ensuing Belfast District Synod which appointed a special committee to study the situation and make recommendations.

Before the synod committee could hold its first meeting Mr Jameson tragically died. That spring he had begun to feel unwell but had made no complaint. He carried on with the work of the Mission and the heavy secretarial work in preparation for the coming Belfast Conference. He had arranged and took part in the official Conference Sunday service in Donegall Square church. When it came his turn to go to the pulpit for the scripture readings, his eyesight failed suddenly. By an amazing feat of memory and complete self-control, he was able to repeat the passages word for word and return to his seat without the congregation having any inkling of what had happened. Two days later he was under strict medical supervision and was confined to bed. He was admitted to hospital in early August and his death took place on 20 August 1955 at the age of fifty-two.

The superintendent's death was a cruel blow and it came at a time of converging problems. The Conlon Street dilemma, mounting concern about the financial viability of the children's home, day-to-day problems of bricks and mortar in the manses, were all compounded by his death and all happened against a background of accelerating social change. The president of the day appointed Samuel H. Baxter to the superintendency until the following Conference. The Mission Committee had no hesitation in welcoming the appointment and requesting its continuation in 1956. Mr Baxter faced up to the unexpected responsibilities with characteristic courage. The Church's committee, which dealt with ministerial emergencies, recognised his need of ministerial back-up and the Reverend A. Ivan Carson was appointed junior minister until the Conference of 1956, when he was succeeded by the present Home Mission Fund general secretary, the Reverend Paul Kingston.

As with his predecessor, it was Conlon Street and Childhaven that engaged Mr Baxter's administrative attention especially. The synod committee had not met and did not do so until November. It was composed of representatives of the Mission and the Carlisle Memorial, Agnes Street, Oldpark Road and Crumlin Road congregations. Its deliberations were reported in full to the Mission Committee on 16 December 1955 and to the ensuing spring synod. The result was a foregone conclusion. The synod directed that all work at Conlon Street should be discontinued. The Mission Committee was told on 22 June 1956 that the closing services would be held the following Sunday and that 'The Sunday School teachers and scholars will join Agnes Street Methodist Sunday School.' It was all probably inevitable but one is left to speculate as to what might have happened in that notoriously difficult social and political area if the building had been erected and the work developed. Undoubtedly Conlon Street was uncomfortably near the Carlisle Memorial and Agnes Street churches, but neither was doing the work or seemed likely to do the kind of work that the Mission had attempted with a good measure of success. Of the four congregations, other than the Grosvenor Hall, participating in the discussions and recommendations, only the one in Crumlin Road survives, and it was on the periphery of the Conlon Street area. As it was, the Mission was left with a non-negotiable plot of ground in Fortingale Street on which it paid ground rent until the whole area was vested for urban renewal purposes.

The children's home at Childhaven took up a great deal of Mr Baxter's time and attention. The willingness of the new welfare services to provide residential accommodation for children in need of care and protection and the financial viability of the home led to discussions with the National Children's Home, the child-care organisation of the British Methodist Church, and a visit from its principal, the Reverend John W. Waterhouse. At one stage it looked as if the Mission Committee might well request this organisation to take over the work at the home.

On top of these heavy responsibilities Mr Baxter and his staff were also coping with the gradual expansion of work at Springfield Road. The Reverend D. Brian Dougall, later to rise to the heights in the chaplaincy department of the British Army, was appointed for the year 1951–2. During the ministry of his successor, the Reverend Benjamin H. Taylor (1952–4), it was decided to replace the old corrugated building with a new church and hall. The congregation had outgrown what was formerly a British Legion club hall. The new buildings were opened in September 1956 during the ministry of the Reverend George R. Morrison (1954–8). Inevitably, however, the scheme added to the responsibilities of the three superintendents who were in post during these years of change.

Meanwhile, the Sunday evening service and the Saturday evening film service were a weekly challenge not to be avoided. Mr Baxter was never more fulfilled than when offering the good news of the gospel but he found the burden of administration militating against the kind of ministry to which he felt he had been called. At the March 1957 committee meeting he intimated a strong request to be relieved of the superintendency. It had not been an easy decision for him to reach and it took considerable moral courage to take it. It was only at his strong request that the committee acceded to his wish. It was fitting that at his last committee meeting in June, prior to his appointment to the Carlisle Road church in Londonderry, Miss Lucy Kerkham, the matron at Childhaven, paid a warm tribute to his work and interest in the welfare of the children. Her report contained these words:

> We at Childhaven are greatly indebted to Mr Baxter and wish to thank him for the many improvements that have been brought about in the last two years. They have greatly aided the smooth running of the Home and added to the comfort of us all.

It was a well-deserved tribute: 'inasmuch as you have done it to one of the least of these. . .' Could any person ask for greater appreciation?

Mrs Robert R. Cunningham lays a foundation stone for the new Springfield Road church on 15 May 1954. The president of the Methodist Church, Dr R.M.L. Waugh is second from left, and to his left are Robert R. Cunningham and A. Benjamin Taylor.

Boys from Conlon Street hall about to set off in July 1954 for the holiday home at Childhaven, Millisle. Sharing the fun is the Mission's superintendent, Joseph B. Jameson, who was to die tragically in 1955.

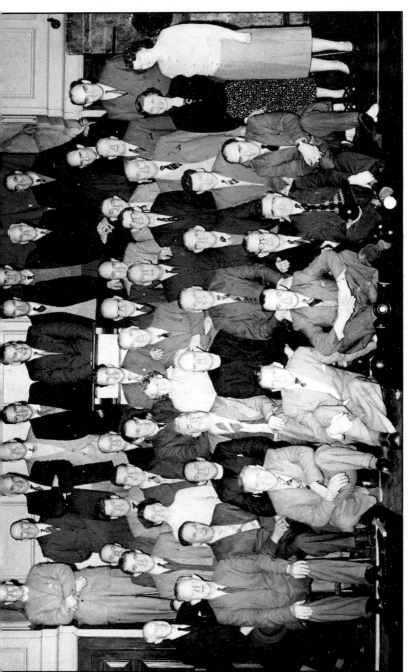

The Grosvenor Hall Bowling Club, 1956, with Dr Samuel H. Baxter (second row, fifth from left) and Richard Greenwood (second row, third from left).

The Mission's anniversary is always a great occasion. In February 1958 the visiting preacher was Dr William E. Sangster pictured here with Mission staff: left to right, Paul Kingston, Jean Richardson, Eric Gallagher, Dr Sangster, John N. Spence, Mary Gihon and Richard

Castle Rocklands, Carrickfergus. The gift in June 1960 of Mr and Mrs J.R. Thomson, executors of Mrs Boyd's will, the house was opened as a home for senior citizens on 6 June 1964.

The Grosvenor Hall stewards and members of the ministerial staff, 1964. The chief steward, William T. Millington, is seated third from left; to his immediate left are Joseph McCrory, Eric Gallagher and John Robinson.

Easter residential conferences for young people were held at Childhaven, Millisle, each year during the 1960s and 1970s; this 1964 group includes two future candidates for the ministry – the late Robert Bradford MP and Leslie Spence.

A Sunday-school anniversary choir, May 1967, at Grosvenor Hall, accompanied by Miss Alice Hutchinson on piano, with Douglas

# IN THE GATHERING STORM
## 1957–69

T he Mission Committee gave anxious consideration to the question of a successor to Dr Baxter. Frequent changes in the pastoral care of any congregation are serious: for a mission they are more serious still. Continuity is essential to public confidence. Eventually they unanimously requested the appointment of the Reverend Dr Albert Holland. They had reason on their side: he knew the Hall and its people; his ten-year spell (1928–38) as second minister was still gratefully remembered. He had made his name as an administrator as general secretary of the Church's Home Mission Fund and the stationing committee considered his continued service there essential to wider Methodism. When the final list of appointments appeared in June 1957, it carried the name of Eric Gallagher at the Grosvenor Hall station instead of Albert Holland. Thus I became the Mission's fourth superintendent within seven years.

I faced the appointment with misgiving. The Mission Committee had asked for someone else. I had no experience whatever of city-mission work and the change in itself was traumatic. I preached my farewell sermons in the quiet dignity of University Road church and two days later I found myself for the first time parading the streets of Bangor, Co. Down, at the head of the Grosvenor Hall band on the 13 July street collection. It was my introduction to the street-collection experience and it was an early lesson in the Mission's need of maintaining a high public profile. It was all unknown territory to be explored with the loyal help of my colleagues, the Reverend Richard Greenwood, later to be principal of Edgehill College, the Reverend Paul Kingston, now the general secretary of the Home Mission Fund, and the two deaconesses, Mary Gihon and Jean Richardson. Gradually I realised I had the confidence of the committee: I had not been in doubt about their good will.

At my first committee meeting in September Richard Greenwood declared that there were twenty thousand people in the Sandy Row area not going to church. It was an indication of the need for a concerted strategy for the inner city that would crop up frequently over following years. The first major worries, however, had to do with property. Springfield Road church had been opened only a year previously but was badly underheated. By December 1957, a tender for a new system had been accepted. The Reverend Thomas A. Hartley (1958–63) instigated the erection of a minor hall and the installation of a pipe organ. He and his successor, the Reverend Arthur D.L. Sleath (1963–9), consolidated the work begun in the new church by Mr Morrison. The omens seemed to be encouraging.

Another problem was lurking round the corner. After years of relief from rates, a rating inspector paid a visit to the Grosvenor Hall premises. The visit was followed by a crippling demand for rates. Recourse was had again to the law. Mr Brian Rankin of Cleaver, Fulton and Rankin, the Mission's solicitor, and Mr John Caskey, valuer, of Martin, Son and Caskey, along with the professionally experienced committee member Mr William H. Patterson, were invaluable advisors. With Richard Greenwood, I spent days listing the precise use to which every room in the vast complex had been put on every day of the preceding four years. We built up a dossier that persuaded the judge at the Belfast Recorder's Court to relieve the Mission of the threatened burden.

There are two big occasions in every Mission year. The first is the Christmas programme with its ten thousand postal appeals, the Christmas Eve street collection, and the social-relief programme, itself then including the Christmas Day dinner and entertainment and the concerts on Christmas and Boxing Nights given by the male voice choir, with the irrepressible Bob Maguire in his role as Mrs Mop. In 1957 it was negotiated successfully, passing all previous financial totals. The other occasion is the anniversary meeting early in the new calendar year. At that time it was always necessary to book the speaker at least a couple of years in advance. The late Dr William E. Sangster, formerly of

Westminster Central Hall, and then the general secretary of the British Methodist Home Mission Department, had accepted the invitation to be the 1958 anniversary preacher. By any standards the weekend could not have gone better. It gave me great encouragement.

Social conditions in Belfast continued to change. In September 1958 Richard Greenwood told the committee 'The Steps are left to the pigeons.' He was of course referring to Custom House Square and the disappearance of the large crowds. Undoubtedly the pigeons were enjoying more room to forage for food but there were still encouraging numbers of people to listen and there was opposition as well. There was another preacher, at the other side of the square, who reminded all and sundry, in a voice that would have awakened the dead, that the road to Hell was littered with the skulls of Methodist preachers. 'Don't listen to them,' he would shout. 'They will tell you about the love of God – I want to tell you about the wrath of God.'

That was not the worst of the opposition. Increasingly, interruptions came from Free Presbyterians and their fellow-travellers. For a long time the late Major Ronald Bunting, for example, was a regular at the meeting. Unfailingly courteous in a way that others were not, at some stage of the meeting he would produce a note book. Then he would read out a number of searching questions. Notes of the answers were taken down and one always suspected that they were dealt with fully in another place before the night was out. In later years major and superintendent were to have a certain respect and regard for each other. More sinister were the attempts by other fellow-travellers to interrupt the meeting altogether. On many occasions they lined up a car battery to microphone and loud speaker at the feet of the Grosvenor Hall audience. They then blasted hymn tunes and other forms of interruptions at the meeting. In the long run the effort was counterproductive for it increased sympathy and support for the speakers. The first time I spoke to Mr Gerry (now Lord) Fitt was when he saw me in Belfast City Hall and said he had heard me the previous Sunday at the Steps. He continued that if that was what the Methodist Church stood for, he liked it. For years afterwards Gerry Fitt's £5 note was as regular as his amble down Donegall

Place in his own inimitable gait on a Christmas Eve. Tragically, community violence and the threat to his own personal safety later made that walk impossible.

From 1959 onwards the movement and decrease of population were recurring themes at committee meetings. Nevertheless, there were still in 1960 full houses at the Saturday evening film service and these continued until the outbreak of civil unrest in 1968. And up until the same date it was possible to count on Sunday evenings on anything between eleven hundred and sixteen hundred people. There was a regular print run of fifteen hundred orders of service for Sunday evenings. Sermons were prepared with particular subjects in mind. Richard Greenwood and I alternated each Sunday evening. We were responsible for several series of special services on such themes as 'Home and family life', 'Marriage', Protestant doctrines and various issues of current concern. One could always identify in the congregation people from different walks of life who had come to hear a particular subject being dealt with. One evening the subject for consideration was a Roman Catholic doctrine with which many Protestants have some difficulty — papal infallibility. The pope had died a few days previously. At the commencement of the sermon I took time to express sympathy with the Catholic people in their loss. I then went on to deal faithfully with the doctrine under consideration. At the end of the service I was called to the phone to be met with a torrent of abuse for daring to offer the slightest word of sympathy to the Catholic Church. I realised how much I had to learn about deeply-rooted prejudice. It is only fair to add that the objection was not typical of the Hall congregation.

Reporters were frequently present at the Sunday evening service. Favourable comment on the sermons in leading articles in each of the Belfast newspapers was not uncommon. Failing the presence of reporters, there was as often as not a phone call on Sunday afternoon or on Sunday evening asking for details of the sermon. The Mission did not suffer in public esteem.

In the summer of 1960 there came the offer of property at Castle Rocklands in Carrickfergus, Co. Antrim, bequeathed for the development of a home for the elderly. This new venture was to take a great deal of time and energy over the next three years.

Meanwhile, other property matters were pressing. They included major renovation at Childhaven, the complete rewiring of the whole Grosvenor Hall complex, negotiations with the late Lord Rank, son of Joseph Rank, which resulted in the gift and installation of screen and cinemascope equipment, and an unsuccessful attempt to purchase adjoining premises on the city side of the main Hall. The Large Hall underwent badly-needed redecoration in 1962. Then came major damage to the brickwork of all the Hall's external walls caused by corrosion of the steel framework. There seemed to be no end to the problems of this kind.

In 1958 I had become, without warning, the fifth superintendent of the Mission to hold the post of secretary of the Irish Methodist Conference. I soon found the combined responsibilities of both positions at times almost intolerable. The General Committee of the Church appointed a strong committee to consider the situation. An hour-by-hour detail of the work done over many months was asked for and considered carefully. Those who examined it recognised the burden that was being carried. As a solution they purchased a dictaphone and presented it to the Mission! Had it not been for the loyalty of the Reverend Thomas Woods, who succeeded Richard Greenwood on his appointment as superintendent of the Mountpottinger circuit, and who in turn was succeeded by the equally loyal Reverend Joseph McCrory in 1963, and that of all their colleagues, the work would have suffered disastrously.

Changes were taking place in personnel with the passing of time. The Reverend Thomas A. Noble had replaced Paul Kingston in 1958 and in turn he was followed by the Reverend Ernest W. O'Neill in 1960. Mr John Young died in 1962. He had brought his long and devoted service officially to a conclusion in March 1951, though he continued to give invaluable voluntary help and advice until the time of his death. Mr Robert J. Stockdale relinquished the superintendency of the morning Sunday school in 1964, after years of self-effacing service. He was succeeded by another of the Mission's faithfuls, Mr John H. Weir, secretary of the leaders' meeting, a wise and dependable counsellor and father of the present secretary of the Mission Committee, Mr Wesley Weir. Youth work was the responsibility of a succession of energetic junior ministers, the Reverend C.G. Walpole (1961–2), W. Brown (1962–3), J. Robinson (1963–5), R.D. Rodgers (1965–8), A. Parker (1968–9), D. Houston (1969–70), and R.D. Moore (1970–2). All of them served well and loyally but undoubtedly the lack of continuity was a liability. Nevertheless, each year saw its quota of constructive work among young people. Early in 1965 Mr Frank M. Anderson brought his long term as secretary of the Mission Committee to a conclusion. The Anderson family had served with devotion and none more so than Frank and his wife Margaret. For many years they had given up the greater part of every Christmas Day to go to Childhaven and share it with the children. Mr Anderson's place was taken by Mr William H. Patterson, who brought to the secretaryship attention to detail and valuable experience in the property field.

The 1960s were the years of industrial expansion and there seemed to be a new hope of better cross-community relations. For the record, it is worth noting that Prime Minister Captain Terence O'Neill's Stormont meeting with the Republic's Premier Sean Lemass in 1965 was commended at the film service on the following Saturday night. There was no sign of any dissent. The support of the Mission staff for better relationships in the community did not go unnoticed. On 6 July 1964 the *Belfast News Letter* reported one of my recent sermons, quoting my conviction that God was not calling Ulster to 'religious guerilla warfare'. Joseph McCrory and I found ourselves again and again calling for courage and resolution in face of the coming storm. In January 1965 the congregation was told that a 'recrudescence of religious extremism' was showing itself in many unseemly forms — in character abuse, in scurrilous and defamatory pamphlets, in political pressure groups and other attempts at coercion. The distinguished journalist, the late Dr John E. Sayers, presided at the 1966 anniversary meeting. He paid tribute to the influence and work of the Mission in the emerging unrest. As he spoke the sound of loyalist bands could be heard parading to a party demonstration in the Ulster Hall. The bands persuaded me to say, when I got up to speak, 'I look out tonight upon a city that needs as it never needed before a gospel of reconciliation.' This too was quoted in the *Belfast News Letter* on 1 March 1966. In June of that year in Dublin the Conference designated me for the presidency of the

Church in the following year. The *Belfast Telegraph,* reporting the designation, made the comment: 'He is the only minister who still speaks at the Custom House steps every Sunday afternoon.'

My presidential year was a heavy one with regard to wider Methodist duties and many public engagements. On top of it all the major renovation scheme at Childhaven demanded a great deal of personal attention. Joseph McCrory, supported by his colleagues, kept the work of the Mission going magnificently. The Reverend James Wisheart, who retired in 1967, brought the wisdom of years and an irrepressibly buoyant spirit to a year of greatly-appreciated pastoral assistance. During my year of office, I made contacts that were to affect not only my own life but inevitably the life of the Mission and its people. On 1 January 1968 I joined with the Presbyterian moderator, Dr William Boyd, the Archbishop of Armagh, Dr James McCann, and Cardinal Conway in a joint appeal to the Irish people that they should pray not only for world peace but particularly for peace in Ireland. That appeal was historic: it was the first such joint initiative.

In the autumn of 1968 my public and inter-Church contacts led to my being caught up week after week in some reconciliation initiative or another with no markedly successful results. At the request of the Queen's University Belfast chaplains I joined a deputation to Captain O'Neill in the interest of calming the growing unrest. During that meeting the prime minister said that Londonderry should be governed by its Catholic majority but the Unionists would not have it: 'It was a sacred cow.' The deluge was coming and was bound to affect the Mission more than it realised. Yet looking back, the Mission congregation seemed to be in good shape at the end of 1968.

The holiday home had provided a resource which was, and still is, invaluable in the building up of the congregation. Every Easter and at other times large numbers of older teenagers and young adults had made their way to Childhaven, sometimes on foot on a sponsored walk, to live and play and think and talk together. Numbers of today's leaders and members can trace their interest in and commitment to the Mission and its work back to the influence of the Easter conferences. Their loyalty to the Hall in the latter years of strain and stress goes back to what they learned and experienced then. As some of them married and set up homes in other areas, they joined other congregations which today benefit as a result. Two of them, Leslie Spence and Robert Bradford, entered the ministry. No one could have anticipated the brutality of the Provisional Irish Republican Army that would bring the Reverend Robert Bradford's young and promising life to a tragic end in 1981.

By 1968 much had been accomplished – the home for the elderly at Castle Rocklands had been opened and work on its bungalow colony had started at a cost of well over £80,000; the holiday programme had been given a new look with its growing emphasis on old people and plans for extension were in preparation. The work with young people had been consolidated; the Mission's organisations were running smoothly; the band was having a run of major successes; the male voice choir was packing the Hall on Christmas Night, Boxing Night and St Patrick's Night, all in the interests of Childhaven; the film service was as popular as ever and the Sunday evening service was still well attended; and financial support was growing every year. A search for increased accommodation had been attempted. Grosvenor Hall could still provide a forum for such diverse religious personalities as Gladys Aylward of the 'Inn of the Sixth Happiness' fame, Cliff Richard, Beverley Shea, Bishop Trevor Huddleston, Dr William Sangster, Dr Colin Morris and other luminaries in the Methodist tradition or otherwise. Conviction and commitment among many young adults were evident.

With the burden of the secretaryship of the Conference and the presidency behind me, I was looking forward to concentrating on the Mission's work with an undivided mind. The committee shared my hope for opportunities to consolidate and also to attempt new ventures. We were of course aware that more movement of population would take place before resettlement in the redeveloped areas but there was no reason for alarm about the future. Not even the most pessimistic suspected the storm that was to come.

# 11

# OF PEACE AND RECONCILIATION
## 1969–79

The autumn of 1968 and the events that followed were a watershed in the history of Northern Ireland. In the worsening situation of marches and counter-marches Prime Minister Captain Terence O'Neill made his dramatic broadcast appeal to the people calling for a halt to disruption. Ulster Television invited the prime minister and the leader of the opposition, the late Mr Eddie McAteer, to take part in a Christmas programme stressing the theme of good will. I was asked to chair the programme. I regarded that as an indication of recognition of what the Mission stood for. When the recording was completed, the prime minister talked about his Christmas plans: 'We are going to England for a couple of weeks. We need to get away.' I understood how he and his wife needed rest and quiet but I had an uneasy feeling that Northern Ireland without him could be a dangerous place.

Events quickly proved how justified that feeling was. The ambush of the civil rights march at Burntollet in January 1969 and the Troubles that followed it were just around the corner. The quality of life in Northern Ireland was changing rapidly and the Hall and Mission were being caught up in the unrest more and more. Before long we realised we were striving not only to preserve the fabric of the Hall but also the very life of the Mission itself. It was also clear that media interest in what was being said in the Hall and reaction to it indicated that a wider public was paying attention as the people of Northern Ireland were being urged to be true to their essential being as children of the one God. After 1968 the word 'mission' took on a wider and deeper meaning. This awareness was reinforced by responses to local and network radio services in which Joe McCrory and I participated, to network *Songs of Praise* programmes and to frequent radio and television epilogues, discussions and interviews. They were followed by a plethora of hostile letters, many of them anonymous, and abusive phone calls (many of them in the small hours) and there was always the worry that my children might overhear the threats. On the other hand there was far more gratitude and appreciation from both sides of the religious divide.

In the January 1969 committee meeting the resignation of Mr Wilfrid Bambrick as honorary treasurer was received with regret. He had brought a keen and penetrating mind to the affairs of the Mission. He continued to serve on the committee until his sudden death two years later. He was succeeded as honorary treasurer by Mr David Montgomery, who had already given valuable service as secretary to the trustees and the housing association responsible for Castle Rocklands. The same meeting also paid tribute to one of its members, Mr Norman Thompson, for many years the dedicated leader of the Brother Man service. His widow, for some years the Mission secretary, and his son, Dr Richard Thompson, are still members of the congregation. Mr Thompson's place was taken by Mr Harold Whitten, whose father had been one of the early members.

This was a time when there seemed to be opportunities for expansion. The Mission was being encouraged by the city welfare officials to contemplate providing an old people's day centre. Unexpectedly in March 1969 the factory premises on the upper side of the Hall came on the market. They were bought with the assistance of a £5,000 grant from the Rank Trust. The architects, Messrs Ferguson and McIlveen, were immediately commissioned to prepare plans for a youth centre on the top floors and a day centre for senior citizens on the lower floors. Other property matters were pressing also. Sister Mary Gihon had been conscious for a long time of the need to modernise and possibly extend the holiday home at Millisle. With the major scheme at the children's home completed, the time was opportune to commission plans for a complete renovation and extension.

Other things being equal, in the spring of 1969 the Mission seemed set for two or three significant steps forward. However, the deteriorating situation put a question mark against many of the hopes. Crisis followed crisis in the political and community life of Northern Ireland. On his resignation in April 1969, Captain Terence O'Neill was succeeded by Major James Chichester-Clark. The marching season was a period of extreme tension. The events following the Apprentice Boys of Derry traditional march on 12 August were the final match to the fuse. In the absence of the president I had returned from holiday for a crisis meeting of Church leaders. Later in the evening of Thursday, 14 August I did a round of the Belfast newspaper offices delivering a joint appeal for peace to be published in the next day's issue. The appeal was out of date before it was printed: during the night, widespread violence had erupted in Belfast and across Northern Ireland.

Before the next day's work was well underway, the welfare authorities had asked for accommodation to be made available in Grosvenor Hall for refugees. By 11 a.m. bedding, food and helpers were being looked for. About the same time the head-quarters of the Unionist Party next door to the Hall requested me to speak to the party secretary, the late Mr James Baillie. For the first time I made my way across the threshold. I found myself talking also to a party of shipyard workers led by Sandy Scott, a shop steward. He told me they wanted me to speak at a peace meeting in the yard at lunchtime – they did not want any trouble there. They were hoping to get Brian Faulkner as well, or one of the other cabinet ministers if he could not come. I replied that I had never addressed a crowd like that in my life, that the workers knew where I stood and that I was worried their peace meeting could 'turn into a rough house'. Nevertheless, the men pressed their request, they believed the workers would listen to me. Their final remark clinched the issue: they said it was time people stood up to be counted. Before I had time to think, I was being driven to the yard by Jim Rea, now superintendent of the East Belfast Mission, who was doing student work in the Hall that summer. As Roy Bradford MP, who had been secured as the political spokesman, addressed the crowd, the shop stewards asked me to conclude my speech with a prayer. Even though I was unsure as to how the crowd of men would take it, I did end with a prayer, after appealing to them to keep things quiet in the yard and to use their influence in their own home areas. And spontaneously the men took off their caps: some of them were even seen to weep.

Back in the Hall Joe McCrory had been busy. The refugee centre had been opened. Over a couple of nights accommodation and food were provided for a total of between fifty and sixty people. In 1969 it was still possible for Protestants and Catholics to share the same hospitality, such as it was. More significant in the long term were the meaningful contacts which the Mission made with the Catholic community. Food and clothing far in excess of what was needed came pouring in. The natural thing to do was to share it with those who had the greatest need, so each morning Joe McCrory, accompanied by my son David, then a boy at school, did a round of other shelters in the adjoining parts of west Belfast and shared with them the clothing and provisions that could be spared.

On the Sunday afternoon after the eruption of violence I spoke as usual at the Custom House. As I arrived home I was called to the telephone. I had never met nor spoken to the caller. He was a former IRA chief of staff. He asked if I could use any influence to get the buses back on the Falls Road and said if men could not get to work, they would find other things to do. I told him that buses were needed on the Shankill Road also and asked why he had come to me. His answer was that he knew what the Mission and I stood for and he was as anxious as me to see the people of Belfast — and that included the 'Shankill as much as the Falls' — living and working together. I responded to his request with a phone call to a member of the cabinet secretariat. The buses were back on the streets by the next day, whether or not as a result of the phone call, I am not aware.

Such was the Mission's introduction to the endless years that lay ahead, during which it sometimes looked as if the Hall would be destroyed. At one time there were twenty-two bomb-damage claims by the Mission with the Northern Ireland Office, some for many thousands of pounds. Members of staff were repeatedly in the building when bombs exploded nearby. One afternoon large chunks of metal from the ceiling ventilators in the Large Hall crashed through the flooring below. Perhaps the most serious incident of all was on Wednesday, 22 March 1972. The women's meeting assembled as usual in the Ker Hall. A massive bomb had been placed in a van parked in the bus station on the other side of Glengall Street. Literally seconds before it exploded, a soldier of the Parachute Regiment realised there could be people in the Hall. The rest of the buildings in the street had been cleared. He looked in and saw between sixty and seventy elderly women. Horrified, he ordered their immediate evacuation. Before they had reached the door, the bomb went off and the huge window frames on the Glengall Street side were hurled on top of the chairs where the women had been sitting. Five seconds sooner, many of them would certainly have been killed. As it was, several of them were taken to hospital suffering from shock or lacerations. I was due that night to speak at a meeting in Dublin. I did not go. A copy of my script had been sent ahead to the secretary of the Church group that had invited me and my speech was read in my absence. An *Irish Times* report on 23 March 1972 quoted from it:

> You can see before your eyes all the clear signs of a Greek tragedy moving remorselessly to its final agony. Reconciliation is the pressing imperative and it can only come from inside the two communities.

From 1969 to 1972 rioting and bombing were frequent and the summers, particularly, seemed endless. Night after night the Hall was on 'stand-by' with a member of staff and volunteers from the congregation waiting for a request from the welfare authority to open up the Hall or for the all-clear about midnight. There were also what Joe McCrory called the nightly 'bomb-runs', when the ministerial staff would make their way to any bombed street or district where Grosvenor Hall members lived. There were funerals of those killed, one of which turned without the slightest warning into a well-organised paramilitary occasion. After that, one realised the need for care before criticising others for having acquiesced in or allowed such funerals to take place.

There were other opportunities for seeking reconciliation – for instance, I was invited to serve on the prime minister's 'Peace Conference' in 1969. The Mission shared responsibility for allocating grants from the large amount of money in the city's Innocent Victims' Fund, initiated by the Labour Government, and many had reason to be grateful for the compassion of Joe McCrory as he dealt with the needs of suffering humanity. There was not a month in the early 1970s that did not produce some crisis, if not tragedy, as far as the Mission and its congregation were concerned. Three of them deserve to be dealt with at length.

The first was in the summer of 1970. On Saturday, 27 June there was widespread trouble in the city. New Barnsley estate, where there had been unrest at Easter (thought to have been deliberately fuelled for political purposes), was reported to be under attack and people were being driven from their homes. We had been alerted some weeks previously to fears of communal violence and the possible need of the Hall as a refugee centre if the situation demanded it. The events of the next two weeks are narrated in a report submitted to the Government. Extracts from it tell their own story:

### REPORT OF GROSVENOR HALL REFUGEE CENTRE
### 27 JUNE—9 JULY 1970

1 The call to open the centre was received at 7.50 p.m. on Saturday, 27th June. It was opened at 8.00 p.m. and by 9.00 p.m. the first refugees began to arrive.

2 We had sufficient voluntary helpers to make the centre operational. Food was delivered by the Welfare Authority in good time.

3 The first big test came with large numbers in the early evening of Sunday. Additional helpers were recruited and by 8.00 p.m. the Large Hall had been made ready. The Kitchen staff had also been alerted and hot meals were in course of preparation. Additional beds and blankets were reported to be on the way.

4 By 11.00 p.m. there was no indication of the beds or blankets. The proprietor of a camping equipment firm undertook to hire us his full supply of beds for whatever period might be necessary. Contact was made with Police Headquarters and arrangements made for an Army truck to collect the business man at his home, bring him to his shop, take the beds to Grosvenor Hall and the man back to his home. Unfortunately he was attacked by a mob when trying to open up his premises and had to be rescued by the Soldiers. In the event the beds and blankets arrived separately in the small hours of Monday morning.

5 Monday morning, 29 June, presented the second major problem. It was that of catering adequately for large numbers of high spirited children. At our request 1/3 Welfare Buses were made

available. These were used morning, afternoon and evening to take (a) to their homes those who could go there during daylight hours and (b) the larger numbers of children (with supplies of Coca-Cola and potato crisps) on excursions and visits to public parks and playing areas.

6 Plentiful supplies of foodstuffs were provided by the Welfare Authority. The voluntary helpers prepared breakfast, tea and supper and 'top-tray' lunches were arranged.

7 Health and general hygiene were seen to. The Welfare Authority arranged for Health Visitors during working hours and the remainder of the 24 hours was covered by Red Cross personnel. The large numbers involved put a strain on the normal cleaning and refuse disposal arrangements. Voluntary helpers co-operated in sweeping the floors of the Large Hall and Play areas, the Ker Hall and all the Lavatories, morning, afternoon and evening.

8 That all the New Barnsley families who requested it were re-housed reflects great credit on Mr David Fraser and his assistants from the staff of the Welfare Department who were seconded to the Centre. The Grosvenor Hall second-hand clothes supply was of considerable assistance.

9 Prayers for the children were arranged nightly and a voluntary Church Service was provided on the Sunday.

10 The R.U.C. were most helpful. Security coverage was always good.

11 Security arrangements were tightened: still more because of an unexploded bomb found in the offices of the Unionist Party next door and unauthorised visitors.

12 At least daily visits to the centre were paid by the City Welfare Officer or some of his senior assistants. Ministry officials also visited.

13 The clergy and ministers of the New Barnsley area received lists of addresses to which their former parishioners had gone.

The full report with comments and appendices, including a complete list of all who had received accommodation, with their former and new addresses, was sent to the Government and to the city welfare officer. A letter of appreciation also went to each of the voluntary helpers. This extract indicates the wide range of volunteers:

> The many helpers and volunteers included house-wives, old age pensioners, school pupils, head masters, civil servants, business executives, ministers of religion, students, office, factory and ship-yard workers, university lecturers, transport operatives, medical graduates, nurses, social workers, commercial travellers and manu-facturers' agents, Lions, VSB [Voluntary Service Belfast], Red Cross, Rotarians and PACE [Protestant and Catholic Encounter] members besides. They crossed the religious divide and their ages ranged from seventeen minus to seventy plus. . .
>
> Then too there were the V.I.P.s – the Minister of Development, Mr Brian Faulkner and his entourage of civil servants and security officers, and Lord Mayor who spent so much time talking to so many, the Chairman of the Welfare Authority, the President of our Church (who insisted on sending me home one night and doing duty for me), the Bishop of Connor, the Clerk of the General Assembly, the Chairman of the Community Relations Commission, the Secre-tary of the Northern Ireland Council of Social Service, press, radio and television reporters from Europe, America, Asia and of course from England and the Republic.
>
> But above all we think of the folk for whose sake the whole operation was mounted – the peak figure reached was 138 and we were around the 100 mark for about a week. Many of you will recall the utter desolation of the little old woman in her wheelchair who was brought in on the Sunday afternoon. She had escaped being burned out of her kitchen house as she sat terrified watching gunmen on the roof outside her back window. We saw the death of a community that had lived happily together for almost a generation. Late one night one of the men folk said to me as he thought of the widely separated areas where they were resettling – Carrickfergus, Antrim, Lisburn, Rathcoole, Glencairn, Bangor, Dundonald, any-where. 'We feel like seeds blown in the wind.' He said it without bitterness and he taught me something all of us need to learn. . .
>
> Was it worth the trouble?
>
> Perhaps the last three minutes before the last families left us give the answer. There were tears in their eyes as they went to new strange homes that afternoon. There was the bouquet of flowers presented with embarrassment but with gratitude, 'on behalf of us all'. That said enough. It said everything!

The helpers to whom that letter was addressed included a Queen's University student, whose graduation day we marked

As the Troubles brewed in 1968 Ulster Television broadcast a special good-will Christmas programme. Prime Minister Captain Terence O'Neill (right) and the leader of the opposition, Eddie McAteer (left), read and commented on Bible passages of their choice. The Mission's superintendent, Eric Gallagher (centre), chaired the programme.

(Photograph courtesy of Ulster Television)

Grosvenor Hall young people about to set out on a sponsored walk to Childhaven, Millisle, for the 1969 Easter conference.

A mass meeting at Harland and Wolff on 15 August 1969, the day after violence erupted in Belfast; shop steward Sandy Scott, cabinet minister Roy Bradford MP, and Eric Gallagher called for restraint. (Photograph courtesy of Harland and Wolff plc)

Refugee children from New Barnsley estate, welfare staff and voluntary workers, returning to Grosvenor Hall after an outing in July 1970.

Great Victoria Street railway station and the bus depot in Glengall Street, Belfast, lie in ruins after a bomb attack on 22 March 1972. Members of the Mission's women's meeting narrowly escaped death in the Ker Hall, severely damaged by the blast; several were taken to hospital.

(Photograph courtesy of the *Irish Times*)

A singsong for guests and workers at the women's meeting Christmas dinner, 1969.
(Photograph courtesy of Century Newspapers)

Mission and Craigmore House (previously Childhaven Children's Home) staff, March 1989. Left to right: David Kerr, superintendent; John Gibson, officer-in-charge, Craigmore House, and his deputy, Miss Cindy Scott; William R. Sharpe, the Mission's director of social work; and Mr Kerr's predecessor, Dr Norman Taggart.

A group of Mission staff and leaders at the new Sandy Row church, opened on 2 April 1988, including its minister, Sydney Callaghan, and the superintendent, David Kerr, (front row, third and fourth from right).

by a cake complete with candles. It was cut and eaten late at night after the refugees had gone to sleep. Today that guest of honour is a well-known and respected senior civil servant. During the week, my wife, Barbara, and I celebrated our silver wedding when, along with our three young people, we slipped away for a couple of hours from our temporary home to the manse where members of our extended family had prepared a meal. It was fitting that Lord Grey of Naunton, the governor of Northern Ireland, should pay tribute to the Mission's work in the community at an anniversary meeting during those years.

The second crisis was the virtual disappearance of the Protestant population from the Grosvenor Road area. The years 1969 and 1970 changed probably for all time the demographic spread in Belfast. The Falls Road curfew of 1970 increased tension in the district. Rightly or wrongly the Protestant people felt vulnerable. The violence following the introduction of internment in the year 1971 was the final straw. In street after street the arrival of a van or lorry signalled a family removal to be followed by another and another until every house had been emptied and then occupied by someone or a family from the 'other side', whatever the 'other side' might be. Within two years or less, the Hall's pastoral as distinct from its social-welfare list had been altered out of all recognition. To take one case in point: in 1969 there were four visiting units or areas on the Grosvenor Road, one on the north side and three on the south. Any one of them had sufficient Mission families on the pastoral list to keep a minister or deaconess busy with visits for one week. Today there is not one Methodist family and probably no Protestant families between the Presbyterian Assembly Buildings on Fisherwick Place and the Catholic Falls Road.

Besides the Protestant exodus out of west and part of north Belfast and the Catholic influx into it, urban redevelopment was responsible for a massive reduction in the overall population of three of the Hall's best 'feeder' areas. The following decennial census figures are self-explanatory:

|                     | 1971  | 1981  |
|---------------------|-------|-------|
| Donegall Road       | 7,789 | 6,227 |
| Grosvenor Road      | 7,385 | 2,235 |
| Shankill Road Lower | 8,337 | 5,811 |

The town planners had a field day. They proposed the demoliton of street after street and their replacement with new housing of modern design and finish. Their proposals were accepted by the Government and housing authorities and then began the total clearance of some inner-city areas. They also dispersed the population, many being offered large sums of money (the Government referred to them as resettlement grants, some called them bribes) as an encouragement to leave Belfast altogether. In the process the Hall lost much of its congregation and if that was not bad enough, there followed the clearance of anything that stood in the way of the West Link, the new urban dual carriageway that was to join the M1 and M2; it literally cut a massive swathe out of the heartland of the Hall's congregation. Its effect on Belfast's religious and social life is beyond estimation.

Exacerbating these difficulties was the infamous peaceline, which was constructed at the start of the sectarian unrest and which obstructed the journey of scores of people who had been accustomed for generations to make their way on foot across Townsend Street or Percy Street or Conway Street on their way via Divis Street to the Hall. That is a journey not to be attempted now. Yet in spite of it all there was still a congregation that remained completely loyal and generous, the spiritual nerve centre of a still-expanding service albeit to a diminished community.

The third crisis was the Ulster Workers' Council strike of 1974, which brought down the Northern Ireland Executive. There was concern regarding food and other supplies for the children and old people at Childhaven and Castle Rocklands and worry as to whether or not the staff could get through the paramilitary picket lines. Fortunately, enough supplies were in stock and without exception the staff managed to get to the homes – the work they were doing was sufficient to warrant a 'pass'. It was a different matter looking after the pastoral needs of a widely-scattered congregation. Joe McCrory and I made it clear that we would not be buying any 'paramilitary' petrol. Everything possible was done on foot or by telephone. Some members of the congregation were recruited to act as local pastors, and what limited supplies of bread and other food the Hall received were distributed strictly according to need.

Throughout it all the Mission's ethos stood the test. The founding fathers had left behind them a congregation of remarkable tolerance and insight coupled with evangelistic and social concern. In 1910 R.M. Ker had paid his tribute to a congregation that could hold opposing political points of view. The same spirit was there in the 1970s when member after member refused to surrender to sectarianism. Few congregations know more of what it means to put the gospel into practice.

In December 1974 the quality and depth of the Grosvenor Hall congregation were seen at their best. Many of them had already shown their concern for reconciliation in the community. Sister Mary Gihon, Marjorie Gill and others were members of a Catholic–Protestant Bible-study group which met regularly in the Springfield–Clonard area. Many of the congregation faced abuse as they refused to bow to paramilitary pressures. One family astounded the commanding officer of a British Army unit by giving bed and shelter to the children of a suspected republican 'on the run'. The security forces had been tipped off that his children were 'in a house across the street' and of course it was raided. The CO wanted to know what was going on and was told that although there was no approval of what the children's father was doing, the children were not to blame and had a right to sleep at night. The officer had little to say except he did not understand and if there were more people like them, his job would be easier. Within the congregation every political party was supported; one young member made it clear that he voted for the Social Democratic and Labour Party. However, an event was about to take place that would severely put their tolerance to the test.

On 9–11 December 1974 I took part in the secret discussions between Protestant Churchmen and representatives of Provisional Sinn Feín and Provisional IRA held in Feakle, Co. Clare, in an attempt to bring about an end to the campaign of violence. Like the other Churchmen, I was acting as an individual, not as a representative of my Church, but I was the only one who had a direct responsibility for the pastoral care of a congregation. The Sunday night before the talks I preached from the text 'Blessed are the peace makers'. I pointed out that the peacemaker was subject to criticism and misrepresentation. Just before I left, I told Joe

McCrory that I was disappearing for a couple of days and that I would be involved in controversial business. I also said much the same thing to Mr Brian Rankin, the Mission's solicitor. With the exception of my wife, no one was told of the meeting or of the arrangements. I myself did not know the venue until I was told *en route* by my travelling companion, Dr Stanley Worrall. That the Feakle Talks with the Provisional IRA leadership aroused controversy is an understatement. Threats and abuse were the lot of all the participants. How would the Mission react? On my return all my colleagues greeted me with approval but what of the congregation? The next Sunday morning the attendance was, to my surprise, somewhat larger than usual and far greater than I expected. I reminded them of what I had said the previous Sunday evening and told them of how we had reasoned with the Provisionals and had pleaded with them to call off their campaign. Then I said: 'I don't expect that all of you will agree with what I have done. I have valued and enjoyed your friendship for the last sixteen and a half years and you have had mine. I sincerely hope that you are still my friends.' At the end of the service on that Sunday morning every member most unusually went out by one door only. Without exception, each shook me by the hand and almost every one of them had a word of approval for what had been done. To serve such a people was the greatest honour the Church could bestow on any of its ministers. That year the Christmas street collection reached an all-time high: it has been beaten since but never before 1974. That too told its own story. In retrospect I have asked myself if the Feakle Talks were worthwhile. At least they resulted in a ceasefire that lasted precariously for some months. That meant that lives were saved.

The expansion of youth work and the provision of the contemplated old people's day centre were now out of the question at least for the time being. It was necessary to put the plans that had been commissioned into cold storage. In the 1970s the priority was to hold the dispersed congregation together and to maintain morale. Sister Ellen Whalley (1969–71) was the last Wesley deaconess to complete a term of service in the Mission and there was no appointment of a junior minister after 1972. The main burden of pastoral work fell on Joe McCrory (and his successors) and Sister Mary Gihon, with the invaluable assistance of a retired minister, the Reverend Jim Pedlow. The office staff were greatly encouraged by voluntary help in the maintenance of the accounting records of the residential homes given by the genial Mr W.A. McFarland, a retired bank manager.

Early in 1974 I intimated my wish to be relieved of the leadership of the Mission. I had not responded to a number of approaches from other circuits but at the beginning of 1974 I accepted an invitation to go to Whitehead in the Carrickfergus circuit in 1975. In the event, a decision was made to leave Whitehead without a minister and knowing I would be available to remain in the Mission, at the request of the committee the Conference that year made no change in the superintendency. Joe McCrory moved to Newtownards, where heart trouble was to bring his energetic and vibrant ministry to an end all too soon; he died on 30 January 1980. The Reverend John J. Nelson succeeded him at the Mission until his appointment as chaplain to Campbell College in Belfast in 1978. He was a loyal colleague.

The film services continued until the beginning of the 1970s. A combination of circumstances made their termination inevitable. With the increasing emphasis on sex and violence, there was a dearth of suitable films. On the galleries teenage indiscipline was more and more in evidence: even the most poignant of episodes could on occasion be greeted with ribald laughter. Finally, at the height of the bombing campaign the deserted inner city out of working hours was the culminating factor that compelled a reluctant staff to conclude that enough was enough.

For some time an attempt was made to hold children's, youth and weekly meetings on the same night so as to ensure protection for both young and old on the way home. There were several school pupils in the band and it obtained accommodation in Methodist College, where it continued to hold its practices until the early 1980s when it returned to the Hall. The male voice choir kept functioning until a particularly bad explosion took place one practice evening just outside the Hall. The vulnerability of some of its elderly members and increasing parking difficulties persuaded it to call off its activities. Its disappearance and the death of one of its founder members, Mr John Matier, were a loss.

Throughout, the Women's Fellowship Guild and the afternoon women's meeting kept going. They were the stuff of heroism. Messrs Ernest Whitten and Joe Culbert and Miss Maureen Weir kept the Boys' and Girls' Brigades going. The Hall's magazine, *Intercom*, proved invaluable and still does. There was a congregational outing to Scotland and numerous other local ones. Social evenings and 'evenings of entertainment and exercise' encouraged the congregation, old and young, to keep together. The balance between Sunday morning and evening congregations changed. The morning congregation became the stronger, though in spring and summer it was still possible to assemble a really large crowd in the evenings.

Springfield Road church had made magnificent progress. By the time the Reverend Malcolm E.G. Redman took over in 1969, the situation there had changed out of all recognition. The church was damaged several times and on occasions there was gunfire on the road as members made their way to services. They allowed nothing to stop them. No praise is too high for the way in which people and minister carried on with the work. Mr Redman was succeeded in 1975 by the Reverend Robin P. Roddie and during his ministry these difficulties continued. They were and are an indomitable congregation, though inevitably they have suffered catastrophically from the migration of population.

Talk of Church structures and inner-city reorganisation marked the closing years of the 1970s. Long and protracted conversations took place with the trustees and the quarterly meeting of Donegall Square church with a view to amalgamation. These negotiations during the period 1975–6 resulted in the fusing of the two circuits in June 1976. It was hoped that gradually the two congregations would grow together.

If there was frustration in some parts of the work there were still opportunities and challenges. The Ulster Workers' Council strike of 1974 had underlined the necessity for alternative power supplies at both Castle Rocklands and Childhaven. Costly emergency generators were installed in each place. The full complement of fifteen bungalows on the Castle Rocklands campus was completed in the 1970s. At Childhaven there was another major development at a total cost of over £63,000 in the erection of a number of bungalows for staff accommodation. All the buildings had been paid for. All through these years Childhaven continued to be greatly sought after by the social services and the additional accommodation and improvements at the holiday home had made it into a much more flexible summertime building.

In 1978 the Reverend John Nelson was replaced by the Reverend Arthur Parker, whose property expertise was quickly evident in the replanning of the front wing on Grosvenor Road for use as a youth centre. The adjoining factory building found a tenant when premises in Glengall Street, occupied by the Rank Organisation, were gutted by fire. The rental income thus acquired was a welcome substitute for the income lost when shops on the Grosvenor Road frontage became vacant.

I brought my superintendency to a close in June 1979. In that year life in Belfast and its demographic spread were far far different from anything that had been contemplated a decade earlier. At one stage the destruction of the Hall and the complete disappearance of its congregation seemed inevitable. I could at least look back with gratitude to colleagues and a congregation who refused even to think defeat. There was still a pulsating viable congregation, much smaller admittedly than in the halcyon days but one which would do credit to many another Church. Their loyalty and courage had been tried in the fire and they had won through. The Custom House meeting had eventually disappeared: bans on public meetings, traffic arrangements and social custom had all played a part. The Brother Man service had a smaller clientele and was in the capable hands of Jack Weir's son, Wesley. After thirty years of the welfare state, there were still calls for help. Childhaven was still in demand and was gearing itself for new ventures. The holiday home had carved out a new role for itself, and the home and bungalow colony at Castle Rocklands were an outstanding contribution to the needs of the elderly.

Congregation and community alike marked my retirement in 1979 at a memorable gathering in the Large Hall addressed by colleagues, members of the congregation and the circuit, Mission officials and representatives of other Churches. I preached my farewell sermons on the last Sunday of June and thus completed twenty-two years in the service of the Mission.

# 12

# NEW CHALLENGES
## 1979–89

T he Reverend Dr Norman W. Taggart was appointed
superintendent in the summer of 1979. The Mission
Committee had requested his appointment. He came with
a proven record in a number of areas: circuit minister, missionary
in India, former secretary of the Irish Council of Churches, a
member of the headquarters' staff of the Methodist Missionary
Society.

His first task was to make arrangements for the over-seeing of
the work at Springfield Road. The Reverend Robin Roddie had
been moved unexpectedly and the Conference had not appointed
a successor. The Reverend David J. Allen, followed by the late
Reverend Walter Bingham, both retired ministers, consented to
give part-time assistance and they gave it generously. It became
gradually clear that Springfield Road could not expect to have a
full-time appointment and the second minister on the Mission
staff became primarily responsible for its pastoral care, thus
involving the Reverend Duncan Alderdice, who had succeeded
the Reverend Arthur Parker, in a period of difficulties following
major vandalism to the church in 1981. Mr Alderdice, who served
from 1981 to 1984, used his patience and negotiating skills to
good effect. He was followed by the Reverend W. Sydney
Callaghan in 1984. Population movement continued in the
Springfield area, resulting in a renewed determination on the part
of the remaining members that the work must be kept going in
spite of the vulnerability of the church premises and the danger to
cars parked in or near the grounds. It should be stressed that
relations with the neighbouring Roman Catholic residents continued to be positive and harmonious.

During his first winter, Dr Taggart realised the near impossibility of heating the Large Hall in the absence of the large audiences anticipated when the building was designed. A high estimate from heating consultants brought no joy and in the winter of 1980–1 the decision was taken to transfer worship to the Ker Hall. It was a brave though hard decision but it increased both the comfort of the worshippers and the quality of worship itself. The congregation very soon came to recognise and value Dr Taggart's preaching and his preparation for worship.

In 1979 discussion had already started regarding the future of Childhaven. The Government had appointed the Black Committee to review the whole field of children's work. The signs were evident that a major reduction in the number of children's homes was on the way. Dr Taggart inaugurated a revised programme of monitoring and supervision that was before long to prove its worth. At the same time rumours were circulating about behaviour and discipline at Kincora, a statutory children's home. More and frequent inspections of homes by the Social Work Advisory Group – now the inspectorate – were directed and in the spring of 1983 Childhaven had the first of these visits. The group's report in January 1984 indicated that Childhaven must find a new role if it was to continue. So the tortuous process of reappraisal and negotiation began. It was all very time consuming.

As Dr Taggart took stock of his new responsibilities he looked for new opportunities. One came unexpectedly when Extern, the voluntary organisation, asked for the use of the upper floors of the factory building on Grosvenor Road to provide a night shelter and a daytime drop-in centre. The result was a partnership arrangement under which the building was extensively rehabilitated with the three upper floors adapted for use as a drop-in centre and night shelter and leased to Extern at a preferential rent. The NSPCC was also granted daytime use of the front wing in the main Hall complex for use as a play school.

In the summer of 1980 open-air work was recommenced with a Tuesday lunch-hour meeting in Cornmarket led by Dr Taggart with the assistance of some ministers. More settled conditions in the city centre brought back the crowds and the Hall was again, for a time, being sought after for concerts. This produced welcome income and at the same time enabled the youth club to contribute to the Ludhiana Medical Mission in India through profits from its sale of ice cream and minerals at the concerts.

Passing years brought the resignation of some of the committee's most valued members. Messrs Frank Anderson and Dermot Johnson had served the Mission well. Mr Anderson's death shortly after his resignation in 1979 was a further loss, as was the retirement of the Reverend James Pedlow in the summer of 1980. His place was taken by the Reverend David J. Allen. The Mission owes much to such as these. Mr William H. Patterson sought relief from the secretaryship in 1985 after twenty years of meticulous service. He was followed by the relatively young but far-seeing Wesley Weir.

At the 1982 Conference the Mission was asked to take the Sandy Row circuit into its membership. The wheel had come full circle. The new amalgamation added to Dr Taggart's work load. It brought with it financial and property problems that were not easily solved. Eventually Mr Alderdice was asked to assume responsibility for both Sandy Row and Springfield Road while being relieved of tasks at the Grosvenor Hall. This made life more difficult still for the superintendent.

Escalating inflation brought further challenges, and the costs of maintaining the residential homes and the Grosvenor Hall-based social work called for greater support. However, the Christmas and summer appeals continued to surpass previous totals. As superintendent, I had long been conscious that the custom of food and clothing hand-outs left a great deal to be desired and I had maintained it because I saw no opportunity to make a change. I had acquiesced in the holding of occasional jumble sales as a way of making some contribution to people's self-respect. At least that way they were able to make a small payment for what they had acquired. The empty shops on Grosvenor Road presented an opportunity which Dr Taggart seized and a Grosvenor Good as New shop was opened. Mrs Muriel Green, who had succeeded Sister Mary Gihon as a community worker in 1975, was responsible for the shop, and with the assistance of a team of helpers from the Hall, Donegall Square and Springfield Road congregations, it encouraged self-respect among the purchasers. She retired in the summer of 1984 and her place was taken by Mr George Minford as a voluntary community worker. Before long he was installed in one of the other Grosvenor Road shops and was using it to good purpose as a social-service advice centre.

As high inflation continued, budgets reached approximately £500,000 per annum and the homes, with a total staff of some sixty persons, required much more detailed accounting methods. All of this increased the burdens of the Mission's small office staff as did recent regulations regarding employment and conditions of service. On 1 January 1984 Mr Alan Addy, of Muir and Addy, took up duty as administrator. He was particularly (though far from altogether) involved with the finances of the homes and this significantly reduced the burdens of the superintendent.

However, there was a major problem that refused to go away. The Large Hall had suffered greatly from Belfast's atmospheric pollution and from the wear and tear of sixty years. As well as the heating problem, ancillary rooms and toilet facilities left a lot to be desired. This, combined with the competition of the many newly-opened leisure centres, made lettings increasingly difficult to secure. The Hall that had once been the heart of the Mission was now rapidly becoming a liability. In a bid to solve the problem the new trustees, who had been appointed shortly after Dr Taggart's arrival, decided during the year 1986–7 to test the market. Leaders and trustees had indicated their willingness to move to a new site in conjunction with Donegall Square if the latter was prepared to contemplate a location which would enable the Mission to continue its cross-community outreach. The Grosvenor Road–Glengall Street site had over the years demonstrated beyond a doubt that the Mission had a role in the service of both communities. Because of their tradition in a prestigious city-centre site, the Donegall Square trustees and quarterly meeting (they had by now reverted to single circuit status) felt unable to agree to the suggestion: it was an understandable decision.

At his appointment in 1979 Dr Taggart had indicated that he did not contemplate remaining in post more than eight years and that he would wish to move in 1987. His term of office came all too quickly to a conclusion in the summer of that year. More of his time than he wished had been taken up in the committee work and negotiation in connection with the future of Childhaven and the resolution of problems that came with the Sandy Row amalgamation. The latter involved complex discussions regarding compensation for property that had been requisitioned at Primitive Street, planning permission for a new building and the commissioning of plans that would not involve expenditure above what was allowed by central Church authorities. It was all far more than should be placed on the shoulders of a superintendent left without a full-time ministerial colleague at headquarters. The retirement of his part-time colleague, the Reverend David Allen, in 1985 had been a heavy loss. In these circumstances at Christmas 1985 he had recruited Miss Daphne Twinem as a full-time pastoral assistant. She had just finished her contract as children's officer with the Church's youth department and her appointment had brought urgently needed help.

Dr Taggart left the Mission with the future of the Grosvenor Hall premises unresolved but with the firm decision taken that in one way or another its work would continue on its present site or part of it. The fact that the market had as yet not shown much interest in the property gave his successor more time to think. Much more significantly, Dr Taggart had ushered in a new era in children's work. His negotiations with the National Children's Home had secured the two-year secondment of Mr Terry McClatchey as a principal social worker and thus the future of the Childhaven home had been assured. He also developed a meaningful and mutually helpful relationship with the St Vincent de Paul Society and he had played a greatly-valued role in the deliberations of the Northern Ireland Council for Voluntary Action. Above all else he left a congregation whose horizons had been widened, whose commitment and worship had been deepened and the quality of whose life had been enriched. They were grateful.

Dr Taggart's impending departure had presented the committee with a major problem. It was necessary to seek a successor with the requisite qualities of leadership and ability to identify and grapple with the multifaceted issues confronting a Mission completing one century and facing another in a period of rapid social change. Moreover, they were desirous of finding someone young enough to contemplate a sufficiently long period of service. The last thing a city mission can afford is frequent changes in leadership. In the event they asked for the appointment of the Reverend David Kerr. He was appointed and took up office in July 1987 as he was commencing his twenty-seventh year in the ministry. He had served in two appointments where co-operation with others had been essential, namely, the joint-Church schemes in Limerick–Shannon in the South, and in Knockbreda, Belfast, where he had shared work with Presbyterians. In addition he was already a respected figure in the Irish Council of Churches. He came with a reputation for a willingness to contemplate change and a readiness to initiate. He was completing an arts degree in Queen's University Belfast, which had relevance for the work he was about to undertake.

David Kerr soon discovered challenges to his resilience and to his ability to react quickly to unexpected situations. As with his predecessor, the main problem immediately facing him had to do with the work at Childhaven: Dr Taggart had achieved the agreements in principle that assured the survival of the home and David Kerr found himself immediately dealing with the 'nuts and bolts' so necessary to produce a smooth and successful operation in the new conditions. This task was complicated by the necessity of finding a replacement for Mr Terry McClatchey, who was transferred by the National Children's Home to an appointment in Wales. Inside two years Mr McClatchey had done a great deal to ensure in Childhaven (now called Craigmore House) an increased professionalism as well as to develop stronger links with the area boards of the Department of Health and Social Services. Clearly his transfer had serious implications. Also to be faced was the future of the Grosvenor Hall complex itself. So far the market had produced tentative enquiries only. David Kerr felt some relief in that no irreparable action had been taken that might not have carried his approval. Thus he had some time to assess the situation for himself. There was also the Hall's centenary programme to be considered: after all the event was now less than two years away. And on top of all these problems was the task of making himself known to the general public and the congregation, and of coming to terms with the pastoral work of a very scattered congregation.

Within weeks he had come to two conclusions: first, to activate his centenary committee; second, to go personally to London for discussions with the headquarters' staff of the National Children's Home and at the same time to establish contact with the West London Mission of the British Methodist Church. The latter was clearly grappling with no dissimilar problems. He carried out the London visit in the early autumn and was thus able to report his conclusions in October. He had negotiated an arrangement for Mr McClatchey to keep in contact with Craigmore and to make occasional visits pending a final decision regarding the future of the home. He saw and learned enough in London to convince him of the advisability of not rushing any decision regarding the future of the Hall and the committee quickly decided to put any question of an immediate sale on the 'back burner'. A decision of the West London Mission to appoint a director of social work led to the committee considering a similar appointment for the Belfast Central Mission. Costings and soundings made it obvious that such an appointment would not only relieve the superintendent of a great deal of day-to-day worry and work, it would also ensure the maintenance of professionalism, and expertise and contacts with statutory bodies which are so essential. By mid-October the position was advertised and the appointment of Mr W.R. Sharpe, then assistant director of the Eastern Health and Social Services Board, was subsequently made to take effect from 1 April 1988.

By 1988 inner-city developments were leading to renewed interest in the Grosvenor Hall property. Discussions with officials of the Department of the Environment responsible for that part of the city led to a decision to commission a feasibility study by a prominent consultancy agency with regard to future options. Soon after, Mrs Aileen Hawthorne, officer-in-charge at Castle Rocklands, tendered her resignation following her decision to open a home for the elderly on her own account. This, coupled with the loss of Mr George Minford's very valuable services as the Hall-based community worker, added to Mr Kerr's worries just as he was coming out on top of the initial problems. Mrs Hawthorne was replaced by Mrs Jennifer Currie, a nursing sister with special experience of working with elderly patients. Mrs Eleanor Mayes, a member of the Hall's congregation, who had been assisting Mr Minford, took on responsibility for the community work.

Meantime, the Christmas appeal and programme had been mounted successfully and Mr Kerr had established a strong and happy rapport with the congregation. The building of Sandy Row church was well underway by the time of his arrival: Dr Taggart, along with the Reverend Sydney Callaghan, who had been appointed to take charge of the Sandy Row and Springfield Road congregations in 1984, had successfully negotiated the financial arrangements. The church was opened on the first Saturday of April 1988 and the steadily increasing congregation since indicates that it is meeting a real need. The whole scheme owes much to the negotiating skills of Dr Taggart and to Sydney Callaghan's drive, determination and refusal to be daunted by any difficulty.

At the 1988 Conference Mr Kerr could look back on a year of successful beginnings and of consolidation. He had won the confidence of his officials and the friendship of his people. His introduction of new emphases in worship had been possibly unexpected but were manifestly gaining acceptance. The congregation was growing again, slowly but steadily. So too was the Sunday school. Its superintendent, the faithful Marjorie Gill, with her colleagues, Alice Hutchinson, Louie Johnston and Wesley Weir, had between them given over one hundred and fifty years of faithful service. They had weathered the years of population movement and had seen the school begin to grow again before they handed over the work in the autumn of 1988 to David Gallagher and a group of younger teachers.

'Time Out', a new form of group Bible study, held monthly in the conference centre in the holiday-home premises at Millisle, had been started and was well supported. Weeknight activities were holding their own and members of the congregation from second, third and fourth generation Mission families, along with others of more recent years, were maintaining the long tradition of worship coupled with practical concern and a willingness to serve; the younger generation having the insights of educated minds that had been denied to many of their predecessors.

Thus by 1989 David Kerr, like his predecessors, was convinced with good reason that the mission of the Hall was to both his congregation and a wider public. In his first year, when occasion called for it, he had not shirked to make his concern known for peace and reconciliation. People 'out there' were watching and listening, evidently with approval.

# PART TWO

# THE HOMES

# 13

# OF CARE AND PROTECTION

W hen the Mission was founded in 1889, Dr Crawford Johnson was appalled at the plight of destitute children and urgently set about providing care and protection for the all too numerous sick, undernourished and homeless waifs scattered throughout the city. Existing state provision for these children fell pitifully short of what was needed to tackle the enormous scale of the problem, offering as it did only the harsh conditions of the workhouse, or the industrial schools and reformatories for the many who fell foul of the law. Providing a humane alternative quickly became a top priority, and its work among children over the last hundred years ranks high in the history of the Mission.

Even as early as 1862 the Irish Poor Law Amendment Act had recognised the unacceptable infant death rate in the workhouses and that 'in other respects the workhouses are not well suited in all cases for the caring and nursing of such children in infancy'. It consequently made it lawful for the Poor Law guardians 'to place any orphan or destitute child out of the workhouse, if they think fit to do so, by placing such children out at nurse'. Later, the Orphan and Deserted Children Act of 1876 gave authority for children up to thirteen years old to be placed with foster parents. However, with the chronic shortage of alternative care arrangements, many unfortunate children remained in the workhouses.

Worse than the grim fate of these children were the sentences imposed on young offenders, who, until 1868, faced the possibility of prison, transportation and in certain cases even the death penalty. The Irish Reformatory Act 1858 and the Industrial Schools (Ireland) Act 1868 brought some improvement in so far as they were designed to remove convicted juveniles from the prison system and put them in reformatories, while children up to fourteen years old, 'who were in danger of being delinquent', could be sent to the industrial schools. In a bid to save these ill-fated children from the full rigours of the law, the Mission workers were to become increasingly involved in court and probation work.

The immediate problem, however, was the crying need for homes which could offer a more secure and caring base from which the children would get a better start in life. In 1896 the Mission Committee opened negotiations with a view to some kind of co-operative arrangement with the British Methodist London-based National Children's Home. Indeed an 1898 issue of the *Methodist Church Record* indicates that a house had been rented in Belfast and some children admitted. It was not a satisfactory arrangement and it was eventually agreed that 'suitable cases should be sent to London'. Later in 1898 the Mission appointed Miss Cockburn to take charge of children's work. With the establishment of Dr Barnardo's Ever Open Door in Great Victoria Street, Belfast, in 1899, and the Elim and Olivet residential homes, then also operating in the city, the pressure on the Mission lessened. Co-operation between the Grosvenor Hall and Dr Barnardo's is attested to by a letter to Dr Johnson dated 28 May 1902 from Dr Barnardo's Belfast agent, Arthur Dedman. In it he paid tribute to the care and thoroughness of the Hall's children's workers who had been responsible for the initial assessments leading to the admission of many children to his organisation, adding that the Hall's referrals totalled more than all others coming from other agencies. However, provision made by all of these agencies fell far short of the need — additional accommodation was required.

## CRAIGMORE CHILDREN'S HOME

Dr Johnson was convinced that the best interests of the children would be served by providing a residential home nearer Belfast than London. It had been his intention to provide that home but the pressures of the earlier years and his declining health after 1900 made that impossible. Nevertheless, his innovative mind and his friendship with T. Foulkes Shillington, the honorary treasurer of the Mission, pointed to another solution: a home under Methodist auspices but linked with the Grosvenor Hall through its trustees and the personnel of its committee. One desk diary disclosure of 'Lunch appointment with TFS to discuss Children's Home' was soon to be followed by the decision early in 1902 of Mr Shillington, by then resident in Belfast, to make a gift of his family home and farm of approximately 140 acres at Craigmore, near Aghalee, Co. Antrim, to the Methodist Church for use as a boys' home. (Girls were provided for by the Methodist Female Orphan Home in Dublin.) The 1902 Conference accepted the gift and appointed ten trustees of whom five were members of the Mission Committee. They included Mr Shillington, Dr Johnson and R.M. Ker. Four Mission Committee members and three wives of other members were appointed to the Craigmore Home Management Committee, with Thomas Shillington PC, a relative of Mr Shillington's, as chairman, a position he held until shortly before his death over twenty years later. The official administration address of the home was Grosvenor Hall and John N. Spence was appointed secretary. The Grosvenor Hall link could not have been clearer.

The house was altered to accommodate twenty boys, and a matron, Miss Gordon, and assistant matron, Miss Schofield, were appointed. The first annual report states: 'Early in 1903 the first children – two boys – were admitted.' By the beginning of 1904, twenty-seven boys were in residence and a year later the total was thirty-four; by that time two sets of further alterations had been necessary.

From the beginning the intention was to provide basic education and vocational training such as carpentry and boot mending. The farm was intended to provide not only food and income but also agricultural training. The Methodist national school at Aghalee was transferred to temporary buildings in Craigmore, in what was formerly the warping room of a linen firm owned by the Shillington family, and permanent buildings were officially opened in October 1908; the school served local children as well as the Craigmore boys.

In spite of the unquestionable business acumen of Messrs T.

Foulkes and Thomas Shillington, the financial position of the home was always precarious. Financial support had been promised by the 1902 Conference but with the exception of modest and far from adequate grants from the Methodist Orphan Society it never materialised. The Belfast Poor Law guardians paid the pitiably small boarding-out rate for children. The only other sources of income were whatever profits might be available from the farm, fund-raising gymnastic displays, and the efforts of voluntary collectors – the Shillington family did far more in this respect than should reasonably have been expected from them. It was clear that more money was required, money that was not forthcoming, and the home struggled year after year to keep its doors open.

After the death in 1914 of Mr T. Foulkes Shillington, who had exercised a personal interest in and oversight of the home throughout, it was decided to ask the Conference to agree to the appointment of a minister to the combined principalship of the home and the pastoral care of the nearby Craigmore Methodist congregation. This resulted in 1915 in the appointment of the Reverend John W. Johnstone to the position.

## WHITEHEAD

Craigmore had been in operation for twelve years when the Mission launched its own initiative during World War 1 to provide residential child care. It was unquestionably the recognition by the magistrates of the Mission's court and probation work, and the contacts the Mission had made with the National Society for the Prevention of Cruelty to Children and the Soldiers' and Sailors' Families' Association, that led to the request in 1915 that the Mission should undertake residential work among soldiers' and sailors' children.

The acquisition in 1909 and 1913 of premises at Whitehead, Co. Antrim, to provide working girls with holidays had been a notable achievement; the matron, Miss A.E. Harrison, and her colleagues had acquitted themselves well and Miss Harrison had the attributes that suggested that she might well face up to a different kind of challenge. The superintendent, R.M. Ker, had discussed with her the request for a new children's home and the proposed change in the nature of her work before he brought it to the committee in October 1915. There were only two conditions to the committee's positive response to the request: the home should not be taxed beyond its capacity and the children's allowances, provided by the War Office, should be payable to the superintendent. The future of the holiday programme was ensured by the acquisition of premises in Co. Down and, remaining in Whitehead, Miss Harrison embarked on her new responsibilities, never contemplating what the succeeding years were to mean in terms of hard and unremitting work.

The committee minutes of the period are short on descriptions but they are always to the point, for example: 'The great need for this work is becoming more apparent from the moral as well as the physical breakdown of the children's mothers. Forty-eight children were in residence. . .' (24 January 1916); 'There were sixty children at Whitehead and forty more in Dublin, Balmoral and Craigmore.' (12 December 1916; the Dublin reference is to the Female Orphan Home of the Methodist Church located in Harrington Street; Balmoral refers to Belfast Corporation provision); 'One hundred and twenty children were in charge, sixty being at the Home at Whitehead, where good health was being maintained.' (3 April 1917). These terse references are fleshed out in many of the details recorded in the log book, 'Soldiers' Children's Records'. There is a newspaper report referring to a court case involving the home of three children accepted in February 1918; 'The room only contained a dirty mattress covered with an old blanket and quilt. [The inspector] had called at the defendant's home on various subsequent occasions but each time [the mother] was away from home.' The court placed the children with the Mission. Every entry tells a story of human tragedy — and much of it caused by poverty and physical breakdown.

Although the Mission Committee had warned against it, over-crowding at the home did become inevitable. R.M. Ker reported to the 1919 Conference that over the previous four years 390 children had been committed to his care. Had it not been for what Whitehead did for them, the alternative of the workhouse would have been too terrible to contemplate. As it was, there was always rehabilitation work going on in the homes of the children, with the aim of restoring them to their mothers. The end of the war did not bring with it an end to the need, and Mr Ker and his colleagues soon realised that it was likely to continue for some time to come. In November 1921 he informed the committee that 'Forty-five children are in residence under happy conditions.'

With the provision of the new Grosvenor Hall buildings, completed in 1927, it was feasible to contemplate improvements in the arrangements for the Whitehead children. It is against that background that Mr and Mrs Hugh Turtle's munificent gift in August 1928 of Templepatrick House must be assessed. Their generosity made it possible to transfer the children from Whitehead to more suitable and attractive accommodation at Millisle, Co. Down. So ended the Whitehead chapter of the Mission's children's work. The property was sold; in spite of its deficiences, it had served the children well.

## CHILDHAVEN CHILDREN'S HOME

Standing on a commanding hillside overlooking the Irish Sea, Templepatrick House provided good playing fields as well as residential accommodation. In 1928 it was in good structural condition but needed an extension, and, when completed, was by the standards of the time adequate to meet the sleeping requirements of approximately thirty children in five reasonably-sized dormitories and a number of smaller rooms. There were three large day rooms, including a dining room which was furnished by the late Mr Robert B. Alexander MP (the maternal grandfather of Church of Ireland Archbishop R.H.A. Eames). Unfortunately, unforeseen sewage problems caused delay but on 5 June 1930 Childhaven Children's Home (or 'Childhaven Orphanage' as it was more frequently called) was opened together with a holiday home on the same site. Miss Harrison and her deputy Miss A.M. Johnston, whose health had concerned Mr Ker, transferred to Childhaven along with the Whitehead children. Both willingly faced up to the challenge of the new work and conditions – indeed they took on a new lease of life. Mr John Young was appointed manager of the campus and took up residence with his wife (appointed housekeeper) and family in a newly-built warden's chalet. By 30 June the committee could be informed that the 'Whitehead children had settled down well'.

By the end of 1932 the total outlay on the Childhaven complex, including the holiday home, was £10,360 of which to date £9,902 had been raised. Those parents or guardians who could afford a contribution towards the maintenance of their children were expected to make it. They did not always do so. Nonetheless, in spite of all the pressures of financial stringency, in June 1932 the committee was of the same mind as the superintendent, John N. Spence, when it learned of his 'refusal to accept an offer of financial assistance from Dunmore Park'. If Mr Spence disapproved of any social evil more than alcohol, it was that of gambling. No gambling profits from Dunmore Park, the greyhound race track, would be allowed across the threshold.

For the first four or five years the numbers of children in residence averaged about thirty but by 1936 the Depression was responsible for the dramatic increase in admissions; in March of that year thirty-nine were being cared for. A year later the pressure for places was still great when the trustees of Craigmore Children's Home made their request for amalgamation.

## CHILDHAVEN—CRAIGMORE AMALGAMATION

Over the years 1925–35 Craigmore Children's Home had had increasing financial problems and a frequent succession of principals had not been conducive to continuity and professionalism. The farm had not fulfilled its donor's expectations and in 1919 about 100 acres had been sold for £2,500; after liabilities had been met, a net sum of £1,762 was available for investment. However, the situation had continued to deteriorate and at the end of 1932 the remaining 33 acres were sold for £700 and the stock and implements for £266.17s.7d. (£266.88). By 1935 the financial position was no longer tenable. A decision was taken to seek amalgamation with Childhaven and Craigmore closed at the end of August 1936. The 1936 Conference had authorised the transfer of the boys to go ahead and the final agreement, approved in 1937, ensured the survival of the name 'Craigmore' in the new title, Childhaven and Craigmore Homes, though the home continued to be generally referred to as 'Childhaven'. Craigmore's few endowments and monies left over after the liquidation of its outstanding debts were transferred to Childhaven. The amalgamation was accomplished just in time – had it been further delayed, the Craigmore situation could not have been salvaged. It was a disappointing end to the home but over three hundred boys had been trained and sent out into the world, many of whom would otherwise have had no chance in life.

Miss Harrison and her deputy Miss Johnston continued to run the children's home after the amalgamation in long and faithful service until their retirement in the first half of 1938. It is impossible to overestimate the generosity with which these dedicated women, who, with no professional training but with evident self-sacrifice and caring concern, gave of themselves to the well-being of hundreds of young people.

Miss Harrison's place was hard to fill. Eventually it was taken by Miss Lyske, who had been secretary at the Hall for twenty years and was well acquainted with the needs, difficulties and administration associated with the home. She also had participated in the holiday programmes. Unfortunately, in the autumn of 1939 she had to retire for health reasons. She was succeeded by Mrs Frances Ludlow, the gracious and kindly widow of a greatly-loved Methodist minister, the Reverend Alexander Ludlow. Mrs Ludlow was in charge until her marriage in the autumn of 1946 to John N. Spence, whose first wife had died four years previously.

The outbreak of World War II in 1939 had its impact on the home: air-raid shelters had to be built; a wind-charger was installed for the generation of a measure of electricity; and there was the ever-present responsibility of ensuring that children did not pull back curtains or let the blinds up during the blackout. After all, light from Childhaven's windows could have been seen by German aircraft, and submarines, known to be active in the Irish Sea. There were of course the casualties – substantial numbers of the boys who had been resident in the Whitehead and Childhaven homes joined the forces; one at least was lost in the Dunkirk evacuation of 1940. During this period, sporadic but acute water shortages made the work more difficult. The numbers of children in the home throughout the war years fluctuated between a low of twenty-four in March 1940 and a peak of forty-one in 1942. The average over the period worked out at approximately thirty and all were for the most part under the age of twelve.

Mrs Ludlow was succeeded by Mrs John Young, who was well acquainted with the problems of residential life. She had been on the Childhaven campus since its opening, initially as housekeeper, and had also been involved in the work at Whitehead and in the holiday programme at Childhaven. In the second half of the 1940s the numbers of children in residence continued to fluctuate; they were at the low figure of twenty-seven in March 1947 but climbed to forty on at least two occasions, with an overall average of thirty-five.

Financial records indicate that all the home's work up to 1950 was carried on with great difficulty. Throughout, there was always dependence on subventions from the hard-pressed Mission's social service account. Monies received from donations, while generous, were never sufficient to maintain the work, let alone keep the building in repair, and support from statutory sources was infinitesimal. Although the Ministry of Home Affairs became the supervising authority for children's homes as early as 1921, the Northern Ireland Government did little to assist the voluntary agencies. New legislation affecting children had been enacted in Great Britain in the early 1930s and the Northern Ireland Government had appointed the Lynn Committee to review Northern Ireland legislation in the light of these changes. Although the committee reported in 1938, there was no hurry on the part of the Government to implement its recommendations. With the outbreak of war in September 1939, the opportunity for change, even if it had been sought or wished for, had passed.

However, in 1946 the Government published a White Paper on the care of young people and in the years following its publication, careful but slow consideration was given to its proposals. With the advent of the welfare state in 1949, new legislation, embodied in the Children's and Young People's Act (Northern Ireland) 1950, was enacted, affecting the whole field of child care. Life for Childhaven would never be the same again. Welfare authorities were established and new regulations were imposed regarding 'care and protection' cases. Henceforth, like other voluntary and statutory homes, Childhaven would be visited regularly by the ministry's children's officers and the numbers of children in residence came firmly under their control. The Mission had no objection to the new regulations – quite the reverse – but they did introduce the era of bureaucracy, which has continued to grow with the passing years.

In some respects one of the most far-reaching provisions of the 1950 act was the setting up of the Child Welfare Council, which advised the ministry on any matter 'affecting the welfare of children and young people'. The council's regular reports had profound effects on statutory and voluntary authorities in the field of child care. All of these developments led to more legislation – the Children's and Young People's Act (Northern Ireland) 1968 – bringing Northern Ireland legislation in many ways into step with that of Great Britain. As far as voluntary homes were concerned, all of this increased the pressure for more adequate funding and it gave the welfare authorities responsibility 'to act in the best interest of the child'. In 1972, at the height of the Troubles, came the Health and Personal Social Services (Northern Ireland) Order which created the health and social services boards with their highly departmentalised district structures. This in turn finally led to voluntary homes being required to take their children for the most part from a given 'unit of management' area and to cater for a specified specialised need.

The effect of these legislative changes, and community attitudes regarding the undesirability of separating children from their parents, gradually led to radical rethinking by the Mission Committee with regard to the work at Childhaven. This was certainly encouraged by Miss Lucy Kerkham, appointed matron on the retirement of Mrs Young. She came from England in 1951 with successful experience behind her and she allowed nothing to stand in the way of the children's happiness and welfare. She also brought new ideas and these gave a new dimension to the work. Her suggestions were increasingly listened to and considered by the committee. Meanwhile, there was the ongoing financial concern regarding the Mission's ability to maintain the Childhaven work in the way it would wish. There were renewed contacts with the National Children's Home in the mid-1950s, which reinforced the conviction regarding the urgent need for more professional training for the staff.

Parallel to these developments, approaches began to come from different welfare authorities for placements in Childhaven. A long discussion on this issue took place during the early months of 1957. Eventually the committee decided that the time was not ripe, in spite of the possibility of maintenance revenue in support for any children so placed. There was the fear that to take referrals from the authorities would inevitably mean an erosion of independence. Another significant discussion took place around the same time regarding the traditional appearance on the Grosvenor Hall platform of Childhaven children at the Mission's anniversary meeting. Their annual participation in that event had been considered good publicity and a help in fund raising. Today the home and Mission can say with pride that it is more than thirty years since any Childhaven boy or girl appeared in public as in any way directly or indirectly a money-raiser.

By 1957 the home was costing at least £5,000 per year to run. By modern standards that does not seem a large amount but the money had to come from voluntary giving. The Ministry of Home Affairs inspector, the kindly and distinguished Miss Kathleen Forrest, on more than one occasion told me early in my superintendency that while the home did not possess the amenities enjoyed by the statutory homes, it nevertheless had a family and non-institutionalised atmosphere that was not always detected in other establishments. However, one concerned committee member, the late Mr Charles E. White, principal of Hoggs, the Belfast gift shop, said the home was the coldest building on the Co. Down coast. His comment reinforced an opinion already held by the committee and central heating was installed.

Increasingly it became necessary for the home to be subsidised from the Mission's social service account. By 1959 the time had become 'ripe' to accept welfare-authority placements and with them the modest maintenance payments. Very soon every placement was at the request of social workers. It was to be a long time before negotiations with the welfare authorities (later the area boards) succeeded in securing a payment which was an adequate rate for the job.

Miss Kerkham was compelled by reason of her mother's increasing years to return to England early in 1960. She was succeeded by her deputy, Miss Lily Cairns, who by that time had served for ten years in one position or another in Childhaven. Miss Cairns proved to be a caring and conscientious matron for the next seven years, which were to see further changes, particularly as far as the building was concerned. She too was conscious, as Miss Kerkham had been, of the need for the modernisation of the home and greater comfort for the residents, as well as the need for an increase of staff, particularly qualified personnel.

Successful negotiations with the welfare authorities and the children's branch of the Ministry of Home Affairs, and a munificent gift from the late Mr Thomas Menary of Lisburn, Co. Antrim, led to the modernisation of the kitchen and a major improvement scheme with complete refurnishing in 1967–8, and independent living accommodation for both adolescents and staff in 1973 (the last at a cost of £63,000). Throughout this period the home also enjoyed welcome financial support from the Northern Ireland Premier International Football Supporters' Club, and from responses to broadcast appeals made on its behalf by Dr Jack Kyle, the late Dr John E. Sayers and myself, as superintendent. The Bangor Lions' Club presented the home with its first minibus. Thus, bit by bit, the physical conditions improved and increasingly younger members of staff were encouraged to seek secondment to training courses.

In 1968 Miss Cairns was succeeded by Miss Madge Harvey, who had been serving as deputy matron at Castle Rocklands. She was in post for the next four years until she went back to Castle Rocklands at her own request to occupy the position of matron there. In 1972 Miss Maud Coulter was appointed matron – she was the first to come from the Northern Ireland statutory services. She came with residential child-care qualifications and under her management the training emphasis was developed. Her deputy, Miss Muriel McMahon, was released for training and came back after two years with a professional qualification in child care. For the first time in its history Childhaven had two professionally-qualified persons as matron (now called officer-in-charge) and deputy. During the 1970s and 1980s, this development was a response to the increasing demand for professional standards and other requirements. Step by step the old familiar concept of the caring, self-sacrificing matron, concentrating on each individual child and not overconcerned about form-filling and the requirements of bureaucracy, was giving way to a new kind of person: 'management' had now become the name of the game.

Dr Norman Taggart, on his appointment as superintendent in 1979, immediately came face to face with the financial and staffing implications of the new emphasis. And another traumatic issue emerged almost without warning. In early 1980 rumours began to circulate throughout Northern Ireland with regard to alleged sexual abuse and deviance in a number of children's homes. What could be termed the 'Kincora factor' (after the name of the home where the scandal first broke out) added to the uncertainties and misgivings experienced by residential staff caught up in contraction and the closing of homes required by Government and area boards. It is not too much to say that residential staff in children's homes all over Northern Ireland became demoralised. The slightest physical contact between a child and a member of the care staff could be suspect and the contemplated grievance procedures, being proposed by Government, made staff feel more and more vulnerable.

All of these issues led to prolonged and sensitive negotiations by Dr Taggart on a number of fronts, including the Eastern Health and Social Services Board, the North Down and Ards unit of management of the board, the Northern Ireland Council for Voluntary Action, and the Department of Health and Social Services itself. It became increasingly clear that no voluntary home could hope to survive without some kind of professional back-up person with qualifications, experience and adequate 'clout', who would be a resource person for the staff in the home. The result was further lengthy negotiations, this time with the National Children's Home, which led eventually to the secondment of Mr Terence McClatchey as a principal social worker to the Mission for a period of two years to conclude in August 1987. Few people can have any idea of the time, strain and extraordinary negotiating skill that all of this required from a superintendent who was already heavily burdened with other matters.

In 1985 a comment made years previously by Miss Coulter had

become more and more to the point. She had said that the name 'Childhaven' would no longer seem appropriate if the home was going to cater, as seemed likely, for an older age group. Today the children's home part of the complex is no longer known by that name. Instead, the home is known as Craigmore House on the Childhaven and Craigmore Homes' complex of the Belfast Central Mission. Mr T. Foulkes Shillington would have been greatly pleased.

In the same year both Miss Coulter and Miss McMahon sought relief from the pressures of management. Essentially each had a caring nature and they found the new management structures, which removed them from the close personal contact they had hitherto enjoyed with the children, far from satisfying. They found more rewarding work in their subsequent appointments, respectively, in the fields of care for the mentally handicapped and care for the elderly. Each had served the home with consummate devotion and self-sacrifice.

By the time of Dr Taggart's appointment in 1987 to the Cavehill Road circuit he had concluded a complete reappraisal of the home's future role in the evolving pattern of state provision for children in care. He had successfully negotiated that role and had secured the financial arrangements that would ensure the home's ability to do the work that was agreed. Henceforth, Craigmore House was to be regarded as part of the eastern board's provision for young adolescents who, because of behavioural or other special problems, required residential care.

In September 1987 Mr McClatchey was transferred by the National Children's Home to a post in Wales. The strength and quality of his contribution to the planning and negotiation of reorganisation cannot be overestimated. In the early months of 1988 Mr W.R. Sharpe, formerly assistant director of the Eastern Health and Social Services Board, was appointed as the Mission's director of social work, a new post created on the recommendation of the Reverend David Kerr, Dr Taggart's successor. He has brought experience and expertise that have strengthened the relationships between the home and the social services. Today the officer-in-charge is Mr John Gibson, a highly-qualified, former member of Dr Barnardo's team of residential workers in

Northern Ireland. He is supported by a larger staff, members of which between them possess more professional qualifications and relevant experience than any previous generation of staff in Childhaven. The annual budget, which in 1957 stood at £5,000, by 1988 had reached a staggering £225,000.

Such is the story of the Belfast Central Mission's children's homes over the last hundred years. Throughout that time every child in the Mission's care was gladly given the food and clothing he or she needed. The homes ensured that each child was provided with the education best suited to that child's need, whether in a primary, secondary, grammar, or special school, and as frequently happened, in some institution of further education. All the children had the opportunity of membership in local youth organisations — one of Childhaven's prized features over the years was the display of cups and awards won in this or that school or youth event. Every child was nurtured in a caring environment, based on Christian as distinct from merely Methodist or denominational principles, and was given a healthy religious education which was never 'shoved down the throat'. In the days before the social workers of the area boards assumed responsibility, no young person ever left without every effort having been made to secure suitable employment and accommodation. Since then, the home has been glad to co-operate with the officers of the boards in the search for work and placements for the young people. No institution can claim 100-per-cent success stories but Craigmore, Whitehead and Childhaven can say truthfully that hundreds of ordinary men and women, or those in the professions or skilled trades, who were given shelter, are grateful for what was done for them. That is reward enough for the Mission.

# 14

# OF SUN AND SEA

'Holidays for children', 'Holidays for young people from tension areas' are among the slogans used by numerous organisations that are now providing cross-community holidays for children. They are slogans that stirred the emotions and consciences in Northern Ireland reeling under the bombs and killings of the 1970s and 1980s. Over sixty years earlier the Grosvenor Hall had quietly set about a programme of doing just that for children, young people and later the elderly from the blighted and crowded areas of the city.

There are no detailed records of the first holidays arranged by the Mission. The records for the years 1905–7 reveal only that holidays of some kind were provided, it is not known for how many or for what age group, and that a small credit remained in the holiday account at the end of the 1907 season. In 1908 a credit figure of £17.13s.6d. (£17.67) was recorded. However, an early 1910 issue of the *Grosvenor Hall Herald* states that during an Easter Monday Mission excursion in 1908 to Helen's Bay, Co. Down, opportunity was taken to 'secure a small cottage' for holiday purposes 'for sick and ill-nurtured young people'. Such was the modest beginning of what was to become and remain one of the Mission's greatest responses to the crying need of an impoverished community.

## WHITEHEAD HOME

By the spring of 1909 the rented cottage at Helen's Bay had given way to a house in Whitehead, Co. Antrim. It was an end-of-terrace property at the corner of King's Road and Windsor Avenue with accommodation on three floors. The vigilant eye of Mr John

Young, at that time resident in Whitehead, had noticed its availability. Miss A.E. Harrison, who had been appointed as a deaconess in 1906, took charge of the first holiday programme. In September of that year R.M. Ker announced to the committee that over five hundred working girls had had a holiday. By deft management of the funds placed at Miss Harrison's disposal from the Mission's social fund and the very small contributions from the girls themselves, the net cost to the Mission was £18.16s.0d. (£18.80). The need was easily seen by the rush of applications for what can have been in fact very spartan accommodation.

The 1909 pattern was repeated in each of the following three years. In 1911 and 1912 the programme was reported as 'self-supporting', operating by means of girls' contributions and specially allocated gifts from the general public. In 1913 a larger and more suitable house was acquired at the corner of Edward Road, also in Whitehead, and during May through August, several hundreds of working girls had holidays; in September 150 'puny children had a week by the sea'. In May 1914 all seemed set for another successful season. In June and July the home was crowded to capacity – but the outbreak of World War I in August brought a premature conclusion to that year's activity.

In 1915 came the appeal to provide residential care for the children of servicemen. The decision to accommodate them in the Whitehead Home presented a double problem. The immediate one was how to cope with the new responsibilities and who was to do the coping; the second was what to do about the future of the holiday programmes. Miss Harrison was the answer to the first question: she became responsible for the servicemen's children. As for the second, all were agreed that the holidays must continue. Thus the Mission was back in the business of procuring whatever accommodation might be available at a price it could afford.

## THE BUTTER LUMP AND ORLOCK

A house was taken at Ballyhalbert near Portavogie, Co. Down, where it still remains at the edge of the village, facing the sea. Because of a large rock near it, the Butter Lump, the house was known affectionately by that name. Volunteer members of the

Mission accepted responsibility for the supervision of holidays there. Another venue was at Groomsport, Co. Down.

Then there was the purchase of an amazing edifice at Orlock, Co. Down, even then a very prestigious location in what is now Belfast's modern commuter belt. It had been erected in the days of haphazard development. Mrs Sadie Nicholson, until 1987 the longest serving member of the Hall's ancillary staff, who with her late husband James provided a home and loving care for the infant Robert Bradford when his mother was too ill to look after him, recalls the Orlock building vividly. She described it as like 'a ship downstairs and a train upstairs. You went upstairs by climbing a straight-up steel ladder.' In point of fact the building consisted of a wooden frame and a timber-walled ground-floor base with an old Co. Down railway carriage placed on top as a second storey. Mrs Nicholson added, 'The upstairs windows were train windows. You opened them with a leather strap.' The 'train part' housed thirty bunks. Flush sanitation was not on offer: there were the inevitable outdoor 'privies'. Today it all seems primitive but it served the Mission well. When the time came to part with it, Mr Edward Howard, one of the Mission's oldest and most respected members and son of the well-known Ned Howard, was glad to purchase it for £40 in 1931 as a family holiday cottage. John N. Spence's stamped and signed receipt is still one of the Howard family's prized possessions.

## CHILDHAVEN HOLIDAY HOME

Mr and Mrs Hugh Turtle's gift of Templepatrick House and grounds at Millisle, Co. Down, in August 1928 opened up new possibilities. On 5 June 1930 Childhaven Children's Home was opened together with a holiday home on the lower slope of the Templepatrick site. The holiday home's layout was simple but very effective: two almost square double-storey blocks, with one room for each floor, joined by a two-storey link, which provided a kitchen downstairs and toilet facilities upstairs. The main rooms looked east across the sea to Scotland. The ground-floor rooms served as a dining room on one block and a multipurpose games and sitting room on the other. Above each of these rooms was a dormitory — one side was for girls and the other for boys and each dormitory held fifteen three-quarter-size beds that could sleep two children comfortably and three if needed. Thus, without any undue concern at that time, it was possible to sleep at least sixty children and sometimes more. Finally, there was the Mission's pride and joy — an underground passage built from the lawn in front of the home, right under the Donaghadee—Millisle road to what was then a very attractive stretch of sand, lined with rocks and pools. Mr John Young was appointed manager of the site and, with his wife and family, he took up residence in the warden's chalet.

The new facility could not have come at a more propitious time for it coincided with the commencement of the Hungry Thirties. Frequently Mr Young reported at the Mission Committee meetings on the malnutrition and frightening physical condition of the children. In most summers a total of at least 700 children had holidays lasting two weeks; in 1934 the total was 730 and in 1937 50 adults were also holiday guests. In retrospect it is difficult to imagine what this stupendous programme must have entailed in the recruiting and transport of parties of children, walking them from Glengall Street to Queen's Quay station, then by train to Donaghadee and by bus to Millisle. At the home there was the sheer hard work on the part of Mr and Mrs Young and their teams of voluntary helpers, recruited mostly from adult friends and supporters of the Mission.

To this day, street-collection helpers on Christmas Eve in Belfast or in Bangor on 13 July are encouraged regularly by the comments of well-wishers, who gladly contribute in recognition of holidays they had so long ago and which they never could have otherwise enjoyed. Perhaps the most articulate tribute appears in *Ulster: A Journey Through the Six Counties* by Robin Bryans, now better known by his pen name, Robert Harbinson. His nostalgic walk in the 1960s, from Donaghadee along the sea road to Millisle, prompted happy childhood memories:

> I came this way many times from Childhaven, a house in Millisle where my boyhood summers were spent, and where I went in and out of the sea like an amphibian or lay on the sands, chin in hand, looking in wonder across the sea to the Scottish hills.

There had been magic in the air then. What would I find now? Surely enough, the sea was still there, quietly edging in and out in a lazy summer way and so, on a rise and set about by trees, was Childhaven itself. . .

I walked to the house up the winding path I remembered so well, to see if my old friends the Youngs were still there. But instead I saw 'This tablet commemorates the faithful, devoted service over a long period of years of Mr and Mrs John Young for needy children both in the Orphanage and Holiday Home at Childhaven.'

As one of the thousands of the needy children on whom the Youngs spent an unstinting love, the least to be done in thanks was to set down the memory of their name. Their name will always be linked in my mind with the golden sands and rock pools and oyster-catchers and swooping sea-swallows. . . with feelings mixed of sadness and happiness I silently hoped that the boys and girls who, in these so-called affluent days, still depended on Childhaven for their fortnight's summer holiday would remember afterwards as gladly as I did.

Many of them do.

At the outbreak of World War II in 1939 the Deaf and Dumb Institute's application for the use of the holiday home as an evacuation centre was agreed in principle by the committee. However, it was not until the autumn of 1941, after the air-raids on Belfast, that the building was required, when the Civil Defence Authority took over the institute's premises in Belfast. Consequently, the normal holiday programme was followed for the first two years of the war. (Indeed in the late summer of 1941 the programme was extended to provide a holiday for a party of 'elderly ladies'. The experiment was regarded as having been very successful and the hope was expressed that it might become a permanent feature.) But when the home was handed over to the institute, the dilemma, which had taxed the Mission in World War I, returned – what should be done about the holiday programme? There was no hestitation regarding policy – it must go on – but where and how? There were wooden sheds in the field behind the children's home and there was the gymnasium attached to it. The latter was converted in summertime into a large dormitory, and the sheds provided kitchen and games-room accommodation and storage area. Throughout the remaining war years these arrangements saved the holiday programme. In the committee minutes of 28 September 1944 there is a reference to some of the holiday children who were referrals from the National Society for the Prevention of Cruelty to Children and the Royal Belfast Hospital for Sick Children. A new and happy development in the recruitment of children had commenced.

After March 1946, the home was available again but social conditions were changing. In 1949, for instance, 30 per cent of the beds were occupied by convalescing children referred by the hospitals. More staff was needed, it was no longer possible, even if it had been desirable, to leave Mr and Mrs Young and their band of elderly volunteer helpers to cope for long summer weeks without adequate back-up. By 1948 the pressure was on for 'good staff' and it was difficult to find.

With the retirement of Mr and Mrs Young in 1950, responsibility for the holidays was transferred to the deaconesses and to Sister Mary Gihon in particular. For the next thirty years and more she organised the recruitment of the parties of children, elderly women and men and subsequently married couples for both the home itself, and the warden's chalet, which had been converted into two holiday flats. Year in, year out she spent most of her summers there assisted in the kitchen by helpers recruited from Grosvenor Hall; many can still recall the excellent meals provided by Mrs Gill.

It was Mary Gihon's joy to watch from her bedroom window the dawn break over the Irish Sea in the early mornings of summer. An early riser herself, she had her young assistants up and about by 7.30. She conducted morning prayers for them and those prayers were always rooted in reality and practicality. Next came the briefing session for the day ahead and who was to do what. Then it was 'action stations': the children had to be wakened; those who could not wash and dress themselves had it done for them; bedclothes were folded back and disinfested, and soiled or wet ones taken away for washing. Down to breakfast, the helpers serving the food and supervising behaviour. About 10 a.m. children and leaders moved off to one of the beaches — sometimes to the beach beside the house, via the underground passage, sometimes to Ballyvester, sometimes to Millisle itself, bathing, romping, exploring the rock pools, with the boys almost certainly in pursuit of 'willicks', so important to any Belfast boy who knew what he was about on a seaside holiday. After lunch, a supervised break on the front lawn, or in the playing fields behind the house, or off on a walk, or an adventure in Donaghadee, or the merry-go-rounds in Millisle.

The secret and purpose of the whole operation was to 'keep them moving'. The day started with washing and it ended that way. Soiled clothing and underwear had to be taken away for washing and, if necessary, dried for the next morning. Fighting sleep, the children would eat their 'piece' and then in the dormitory the students waited until 'every last child' was out for the count. With a bit of luck all was quiet by 10 p.m. and the helpers could relax, knowing, however, that all would start again early next morning. Meanwhile Mary Gihon herself would tackle the unpleasant tasks she would not ask or expect anyone else to do. Anyone who saw her at work would be hard put to forget the look of fulfilment and kindly affection that came from her brown eyes as she gave herself to the children. So the work went on through the three long summer months each year. There was a momentary break every other Monday between the time one party left after breakfast and the next arrived just before lunch. In this way the voluntary helpers, many of today's professionals — teachers, social workers, civil servants, ministers of religion and lawyers — learned something in face-to-face encounter with the less privileged side of life.

In the mid-1950s the statutory services began to seek the use of the home out of the main holiday season. This inaugurated a greatly-valued exercise in co-operation with Purdysburn Hospital particularly, that continued until 1988. In 1952 parties had been limited to fifty and in 1959 a decision was taken to replace the two-week holiday with ten-day breaks. One party would arrive on a Monday morning and return on the following Wednesday week. Another would arrive the next day, Thursday, and return on the following Saturday week. This gave the staff a modicum of free time. Perhaps no single change over the years was more welcome to staff and helpers.

It became increasingly clear that the welfare state was doing more for children than for the elderly. Miss Gihon told the committee in June 1956 that old people needed every bit as much attention as children and possibly more. By 1959 a regular pattern had emerged of offering holidays to parties of elderly men and women. For the next fifteen to twenty years holidays were provided for approximately 30 men, 70 women and 150 children per year.

Over the years the Grosvenor Hall Sunday school and youth organisations made regular use of the home at weekends for conferences during the winter or spring. In the late 1950s and early 1960s there were frequent requests from other youth groups and organisations for its use also at weekends. However, because of damage to doors, windows and other equipment, supervision by resident staff was becoming necessary. And because the home was being sought for conferences, the building's adequacy was brought into question. More importantly, was it adequate for the Mission's own work? Large dormitories were no longer desirable. There were other needs as well – a purpose-built indoor play area for wet weather and more up to date washing and toilet facilities. Messrs D.W. Boyd, architects, submitted plans for increasing the size of the dining room, turning the dormitories into small bedrooms and for a new wing providing a warden's flat, a flexible conference/games/devotional room or chapel downstairs and a suite of single or double bedrooms and bathroom and toilet facilities upstairs. In June 1970 a tender of £18,999 was accepted for the whole scheme and by the summer of 1971 the extended and modernised home was operational. Mr and Mrs Trevor Hill were appointed resident wardens, with Mrs Hill combining her duties as warden with those of cooking and housekeeping. Hers was a magnificent appointment for it enabled Miss Gihon to concentrate completely on the children and old folk. The home, now referred to during the winter months as the 'Conference Centre', became more and more sought after for youth training courses and the like. It was yet another response to community need, with the added bonus that the weekend residential conferences kept the place heated and paying its way throughout the whole year, not just the summer months.

Sectarianism has never featured in the Mission's scheme of things and so, when requests and referrals became more frequent, no questions were asked as to whether the children were Protestant or Catholic. The children were accepted gladly if there was a need. In 1987 one former student helper said: 'I knew there were Catholic children but no difference was made. I hardly knew who they were. They were all children who needed a holiday.' The Mission was giving part of the answer to the agonised question posed by Barbara Gallagher in her book of poetry, *Embers: From the Fires of Ulster*: 'Ought we not to pray and play and live together?'

During the early years of the Troubles, shelter and respite were occasionally provided for persons or families who had suffered from intimidation or from violence itself. Dr Norman Taggart developed the concept and initiated a number of shared and guided cross-community holidays in the summertime for family groups. The proliferation of holiday schemes for children of both communities, which have been a feature of the years of violence, has certainly reduced the pressure on the home. Indeed so many holidays have been on offer that it has been advisable to ensure that children, whose parents were more astute, did not enjoy more than one holiday while others went without. This has made it possible to offer holidays to the elderly without depriving the younger folk.

Mary Gihon retired officially in 1974 but continued to give her services voluntarily until her sudden death in 1985. Mr and Mrs Hill served until they reached retirement age in 1985. Their departure was keenly felt and their place proved most difficult to fill. So difficult indeed, that conference bookings had to be refused and the holiday programme curtailed during the summer of 1985. It was resumed with the appointment of the present warden and housekeeper Mrs E. Livingstone in 1986. There still is need and so the home still serves.

# 15

## OF PEACE AT EVENTIDE

The Mission's concern for the elderly goes back to the start of the Mission's work. However, there are no records of any suggestion that permanent residential care should be provided for old folk. Before the 1960s, the holiday programme was considered to be a sufficient contribution. A surprise intervention from an unexpected quarter was to change all that. In May 1960 I received a phone call from the late Reverend James Wisheart, at that time stationed in Carrickfergus, Co. Antrim. Two members of his congregation, Mr and Mrs J.R. Thomson, were executors of a will in which the testatrix, Mrs Boyd, had bequeathed her home at Castle Rocklands, Carrickfergus, Co. Antrim, to another party for development as a home for the elderly. The named beneficiaries had waived their right to the legacy and Mr Wisheart had been asked if his congregation in Carrickfergus would be interested. He and his officials felt that the project was beyond local resources. I was attracted to entering this field of residential care but advised Mr Wisheart that the North Belfast Mission, already in the field, should have 'first refusal'. Its response indicated that it already had sufficient challenges on hand. So Castle Rocklands was offered to the Belfast Central Mission. It was gratefully accepted.

As it stood, Castle Rocklands was a magnificent property set in its own grounds of approximately 3.5 to 4 acres. Situated about 400 yards (368 metres) from Carrickfergus Castle on the main Belfast Road, it looks south across Belfast Lough to the Holywood hills and Bangor in Co. Down. However, it needed alteration and enlargement if it was to meet the conditions of the bequest, and the search for money and the preparation of plans began. It was agreed that to alter the gracious dimensions of the large reception rooms and bedrooms would be an act of architectural vandalism. Available social-work information pointed to the need to have at least thirty paying guests if the scheme were to be financially viable. Consequently, the architects, Messrs Ferguson and McIlveen, were asked to draw up plans for a major extension, leaving the large rooms as far as possible as they were. Building costs alone were projected at £60,000, not to mention furnishings. Interest and good will were in plentiful supply but hard cash was difficult to come by. Eventually, on the advice of Mr J.A. Wilde, then Co. Antrim's chief welfare officer, an approach was made to the appropriate government department. A housing association was constituted, generous grants were offered, and the way ahead made possible. A successful fund-raising campaign was launched and by March 1961 the plans had been completed and approved.

When all seemed set to go ahead, unexpected problems presented themselves. In June 1961 the Mission's solicitor, the late Mr W. Brian Rankin, advised that the transfer was not as simple as had originally seemed to be the case. The property had been bequeathed to another party. It was questionable if the executors could vary the bequest or interfere with the wishes of the testatrix. The executors' solicitor had the same misgivings. After lengthy discussions, Mr and Mrs Thomson were eventually to seek a ruling from the High Court. The case was heard before the late Lord Justice McVeigh early in the autumn term of 1961. At one stage during the morning session, the judge intervened to say that if the case went on the way it seemed to be going, it would finish in the House of Lords. When counsel had completed their submissions, he was incisive. There had been a great deal of difficult law in the case, he said, and he was grateful for the trouble to which counsel had gone to elucidate it. He said he would make short law of it and ruled that the Castle Rocklands property should go back to the estate and the executors could do what they liked with it.

Nevertheless, the Mission's representatives left the court with mixed feelings. They were to some extent relieved, but would the offer be renewed? They need not have worried. The offer was most generously renewed and with the house an opportunity to purchase for £2,500 the two paddocks that lay between it and the

Belfast Road; they were approximately 2.5 acres in extent and had not been part of the original bequest. The offer was accepted forthwith: the Mission never made a better bargain. By January 1962 the property was in the hands of the Mission and in June a tender in the sum of £60,739 was accepted for the building contract. Building operations were deferred until the beginning of 1963 while the builders completed another contract. Meanwhile the housing association was registered and by April 1964 a matron, Miss Jean McCluney, and a full complement of staff had been appointed.

The news of an attractive new home quickly attracted enquiries and applications. For the sake of residents and staff alike, it was decided to phase in new arrivals gradually. By the end of May the first three residents were happily settled in. The official opening took place on 6 June 1964, one of the wettest Saturdays that year. In the presence of the Minister of Health and Social Services, William Morgan MP, the lord mayor of Belfast, the mayor of Carrickfergus and many other dignitaries from Church, civil service and community, the home was dedicated by the president of the British Methodist Conference.

The Mission Committee had been greatly concerned regarding the weekly charge for the maintenance of residents. Eventually, the sum of £6.5s.od. (£6.25) per week was arrived at. There were critics who, when they heard the figure, suggested that the Mission was going to run a luxury home for people with luxury incomes. In point of fact the figure was far too low; within a year or two it was raised to £8 and that again did not keep pace with the soaring running costs caused by inflation.

Castle Rocklands quickly established itself. From the outset it has had the benefit of the closest and most harmonious co-operation with and support from the staff of the Northern Health and Social Services Board, and consequently the home has been able to develop a standard of service of which it can be justly proud. There has also been the closest co-operation between the staff and the local medical practitioners and hospitals. This has ensured the peace of mind of residents, staff and the Mission itself as far as medical care is concerned. Dr Nessie Maybin, the wife of the Reverend Malcolm Redman, for many years gave her professional services voluntarily as medical consultant, interviewing applicants and assessing their suitability for residential accommodation. The home has never been without a lengthy waiting list – as the numbers of old people have increased, so too has the pressure for places. There has also been a marked increase in the age of residents on admission, today it is unusual to accept anyone on the lower side of eighty. And since the home's policy is to accommodate residents right to the end of the road (unless the medical officers order otherwise), the staff have had the great joy of felicitating more than one centenarian and caring for people remarkably active in their nineties.

Successive matrons, now known as officers-in-charge, have brought their own characteristic gifts to their work. The first of them, Miss McCluney, set the pattern, which was maintained in turn by her two immediate successors, Miss Madge Harvey and Mrs Edna Kerr. Miss Harvey, herself now a resident in Castle Rocklands, had already demonstrated her caring qualities as matron in Childhaven and Mrs Kerr had returned to the Castle Rocklands' staff after living for a time in Australia. Mrs Peggy Boyd, in all too short a tenure before going to live in Portugal, brought a dimension of expertise and experience gained in the statutory services and was succeeded by her deputy, Mrs Eileen Millar. On her retirement, Mrs Millar was succeeded by Mrs Aileen Hawthorne, herself a former member of the staff, who had gone to social services and had obtained professional qualifications in residential care for the elderly. Mrs Jennifer Currie took over from Mrs Hawthorne in the early weeks of 1988 when the latter left to take responsibility for her own residential home for elderly folk. All of them and their colleagues, who have served alongside them, have regarded their efforts as something more than work. This was never more evident than during the Ulster Workers' Council strike in 1974. During those agonising two weeks, the staff allowed nothing to come between them and their service to the old folk, who felt so vulnerable.

A quarter of a century has seen additions and alterations to buildings and equipment. A massive auxiliary electricity generator was installed following the 1974 stoppage. More recently, double-glazed windows were fitted to all bedrooms facing the sea, and in order to comply with health and safety regulations, a new laundry was provided and the kitchen quarters completely replanned and re-equipped during the years 1986–7 at a cost of over £40,000. The exposed position of the building requires a regular programme of external painting and until the acquisition by Carrickfergus of its new marina, which entailed altering the line of the sea wall, the home had each year to face extensive and costly repairs to the wall damaged by gales.

Easily the most interesting and significant addition since 1964 has been the erection of a purpose-built colony of bungalows for elderly folk. Its origin is a story in itself. In the spring of 1963, at the invitation of the Board of Evangelism of the American Methodist Church, I undertook a lecture and preaching visit to the United States. I made a point of visiting a number of homes for senior citizens run under the auspices of the American Methodist Church. In the grounds of almost every one of them there were attractive bungalows occupied by elderly persons. They had been built to the order of their occupants, who donated them to the home in return for life occupancy. It seemed to me that the two paddocks might be used for such a development, but would traditionally hard-headed Ulster people be willing to participate in such a scheme? I was not too sure.

Very soon after my return my late father told me that while I had been away he had received several phone calls and visits from a lady who had 'some strange idea' that she could build a house in Castle Rocklands. She wanted to live in it and she would give it to the Mission when she died. He advised me to see her as soon as I could. She was contacted and with the understanding co-oper-ation of the late Mr Rankin, a proposal was agreed through her legal advisers whereby she paid a significant proportion of the contract price of a bungalow and in return she obtained a licence to live in it for her lifetime, with the assurance that she would be provided with services, as and when required, and that there would be a place for her in the home itself, should she no longer be able to live independently. The idea caught on and before long other bungalows were being erected. However, the project was viewed with some initial hesitation by senior officials of the Department of Health and Social Services, who felt anxious about the nature of the scheme. They were not sure that we were doing the right thing but said that while they had no authority to require us to stop, they asked us to think carefully and perhaps find some other use for the ground. After lengthy and careful consideration, the scheme went on and before long the department was sending social workers and others to see it in the hope that it might be copied. Today those paddocks have been changed out of all recognition into a landscaped campus of fifteen bungalows.

Since it opened in 1964, Castle Rocklands has given care and peace of mind to nearly three hundred residents. It has been far from easy to keep the project running on an even financial keel. In the 1970s rampaging inflation at one time made the financial situation precarious, a time when the support and advice of the northern board officials were never more valuable. Inexorably the weekly charge rose higher but the Mission had some comfort in the thought that its charges were never higher than those of the statutory homes. Naturally fewer people today are able to meet the full charge of £159 per week but the state so far has not jibbed from meeting its obligations to those who have borne the burden and heat of the day. The Mission has been conscious all along of its responsibilities. A budget of well over £280,000 in 1988 for Castle Rocklands alone demands nothing less.

The spiritual well-being of the residents has always been a priority and a small chapel was provided when the home opened because of the conviction that more than physical care and food and heat are needed. Contact was established from the start not only with the Carrickfergus Methodist ministers but also with the other Churches and their ministers. On any day of the week a visitor will see this or that minister going to call on one of his flock. Each Wednesday afternoon and on other special occasions a devotional or communion service is conducted by one of the local ministers or by a member of the Grosvenor Hall staff. It has been all worthwhile.

# PART THREE

# PEOPLE AND PROSPECTS

# 16

# THEY ARE THE MISSION

To the general public the Mission may have been Crawford Johnson, Robert M. Ker, John N. Spence, or any of their successors. They and their ministerial colleagues, however, would readily acknowledge that there were others whose devotion went far beyond the bounds of commitment. They were 'the Mission'. In my last report before retirement in 1979 I wrote of my colleagues: 'In the darkest and most dangerous days, their physical courage, their endurance which went beyond reasonable expectation, their unfailing cheerfulness and loyalty kept the work going and carried me along with them.' That tribute to the staff of the 1970s could well have been written by any of the Mission's superintendents.

In the early years the reports carried frequent references to the work 'in slumdom'. That description was no exaggeration. There were the narrow cobbled streets of 'two-up-and-two-down' terraced houses, where the front room was so small any average-sized person could touch the fireplace wall and the opposite one at the same time, and where less than three strides would bring you from the front and only window to the poky little back room, just large enough to hold a small bed, and the passage (alias the kitchen) beside it with its gas cooker, cold water tap and 'jaw box', which was wash basin as well. And of course there was the cold and drafty outside toilet with its three-quarter door. Many of those houses were scandalously overcrowded but thousands of them had a dignity all of their own because of the human dignity of those who lived in them. But in those early days there were many other thousands where dignity had long since disappeared, where the urge to live meaningfully had been crushed by the relentless forces of poverty and slum conditions, where drunkenness, child neglect and prostitution were all too prevalent. That was where the Mission deaconesses were to be seen day in, day out, all year round.

Their insights into the human misery and the degradation they found still make poignant reading and never more so than when they refer to their work among children so often referred to by R.M. Ker as 'His Majesty's Most Helpless Subjects'. There was the three-year-old found drinking whiskey while her mother was in a drunken stupor, or the emaciated and vermin-ridden child wrapped up in a blanket and carried to the children's hospital. Or the physical threats in trying to reason with drunken and dangerous women – and men. The Epistle to the Hebrews has its roll of honour: the Grosvenor Hall has its also and on any count the deaconesses rank high in it. The combined work of seven of the longest serving gave a total of almost two hundred devoted years to the Mission's service. The remainder gave of their all; more than one deaconess's health broke down irreparably.

What made them do it? One thread runs constantly through the story. It was concern for others. In the early years they wrote and talked about the girls who were driven to make their living on the streets. The Mission's deaconesses believed that each of these girls had a God-given dignity destroyed or damaged and it was their task to help them rediscover it. Miss M. Hoey served from 1895 to 1923. What was later written about her in the 1939 report could have been written about almost every one of them: 'She was in every way and at every hour at the disposal of God and suffering humanity.'

Miss Curran (1900–19) was a familiar figure in the police courts. Her efforts to help wayward girls and boys frequently went far beyond the comprehension of the law. Almost fifty years before the advent of professional child-care services she had put herself on record: 'the problems of child life are fundamental. They lie at the root of all social well-being and social progress.' (*Grosvenor Hall Herald*, September 1913). It was the same with Miss A.E. Harrison (1899–1938): she had fifteen winters dealing with human fallout and fifteen summers helping underpaid working girls to enjoy God's fresh air and to renew their vitality. After that she spent twenty-five long years providing care and shelter for the children who needed it in the children's homes. There were those who toiled between the wars and after: Miss Elizabeth Allen (1919–51), small of stature and great of heart, who 'for some thirty years was the friend of the poor and the counsellor and guide of the youth of the Mission' (1951 report); Miss Wilson (1917–48) was quiet, retiring but utterly faithful for more than a quarter of a century. She was a contemporary of Miss H.M. Cathcart's (1920–42), tall and dignified, for more than twenty years the 'financial Deaconess' whose work entailed far far more than obtaining monetary support from businessmen. For more than three decades Mary Gihon (1948–74) carried the burden of many of the Mission's people on her willing shoulders. What she did for them can never be overvalued. She retired in 1974 but until her sudden death in 1985 she loved and toiled and prayed for others.

From the beginning the Sisters shared the philosophy of the early superintendents. Miss Black (1895–1905), Miss Cully (1902–8) and the others, as they toiled in the soup kitchens and provided meals and sustenance for starving children, regarded themselves as more than social workers or mere evangelical 'do-gooders'. They were imbued with R.M. Ker's convictions. Shortly after he succeeded to the superintendency, he recorded his thoughts about relief work:

> What has a soup kitchen to do with religion? There are those who split up life into compartments and label one social, another, spiritual. Grosvenor Hall and its workers countenance no such partition.

That was the stance of all.

There were those whose service came officially to an end with matrimony: Miss Evelyn Williams from far away Tipperary (1910–15), destined as Mrs Lindsay, to be well known in Irish Christian Endeavour circles; Miss Sybil Thompson from Co. Wexford (1941–5), still remembered for her work with children and now, with her husband Mr George Megahey, a member of an early Grosvenor Hall family, though members of the East Belfast Mission, vitally interested in all that happens in the Hall; Miss Nellie Meechan (1935–9), kindly and gratefully remembered, who became the devoted wife of the Reverend Dr Albert Holland, himself on the staff for ten successful years; and Miss Hanna Crothers (1948–56), to become Mrs Hanna Hanna and, with her husband, for many years a loyal member of the evening choir.

From 1951 to 1971 there was not a year when a member of the Wesley Deaconess Order was not working in the Hall. Sister Bettina Bridges (1951–3) left a mark that is still remembered. Sister Jean Richardson (1953–60), later killed with her husband in a tragic motor accident in England, gave seven years almost entirely in the service of young people. There were Sisters Iris Porter (1960–4), eminently geared for work with the young, and Joan Stidworthy (1964–6), steady and loyal. Finally, there was Sister Mavis Hamlin (1966–9), whose caring service terminated with matrimony, and the able Sister Ellen Whalley (1969–71), now the Reverend Ellen Whalley, Irish Methodism's first woman minister. For all of these and others whose service was shorter but equally loyal, the Mission has every right to be grateful.

In addition to the Sisters of the Mission there were lay workers ready to help. The name of James Dixon (1889–1919), often referred to as the 'Soldier Evangelist', appears on every report from the year the Mission started until he responded to a call in 1918 to work in Canada. No one can compute the measure of his contribution. He was open-air preacher, successful evangelist, manager of the labour yard, Boys' Brigade captain and a host of other things as well. There were other male helpers also, notably George Poolton (1890–1), and Robert Norris (1893–4), later to be ordained in another Church.

All of these worked in the city streets by day and in the Mission's various activities by night. By the mid-1970s, to all intents and purposes, downtown Belfast after working hours was a ghost town. There was a need to look after the old and frail during daylight hours, and to be ready, if necessary, to go to their assistance by night, wherever they might be. Thus the first community worker, Mrs Muriel Green, was appointed in 1975 to succeed Mary Gihon. She served with enthusiasm until 1984 and on retirement she was succeeded by George Minford (1985–8). His understanding of human nature, his patience and his belief that lives of human beings can be transformed helped many.

What too of the service given by successive generations of the evening choirs under organists and choirmasters such as Joseph McIlveen, Alfred Johnson, Dr Jim Breakey, and Douglas Armstrong; and by the male voice choir conducted by Albert McClenahan or William (Billy) Thompson; and the other choirs under Miss Annie Coulter and Mrs Coey? All of them sang, and helped others to sing, to the glory of God, enriching the worship and widening the musical appreciation of the congregation. What of the contribution to the lives of girls and boys that came from the devoted service of Girls' Brigade and Boys' Brigade officers over many years? Girls' Brigade captains like Mary Gihon, Marjorie Gill and Maureen Weir, and Boys' Brigade captains such as James Dixon in 1895 and his lineal successors, Hugh Meharg, Edward Maynes, Dr William L. Northridge, J. Wright, A. Stranix, Robert Ferris, John McKeaveney, Tom Pakenham and Ernest Whitten and Junior Brigade stalwarts such as Joe Culbert all left their mark of worth on successive generations.

Throughout, one superintendent after another has been supported, encouraged and protected by successive secretaries. The secretarial work was originally seen to by a deaconess or on a part-time basis by volunteers. However, as the work developed it was no longer possible to operate in that way and the permanent position of secretary was established. The confidences of the Mission, its staff and congregation were safe in the keeping of people like Mrs Eileen McCann, later Mrs Lawrenson (1941–55), and Mrs Pearl Thompson (1955–62). Miss Lyske (1926–41) left the Hall after nearly twenty years to face the demands and challenge of Childhaven. Miss Esther Fyffe (1962–), ably supported by her colleague Mrs Margaret Jones (1962–88), has carried a load that few would have tolerated. Their cheerful efficiency, loyalty and courage over years of bombs and blasts, and their ability to maintain discreet confidentiality have served the Mission well and have won the admiration of many far beyond the Hall. Mrs Jones retired in December 1988 and was succeeded by Mrs Eleanor Mayes when responsibility for community work was added to Miss Daphne Twinem's duties.

The work of caretakers or sextons is often taken for granted. Not so in the Grosvenor Hall. Over a hundred years there have been very few caretakers for the simple reason that they gave long service. Charlie Ferguson, Ned Watson and Billy Patterson were names to conjure with and there were others for shorter periods like David Reid or Sam English. All were known and respected as people in their own right far beyond the Mission and Methodism. Wallace McCormick has been the helpful maintenance officer for many years and behind the scenes there has been the loyalty of people like Mrs Sadie Nicholson and Mrs Maisie Watson, who between them chalked up seventy years and more of unremitting toil. The memory of Billy Bryson comes back too from the past. He was the night caretaker, diminutive of stature but always at his post, in good weather and in bad. All these and many more gave and served, not so much for the money they earned as for their belief in what the Mission stood for.

So too did generations of manse families, who, year in, year out, knew what it meant to be at home mostly on their own: wives and mothers — and children, who rarely ever had a Christmas Day or Evening in their own homes, who opened their Christmas presents and played their games in an upstairs room of the Ker Hall, or in the homes of friends or relatives, while their parents were busy with all that had to do with the Christmas Day dinner for men who were homeless or living in the city's lodging houses. The price for family life was high.

R.M. Ker drew up a roll of honour, which paid tribute to members who had died, when the old Hall closed: he could have made another of those still living. Crawford Johnson could have done the same, and to this day so could all of their successors. But all those rolls put together would be incomplete. For there were many others also. They have laboured in the Hall, in the homes, in Springfield Road, and now in Sandy Row. Along with the named and unnamed, the remunerated (but never fully paid), and the unrewarded, as 'apostolics anonymous', they all served because of their belief in what it was all about. They were or are and will continue to be 'the Mission'.

# 17

# THE ROAD AHEAD

S uch is the story of the Belfast Central Mission at points of
need throughout one hundred years. Today the Mission's
congregation bears no comparison with that of the halcyon
days but its numbers are growing, even if slowly. Its leadership,
and that of the Mission itself, is increasingly found from among
the families with long connections with its work. When the
original Grosvenor Hall closed its doors in 1926, it was reckoned
that five million people had crossed its thresholds; a conservative
estimate indicates that the present Hall has seen at least as many
and probably more. A Mission that has catered for the spiritual
and social needs of numbers like that has a proud tradition. That
tradition will enable it to face the different challenges of the next
century – not least, among those who are returning from the
suburbs in search of more convenient living accommodation. The
informality and fellowship of the Hall can still mean much to the
lonely and rootless of the inner city.

In its day the Hall has hosted many important meetings that
never hit the headlines, for instance: the Churches' Industrial
Council met there with Falls Road community leaders and helped
defuse the 1965 sectarian riots; it was the venue in the spring of
1965 for discussions between representatives of the Roman
Catholic Church on the one hand and of the Church of Ireland,
and the Presbyterian and Methodist Churches on the other that
led to a historic joint deputation of Church leaders to Prime
Minister Captain Terence O'Neill regarding religious provisions
in the charter of the New University of Ulster; there too the initial
discussions took place that brought to birth the Columbanus
Community of Reconciliation in 1983.

Who can quantify the relief and rehabilitation programmes of the children's homes, the holiday homes and the home for the elderly at Castle Rocklands? The service they render today is as valuable as ever. Who can evaluate the mission to the sick by successive generations of chaplains at the Royal Victoria Group of Hospitals? How many thousands found a better quality of life because of the Happy Evenings, the lecture programmes and all that went with the weekly timetable of the early years? What too of the memorable evenings with Cliff Richard, Paul Robeson, Kenneth McKellar, W.H. Jude and many another artiste of merit?

The Mission has not only maintained its own work, it has also made a significant contribution to the Christian ministry. The names of members and former members of the Hall and the Springfield Road church, who offered for the ministry, tell their own story: Robert J. Bradford, Samuel Burch, Eric Carson, Ivan Carson, Wilfred Carson, Brian E. Chambers as a boy, William Cowden, Stuart Heaney, Thomas A. Johnston, Ernest Ker, Charles Keys, Francis McBrien, John A. McClintock, William Megahey, Robert Norris, Leslie Spence, Richard Taylor, John Wilkinson and John W. Young. Among them were a president of the Irish Methodist Church, a principal of Edgehill College, chairmen of district synods, a superintendent of Londonderry City Mission, an acting secretary of the Irish Methodist Conference, a senior chaplain in the Royal Air Force, and one who was nominated as the only white bishop-elect in the aborted United Church of Nigeria.

The Mission is very conscious of the service it has given to the community at large since 1889. It realises, however, that changing conditions will demand different accommodation and different methods. By the spring of 1989 preliminary reports and findings from the feasibility study indicated that the professionals were recognising what the superintendent and his predecessors had contended regarding the short- and long-term value of the Grosvenor Hall site, placed as it is at a community interface. Civic proposals for Laganbank and the availability of other better-serviced venues have been seen to reduce the attractiveness of the main Hall for the 'bread-and-butter' lettings that had hitherto been of such advantage, and in any case the ancillary facilities and amenities fall far short of what is now considered necessary. Furthermore, the day of the fifteen-hundred-plus congregation has gone. Purpose-built reconstruction is called for.

The appointment of Mr W.R. Sharpe as director of social work has opened up new possibilities for further programmes of social action. The day of the mass-feeding operations has disappeared, so too has that of food and clothing hand-outs. But the late twentieth century has its own problems. High unemployment, low wages and inadequate welfare benefits mean there are still many for whom the battle for survival will continue to be hard. In addition there will always be those whom society calls 'socially inadequate' but who must be provided for by the Mission's caring programme. Increased longevity has meant an expanding field of work among the very elderly in reduced circumstances. There are the lonely and the ever-increasing numbers of one-parent families. There are deficiencies in specialised residential provision for certain groups, like the mentally handicapped and discharged prisoners, that demand attention. All these areas are making new demands on the voluntary agencies and the full implications of recent social-welfare legislation have yet to be taken on board. Already there is evidence of the new pressures with which the Mission's community worker will have to grapple. The advice centre will continue to cope with the challenge of assisting more people to achieve the full potential of lives that do not need to lose their human dignity.

As its centenary approaches, future developments in the Mission's social-work programme have been decided upon. The first was to adapt, as soon as possible, the holiday home and Conference Centre after two decades of intensive usage since their last renovation and to refurbish them in order to cope with the demands of changing needs and programmes. Thus they would be of greater service still to both the Mission and the wider community. Craigmore House is also calling out for work to be done to meet the requirements of its older teenage group and a renovation contract for £50,000 was accepted and the builders moved in at the end of March 1989. A proposal was approved to initiate a counselling service for elderly people with concerns regarding their future housing and care and related problems. Also, the attention of the superintendent was drawn to the availability of a substantial house and grounds in suburban Belfast. With the assistance of a large grant from a charitable trust, it was purchased with a view to meeting what is now regarded as one of the most urgent social needs, namely 'housing with care' for the elderly. In this way the social and community outreach and agenda for the next century are taking shape. And as the plans for redevelopment of the buildings are finalised, they will facilitate the outreach to the inner city's needs, which is very much part of the Mission's concern.

John Wesley advised his followers to go to those who needed them and to those who needed them most. For one hundred years the Mission has sought to serve at points of spiritual and social need in the life of Belfast. It still does so today, though the conditions are far far different from those facing the founding fathers. Now it finds itself at a community interface and it is happy to be there. Service in the days to come will present its challenges and difficulties but superintendent, colleagues and committee will gladly continue the Mission's work, reminding the men and women of a divided city of their need to be reconciled not only with the God who made all of them but with each other.

# APPENDICES

### 1
Belfast Central Mission,
superintendent ministers, 1889–1989

### 2
Belfast Central Mission,
honorary treasurers, 1889–1989

### 3
Belfast Central Mission,
honorary secretaries, 1889–1989

### 4
Grosvenor Hall Leaders' Meeting,
honorary secretaries, 1951–89

### 5
Belfast Central Mission,
ministerial staff, 1889–1989

### 6
Grosvenor Hall,
full-time lay workers, 1889–1989

### 7
Lay members of the
Belfast Central Mission Committee, 1889–1989

# Appendix 1
BELFAST CENTRAL MISSION, SUPERINTENDENT MINISTERS,
  1889–1989

| | |
|---|---|
| 1889–1905 | R. Crawford Johnson |
| 1905–26 | Robert M. Ker |
| 1926–50 | John N. Spence |
| 1950–4 | Robert R. Cunningham |
| 1954–5 | Joseph B. Jameson |
| 1955–7 | Samuel H. Baxter |
| 1957–79 | R.D. Eric Gallagher |
| 1979–87 | Norman W. Taggart |
| 1987– | David J. Kerr |

# Appendix 2
BELFAST CENTRAL MISSION, HONORARY TREASURERS,
  1889–1989

| | |
|---|---|
| 1889–1914 | T. Foulkes Shillington |
| 1915–25 | David J. Lindsay |
| 1925–39 | Henry M. Johnson |
| 1939–47 | Henry M. Anderson |
| 1947–53 | Dermot P. Johnson |
| 1953–69 | Wilfrid T. Bambrick |
| 1969– | David H. Montgomery |

# Appendix 3
BELFAST CENTRAL MISSION, HONORARY SECRETARIES,
  1889–1989

| | |
|---|---|
| 1889–91 | Rev. G.R. Wedgwood and Rev. James Harpur |
| 1891–4 | Rev. Richard Cole and Rev. James Harpur |
| 1894–8 | Rev. William S. Carey and Rev. James Harpur |
| 1898–1902 | Hugh Anderson |
| 1902–39 | Henry M. Anderson |
| 1939–47 | Dermot P. Johnson |
| 1947–65 | Frank M. Anderson |
| 1965–85 | William H. Patterson |
| 1985– | J.R. Wesley Weir |

## Appendix 4
GROSVENOR HALL LEADERS' MEETING, HONORARY
SECRETARIES, 1951–89

| 1951–80 | John H. Weir |
| 1980–7 | Pearl Thompson (Mrs) |
| 1987– | Mervyn Farley |

## Appendix 5
BELFAST CENTRAL MISSION, MINISTERIAL STAFF,
1889–1989

Agnew, Wilfred A.     1947–8
Alderdice, Duncan     Springfield Road and Grosvenor Hall     1981–4
Allen, David J.     Springfield Road and Grosvenor Hall     1979–85
Allen, Hugh     1926–7
Alley, George (retired)     1894–5
Bagnall, Robert G.     1948–50
Baxter, Samuel H.     1954–7
Bingham, Walter     Springfield Road     1979–81
Booth, Alan R.     1938–9
Brown, William     1962–3
Burch, Samuel     Cornerstone Community     1986–
Callaghan, W. Sydney     Springfield Road and Sandy Row     1984–
Carson, A. Ivan     1955–6
Collins, Alfred     1938–43
Crooks, Louis W.     1897–8
Cunningham, Robert R.     1939–40; 1943–54
Daly, John J.     1919–21
Dougall, D. Brian     Springfield Road     1951–2
Duke, John A.     Springfield Road     1944
Elliott, John W.P.     1905–6
Ferguson, Samuel D.     1940–7
Gallagher, R.D. Eric     1957–79; retired, 1979–
Gamble, Albert W.     1927–8
Good, George E. (retired)     Donegall Square     1981–3
Greenwood, Richard     1956–60
Grubb, James     1889–95
Hartley, Thomas A.     Springfield Road     1958–63
Holland, Albert     1928–38
Houston, David     1969–70

173

Hunter, W. Johnstone    1914–17
Jameson, Joseph B.    1954–5
Johnson, R. Crawford    1889–1905; retired, 1905–14
Jones, Aelfryn E.    1952–4
Kelso, Herbert    1982–3
Ker, R. Ernest    1927–8
Ker, Robert M.    1898–1926
Kerr, David J.    1987–
Kingston, Paul    1956–8
McCrory, Joseph    1963–75
McIlwrath, George A.    Springfield Road    1945–7
Maxwell, Robert    Springfield Road    1943–4
Moore, R. David    1970–2
Morrison, George R.    Springfield Road    1954–8
Nelson, John J.    1975–8
Nelson, Robert A.    1924–5
Noble, Thomas A.    1958–60
Northridge, William L.    1920–4
Oliver, William J.    1931–7
O'Neill, Ernest W.    1960–1
Parker, Arthur    1968–9; 1978–81
Plunkett, Hedley W.    1950–1
Redman, Malcolm E.G.    Springfield Road    1969–75
Robinson, John    1963–5
Roddie, Robert (Robin) P.    Springfield Road    1975–9
Rodgers, R. Donaldson    1965–8
Sleath, Arthur D.L.    Springfield Road    1963–9
Spence, John N.    1902–14; 1925–50; retired, 1950–61
Taggart, Norman W.    1979–87
Taylor, Benjamin H.    Springfield Road    1952–4
Teasey, Robert J.J.    1928–31
Thompson, George W.    1896–7
Walpole, Christopher G.    1961–2
Whittington, T. Stanley    Donegall Square    1976–82
Wisheart, James    Grosvenor Hall    1967–9
Woods, Thomas    1960–3

The following retired minister, resident on another circuit, also
    served as indicated:

Pedlow, James    Grosvenor Hall    1972–80

## Appendix 6

GROSVENOR HALL, FULL-TIME LAY WORKERS, 1889–1989

Adams, John     1889
Allen, Miss Elizabeth     1919–51
Atherton, C.F.     1894
Bambrick, Miss     1924–7
Black, Miss     1895–1905
Blair, Miss     1927–34
Bridges, Sister Bettina     1951–3
Bryans, William     1890
Buchanan, Miss     1895
Cathcart, Miss H.M.     1920–42
Cockburn, Miss     1898
Coulter, John     1889–90
Crothers, Miss Hanna     1948–56
Cully, Miss     1902–8
Curran, Miss     1900–19
Dixon, James     1889–1919
Elliott, Miss     1909–12
Fyffe, Miss Esther     1962–
Gihon, Miss Mary     1948–74
Gillespie, James     1905–6
Green, Mrs Muriel     1975–84
Hamlin, Sister Mavis     1966–9
Harrison, Miss A.E.     1899–1915; in children's homes, 1915–38
Hoey, Miss M.     1895–1923
James, W.     1921–4
Jones, Mrs Margaret     1962–88
Ker, R. Ernest     1925–6
Latchford, Miss     1895
Lyske, Miss     1926–41
McCann (later Lawrenson), Mrs Eileen     1941–55
McMaster, Thomas     Springfield Road     1949–51
Martin, Miss H.     1911–14
Meechan, Miss Nellie     1935–9
Munro, Miss M.     1889–97
Norris, Robert     1893–4
Porter, Sister Iris     1960–4
Poolton, George     1890–1
Reilly, Miss     1946–7

Richardson, Sister Jean 1953–60
Rutledge, Miss M. 1909
Shannon, Miss 1892–3
Sharpe, W.R. 1988–
Shillington, Miss 1945
Spence, Miss 1899–1903
Stidworthy, Sister Joan 1964–6
Thompson, Mrs Pearl 1955–62
Thompson, Miss Sybil 1941–5
Turner, John Springfield Road 1944–5
Twinem, Miss Daphne 1985–
Whalley, Sister Ellen 1969–71
Whitehouse, Percy 1902
Williams, Miss Evelyn 1910–15
Wilson, Miss 1917–48

## Appendix 7
### LAY MEMBERS OF THE BELFAST CENTRAL MISSION COMMITTEE, 1889–1989

Addis, Richard 1904–22
Addy, Alan 1985–7
Alexander, Robert B., JP, MP 1928–54
Allen, John 1934–5
Anderson, David, JP 1915–29
Anderson, Frank M. 1936–79
Anderson, Henry M. 1902–52
Anderson, Hugh 1897–1901; 1926–45
Anderson, Robert H. 1951–
Armstrong, William 1943–6
Aston, H. 1896–8
Bagnall, Mrs Ann 1988–
Bambrick, Wilfrid T. 1937–70
Baskin, W. Haughton 1928–30
Belch, Nat 1983–8
Bell, R.J. 1899–90
Bigger, Mrs D. 1896–8
Blair, John 1970–1
Boland, Miss Heather 1988–
Bourke, Charles E., JP 1934–44

Brandon, H.B., JP    1898–1923
Brandon, W. Harold    1923–41
Brown, Samuel    1985–
Capper, Grahame    1977–84
Charlton, J.R.    1940–57
Clarke, G.W., JP    1945–6; 1950–1
Clarke, Robert    1904–8
Collins, Mrs Mary    1939–43
Coulson, John H.    1929–30
Cowdy, F. Charles, JP    1914–16; 1927–39
Crawford, Mrs Robert    1896–7
Culbert, Mrs Joan    1983–
Culbert, S. Joseph    1975–6; 1980–3
Cunningham, Frank    1978–84
Curtiss, William    1983–4
Dixon, Alfred C.    1914–31
Dixon, Hal    1970–3
Dixon, James    1899–90; 1905–19
Dobson, Adam    1896–1900
Doran, William J.R.    1952–75
Dumican, Hugh    1904–5
Dunn, William R.    1912–14
Elliott, Noel C.    1934–40
Farley, Mervyn    1986–
Ferris, Robert, jun.    1937–44
Fitzsimmons, John    1905–8
Fullerton, T.A.    1896–1905
Fulton, David    1924–34
Fulton, George H.    1911–31
Fulton, John    1897–1916
Fulton, William    1931–47
Gallagher, Mrs Barbara E.S.    1969–88
Gallagher, David R.S.    1988–
Geddis, William    1904–10
Gihon, Miss Mary    1947–85
Gill, Miss Marjorie    1972–88
Graham, J. Stanley    1988–
Hall, Mrs Valerie    1986–8
Hamilton, Kenneth    1971–3
Hamilton, Mrs T.C.    1976–

Harrison, Herbert    1981–3
Hawthorne, Mrs R.    1976–
Heaney, Andrew    1899–1904
Heaslett, David, jun.    1905–14
Hill, John L.    1978–83
Hinds, J. Eric    1963–85
Hodges, Thomas    1946–55
Hoey, Miss    1896–1923
Hooks, Mrs Hessie    1981–
Howard, Edward    1967–9
Jefferson, W.J.    1896–1906
Jefferson, W.J., jun.    1906–10
Jeffery, Frederick    1977–83
Johnson, Alfred W.    1908–30
Johnson, Mrs Alfred W.    1929–30
Johnson, Dermot P.    1936–80
Johnson, Henry M.    1904–39
Johnson, Robert    1896–1917
Johnston, Gerald    1977–
Johnston, Miss Louie    1971–4
Kelly, Mrs Beryl    1981–
Kelly, John    1896–1905
Ker, R. Alan    1980–4
Ker, Mrs Selina    1927–69
Kevin, Dr H.    1896–1903
Kirk, Miss M.    1976–81
Kirkpatrick, Mrs E.    1981–
Kirkpatrick, G. Hunter    1974–88
Kirkpatrick, Samuel T.    1921–34
Kirkpatrick, William H.    1937–63
Lindsay, David J.    1915–24
Logan, Arnold    1944–6
Lowe, Alfred    1896–1912
Macauley, W. Alan    1983–4
McCleery, Frank    1967–71
McCluskey, Mrs Samuel    1984–7
McIlroy, Miss E.    1976–81
McIlveen, Joseph    1896–9
McKee, Alex    1974–80
McKee, William    1955–8

McKinley, Adam  1983–8
McKinney, William  1977–8
McKinstry, Samuel  1948–53
McMeekin, Alex  1977–83
Magee, John  1943–4
Maguire, John  1896–9
Matier, John  1942–73
Mayes, Mrs Robert  1984–
Meegan, Mrs Jennie  1986–8
Megarry, F., JP  1896–1903
Menary, Frederick H.  1928–39
Menary, Thomas H.  1931–46
Mercier, James J.  1903–4; 1908–10
Mercier, Samuel  1897–1926
Mercier, W.T.  1896–1909
Metcalfe, Arthur W.  1910–30
Minford, George  1986–8
Moffitt, Miss Frances  1987–
Montgomery, H. Trevor  1930–61
Montgomery, David H.  1951–
Moreland, James  1977–83
Murray, Edward J.  1934–42
Musgrave, Mrs Leila  1988–
Newell, James  1983–
Nixon, James  1902–8
Nixon, W. Herbert  1931–8
Pakenham, Thomas, JP  1967–70
Parker, William  1899–1900
Patterson, William H.  1951–
Phenix, Samuel  1950–71
Phillips, James J.  1904–14
Philpot, Mrs W.  1896–1916
Prenter, Richard J.  1914–24
Rainey, Miss Rosemary  1977–83
Rainey, William  1977–83
Reid, Norman C.  1932–41
Robb, W. Norman H.  1928–76
Robinson, D.  1896–8
Robinson, James  1908–10
Shannon, David  1899–1900

Shaw, John S.    1897–1900
Shaw, Lancelot    1896–1907
Sheridan, John C.    1914–17
Shillington, Arthur F.    1931–41
Shillington, T. Foulkes    1896–1914
Shillington, Mrs T. Foulkes    1910–60
Shipway, Stanley R.    1963–85
Skelley, J. Bell    1904–8
Smiley, Dr James A.    1977–82
Smiley, John    1980–3
Smith, Mrs Marie    1983–4
Smyth, Walter    1951–85
Spence, Alex    1984–
Spence, Mrs Jane    1929–42
Stafford, Benjamin    1908–28
Stafford, Frederick    1911–36
Stafford, Mrs Frederick    1938–40
Stafford, Malcolm A.    1937–8
Stephenson, John    1896–1906
Stephenson, Robert G.    1906–8
Stewart, John    1923–34
Stockdale, Robert J.    1947–57
Storey, Miss    1910–16
Sullivan, James    1933–58
Taylor, Alexander    1900–6
Thompson, David J.    1925–53
Thompson, Frederick, MP    1931–52
Thompson, James B.    1904–21
Thompson, Norman    1952–60
Thompson, Robert    1906–10
Tinman, Lindsay    1980–4
Tomlinson, Kenneth    1963–85
Turtle, Hugh    1925–53
Twinem, Miss Daphne    1987–8
Unsworth, John    1988–
Walker, John W.    1955–6
Wallace, William H.    1904–14
Watson, David H.    1953–85
Weir, John H.    1952–
Weir, J.R. Wesley    1984–

White, Charles E.  1939–70
Whitla, Sir William  1908–9
Whitten, Harold  1969–72
Whitten, Ernest  1980–
Worrall, A. Stanley  1963–83
Young, John  1905–18; 1927–62

# INDEX OF PEOPLE

# SELECT INDEX OF PLACES

Although the Belfast Central Mission has been based at the Grosvenor Hall, at different times and for varying periods it has witnessed at points of need in many places. Square brackets indicate that the venue was not part of the Mission at that time.